The Dawning
of the Day

LIAM NEVIN

The Dawning of the Day
Copyright © Liam Nevin, 2021
The author has asserted his moral rights

First Published in Ireland, in 2021, by The Manuscript Publisher
ISBN: 978-1-911442-36-3
A CIP Catalogue record for this book is available from
the National Library

Front cover photo used courtesy of the National Library of
Ireland: *Sackville (O'Connell) Street, May 1916*. Recoloured and
designed by Brendan Nevin.
Back cover photo: *Rural Kildare Scene* by Oscar Duggan

Typesetting, page design and layout, overall cover design by
Documents and Manuscripts

The Dawning of the Day

DEDICATION

To my youngest grandchildren, Sadie and Liam,
whom I love very much.

FOREWORD

As a boy, it was a family tradition, on a Sunday afternoon, to take a walk to the local cemetery, less than a mile from our house. In the cemetery, my mother's parents were interred. Being a child, I was not very interested in my family tree but the walk was always enjoyable.

My mother often related the story of a soldier who was fatally wounded in a field that we passed on the way. She said it happened in 1922, when she was twelve years old. She could recall the talk of her family and the neighbours at the time: how shocked they were, etc.

Not very long ago, I was reading a book on the Irish Civil War when I came across an account of the incident. It transpired that the soldier was a member of the Free State Army. Apparently, an anti-treaty IRA column from Leixlip had ambushed a train on its way to Dublin, on the line close to the cemetery. The Free State Army had been informed of the impending attack and were soon at the scene. Fighting broke out. The IRA men – five of whom had deserted from the National Army and would later be executed by the Provisional (Free State) government – retreated and commandeered the local manor house, where the battle continued. The soldier whom my mother spoke of, was killed crossing the field to the house.

Further research into that period revealed incredible accounts of atrocities on both sides. Families were torn apart and neighbours became bitter enemies. I never remembered being taught much about that time when I was at school in the sixties. It was probably too painful or too embarrassing for those who lived through it. Most history books went only as far as the Anglo-Irish War, when Ireland had 'won her freedom'. I remember the enmity that existed between neighbours when I was growing up in the fifties and sixties. I struggled to understand why some families were for and others against the Treaty of 1921. My research would lead me to the answer.

I decided to write an historical novel about the events that occurred in the early part of the 20th century in Ireland. Before the first quarter was over Ireland, politically, had been through a tumultuous time. It moved from being part of the British Empire to being granted Home Rule in 1912. This emancipation was delayed due to the outbreak of the First World War. Finally, in 1921, the Anglo-Irish Treaty was signed, which led to the partition of the country, the Civil War and the birth of Saorstát Éireann (the Irish Free State). I fictionalised the characters and families in my story but included actual events, which I thought were appropriate for the time.

I would like to thank my dear wife, Marlene, for her patience and support while I worked on my project. I would also like to thank my son, Brendan; my daughter, Pauline; my stepson, Tony; my family and especially my brothers John, Peter and Seamus and my good friend Colm Nelson for their encouragement and support. My dear friend Michael O'Shea also encouraged and helped me considerably in putting together the storyline for which, I am very grateful.

Finally, I would like to thank Oscar Duggan for editing and preparing my book very professionally.

CONTENTS

NOTES ON TEXT

*Abbreviations and initialisms used in this text
denote the following terms:*

ADRIC – Auxiliary Division of the Royal Irish Constabulary (RIC – see below)

AOH – Ancient Order of Hibernians

BE(F) – British Expeditionary (Forces)

DMP – Dublin Metropolitan Police

GHQ – General Headquarters (used in connection with the IRA – see below)

GPO – General Post Office. Located on Dublin's O'Connell Street (formerly Sackville Street), it served as the rebel headquarters during the Easter Rising of 1916.

IRA – Irish Republican Army

IRB – Irish Republican Brotherhood

IRP – Irish Republican Police

ITGWU – Irish Transport and General Workers Union

IV – Irish Volunteers (Óglaigh na hÉireann)

MP – Member of Parliament

OC – Officer Commanding

PM – Prime Minister

RIC – Royal Irish Constabulary

SMLE – Short Magazine Lee Enfield

TD – Teachta Dála (*plual*: Teachtaí Dála) referring to a member of Dáil Éireann (the Irish parliament)

USA – United States of America

UVF – Ulster Volunteer Force

DRAMATIS PERSONAE

It is November 1920.

John and Mary Brennan are living in Barrow Street, Dublin along with their children: Michael (b. 1912), Bridget (b. 1914), Sean (b. 1916), Patrick (b. 1919) and their newly born daughter, Joan. Previously, John had joined the British Army, in 1915 and was wounded in the war.

Brian and Margaret (Mags) Byrne live in Rathangan, Co. Kildare with their two boys, Joseph (b. 1916), Thomas (b. 1918) and their new-born son, Seamus. A baby daughter was still born in 1915.

Brian's employer is Major George O'Kelly, a Boer War veteran. His wife is Elizabeth and they have a daughter, Martina; a son, John (killed in war) and another son, George living in London where he works as a barrister.

Brian's brother, Bill joins the Dublin Metropolitan Police (DMP) in 1912. While based in Dublin, he meets Kathleen O'Connor. Her digs are in Dame Street. She has a sister, May, with digs also in Dame Street. Bill suffers injuries during the Lockout riots of 1913.

CHAPTER ONE

Uncertain Times

*A Dublin working-class family welcome their newest member
into the world. Times are hard. The country is in turmoil.*

On the first of November 1920, Mary Brennan gave birth to a
baby girl. She laboured all through the cold frosty night and the
elderly lady, Josie Smith, who was the unofficial midwife for
Barrow Street and the surrounding area of Dublin, did her best
to give Mary some relief from her painful birth pangs. Mary
already had four children: three boys and a girl. She'd had one
miscarriage.

Her husband, John, worked hard as a casual labourer to keep
the family fed and watered and the rent paid on their two-up,
two-down little house. He worked in the Graving Dry Dock
in Ringsend but some days, he was not required due to the
'troubles' in the city. He found the work painful at times, owing
to the wounds he suffered in the war. The baby was christened
Joan.

The house that the Brennans rented in Barrow Street was very
basic but at least it had four rooms. Michael and Bridget slept
with their brothers, Sean and Patrick, in the back bedroom.
John and Mary had the front one. Patrick was aged 18 months.
The other three children were at school in Great Brunswick
Street, which was the birthplace of Patrick and Willie Pearse,
the executed Irish revolutionaries of the 1916 Easter Rising. The
street would be renamed 'Pearse Street' in later years.

Downstairs was the parlour at the front but this was only used
at Christmas, or when there were visitors. The back room was
the kitchen/lounge and washroom. It had a large dresser filled
with the delph and other bits and pieces. There was a large
table and four chairs. John and Mary each had ancient well

used armchairs, which they bought in a pawn shop. Over the open fire, a mantle clock resided with a china dog on each side. The picture of the Sacred Heart hung above these. Out in the back yard, there was the dry toilet and a coal scuttle. Water was available up the street from a communal pump.

Later in the same day, the sad news came through that a young medical student by the name of Kevin Barry was hanged in Mountjoy Prison. He was only eighteen years of age. He was convicted of being involved in an operation by the Irish Volunteers, which resulted in the deaths of three British soldiers. He was the first Irish Volunteer to be executed since May 1916. Mrs Wilson had come in to see the new-born baby and related the events of the morning in Mountjoy.

'Did yis hear the terrible news?'

'No, Mrs Wilson. What happened?' replied John and Mary together.

'The bastards murdered the poor young Barry lad in Mountjoy this morning. He was only a gosoon of eighteen, God rest him.'

'Lord save us!' came the affirmation in unison.

'Yeah, they pulled him out from under a lorry, and nearly tortured him to death, as he wouldn't tell on his comrades.'

'That's shockin'. Wasn't he going to be a doctor?'

'That's right, and his poor mammy was heartbroken. They should have shot him like a soldier and not hang him like a dog.'

'Very true Mrs Wilson, very true.'

John Brennan had volunteered to join the British Army in 1915, on the advice of John Redmond MP. One slogan read:

> *Follow Mr John Redmond's advice and join an Irish regiment today, and make yourselves fit to join your gallant countrymen in Belgium.'*

John Redmond believed that the war would be short lived, thinking in 1914, as many others did, that it would be 'over by Christmas'. He had a vision that the Irish Army, formally known as the Irish Volunteers (IV), would be honoured in a victory parade down Sackville Street in Dublin and that Home Rule would be conceded to Ireland, or at least twenty-six counties of it. However, Lord Kitchener, although born in Ireland like Wellington, had no time for nationalism and never wanted to see anything that looked like an Irish Army in the war, even though the UVF were allowed to be members of their own regiment, the 36th (Ulster) Division.

John had been out of work for several months and struggled to feed his wife and two children. Yes, the soup kitchens kept the family from starvation but more and more families were beginning to rely on them almost entirely. This meant there was often not enough food to go around, so things were getting desperate.

Over a few pints in the local pub John was talking to friends and fellow labourers, mostly out of work too. They were discussing joining the British Army and perhaps agreeing to 'take the King's shilling.'

The Home Rule Bill was introduced in 1912. The Ulster Unionists had campaigned against Home Rule from Dublin believing that 'Home Rule was Rome Rule'. In September that year, 250,000 of them signed a Solemn League and Covenant, pledging themselves, before God, never to accept it. The Ulster Volunteer Force (UVF) was formed in 1913. They imported 25,000 rifles and five million rounds of ammunition, purchased illegally in Germany, in April 1914. They were landed at Larne, Bangor and Donaghadee. The UVF became the best equipped force, outside the British Army, in the United Kingdom.

Although the guns and ammunition had been imported into Ireland illegally, James Craig and Edward Carson, together with many Conservative MPs, not only condoned the importation but positively celebrated it. They believed that the key weapon – namely, the UVF – that would scotch Home Rule for all

Ireland was in place. Redmond and Prime Minister Asquith's reaction to the arming of the Ulster Unionists was hesitant and indecisive. British officers in the Curragh Camp declared that they would resign their commissions rather than act against the UVF.

The nationalist Irish Volunteers was set up in 1913 in response to the setting up of the UVF. The nationalist and author, Erskine Childers, attempted to import 900 (obsolete) German rifles plus ammunition for them in June 1914, through Howth on his yacht, *Asgard*. However, they were intercepted in Bachelors Walk in Dublin by the King's Own Scottish Borderers regiment and, in the confusion, four people were shot dead, including the wife of a 'British' soldier.

The Home Rule bill was passed in September 1914 but was formally postponed under an amending Act for a minimum of twelve months and 'no later than' the end of the continental war. The soon-would-be partitioned Ireland was taking mental shape as early as the first months of 1914.

John Brennan was more worried about looking after his family than discussing politics.

'What do yis t'ink lads about joinin' up?' he asked his companions, as he took a sup out of his pint of plain.

'Ah jayus, John. If it means Ireland will be free, I t'ink maybe we should go for it,' said the 'skinner' Black as he nursed his pint of plain, trying to keep it as long as possible due to financial difficulties (porter had gone up 50%, from two pence to three pence a pint in 1914).

'Yeah, lads but will dem bastards in fucken England set us free?' asked Johnny 'the Hopper' Treacy.

'Well, me missus and the kids will get a regular few bob if I go for it?' remarked John, hoping for a unanimous 'yes'.

The group discussed the issue further. There were many 'ifs' and 'buts' and heated argument was not excluded.

The churches generally encouraged men to join up and fight for the freedom of small nations. It was subtly suggested that if Irishmen enlisted, then Home Rule would definitely be implemented in the whole of Ireland. Then Ireland would certainly be free!

However, in the early days, the Catholic Church was not very enthusiastic about Home Rule. It considered it to be a movement launched by Protestant conservatives, including Charles Stewart Parnell. In 1872, the then Archbishop of Dublin, Cardinal Paul Cullen, (the first Irish Cardinal, who spent many years in Rome and was sent back by the Pope to Ireland, to 'Romanise' the Irish Church), launched a rival movement known as the Catholic Union, in response to similar movements being launched in England and Scotland. It was a 'specifically' Catholic organisation. However, it was said that the Irish Catholic hierarchy was less worried about constitutional Irish nationalism than latent Fenian sympathies.

The Catholic Church also was uncomfortable about families taking relief from soup kitchens that were not organised by Catholic charities, for fear that they may be exposed to Protestant beliefs. People who availed of these kitchens were often nicknamed 'soupers'. This dated back to the time of the Great Famine, when a condition for obtaining soup and bread was to convert to Protestantism.

John Brennan thought long and hard about leaving his family and going to the Front. He knew some of the men who had gone and learned that their families were now receiving a considerable remuneration, known as 'separation allowances', from the British Army. The allowances were one shilling and a penny a day, together with two pence a day for each child and three shillings and six pence from compulsory allotment out of their husbands pay if they were serving abroad. He loved Mary very much, as well as his two children but food had to be provided and rent paid. He also knew that 'separation wives' were often targeted by single young men who offered them 'comfort'. Some unscrupulous women accepted the offer. That worried John a little but he brushed the thought from his mind.

He brought up joining the army with Mary one evening, which very upset her.

'But John, you will be away from us in a foreign land and war is dangerous,' said Mary trying to hold back the tears.

'I know, Pet but the war will be over very soon and we will lose out on a handy few bob,' John replied as he lit a Woodbine and sucked hard on it, blowing smoke through his nose.

'T'ink of the t'ings we could have on a regular income,' he added.

'I know John but what if you don't come home?' pleaded Mary, as tears began to flow down her cheeks.

'Of course I'll come home, Pet. Sure all I'll have to do is hop on the boat to France and fire a few shots at the Germans and keep me head down,' said John, not really convincing himself.

He reached over and held his wife's hand and tried to console her. They both wept.

John was upset about leaving his family but, secretly he looked forward to a new adventure and a change from the troubles of everyday life in Dublin. He felt guilty about having that feeling but still hoped the war would end after about six months.

Yes, Mary knew of women whose husbands had already gone to France and she also knew of the money they received every month. Over the first two years of the war, the cost of living in Ireland and Britain had increased by about 50%. Already there was industrial unrest in Britain, which worried the government but, she also knew of the pain they held in their hearts. They worried every day if their loved ones were safe and dreaded the knock on the door when the telegram boy with the envelope edged in black came. Some families had already had that experience of getting the dreadful news that their husband or son would never return home. However, the newspapers of the day, such as the *Irish Independent*, the *Dublin Daily Express* and the *Dublin Evening Telegraph* did not print the true story of what was happening on the Western Front. The government did not want potential recruits to change their minds and so, reports of the carnage on the Western Front were severely censored.

CHAPTER TWO

The New Century Maturing

In rural Kildare (not far from Dublin but a somewhat different world) a child is also being born to a family of farm labourers.

On the first of November 1920, a son was born to Brian and Margaret Byrne. He was born in their little rented 'gatehouse' in Rathangan, County Kildare. The local 'midwife' came to assist as usual. The house had two bedrooms and a kitchen. There were no toilet facilities, apart from chamber pots under the beds and Brian and the children used a neighbouring field and/or ditch to relieve themselves in the summer months.

Brian worked as a farm labourer in the 'big house' owned by Major George O'Kelly, which stood about 300 yards away from the gatehouse at the end of a winding, tree-lined avenue. It was a large manor house consisting of ten bedrooms, two reception rooms, a large dining room and four bathrooms. There was a large kitchen to the rear of the building. The front entrance had three steps leading to large oak door with a pillar at each side, supporting a stone canopy. The front of the house was covered by colourful wisteria that flowered every late spring. The estate had 500 acres of finest Kildare land. Major O'Kelly lived there with his wife, Elizabeth and one unmarried daughter, Martina. Sadly, his eldest son, John, was killed in the Great War. He was an officer with the Royal Dublin Fusiliers. His death occurred at the Western Front on the first day of the Battle of the Somme – the first of July 1916. His second son, George junior, lived in London and was a barrister.

By 1920 the servants were reduced to three. Before the war ten were employed. Four men were employed on the farm including Brian. These houses were getting more expensive to run and maintain. The Major was, unusually, a Catholic and was an officer in the British Army. He fought in the Boer War and won several military medals.

Part of Brian's job was to open and close the large black iron gates to visitors in the evenings. The gates hung on stone clad pillars and were sometimes left open during the day. At the lodge side there was a smaller gate, which was a pedestrian entrance. Margaret sometimes assisted Brian in opening the larger gates. The couple already had two children, both boys. They were named Joseph and Thomas. They thanked God for their children and believed that He had sent them. There was no thought or discussion about family planning, the babies 'came' or didn't come and that was the end of it. The Catholic Church encouraged couples to have children, whether they could afford to feed and clothe them was another matter.

The house came with a kitchen garden. Brian sowed his own potatoes, cabbage, onions, carrots, etc, which helped enormously with feeding his growing family. They also kept chickens and ducks. These provided welcome Sunday dinners from time to time and, of course, eggs. The potatoes usually lasted till April or May. Before the winter set in the remaining spuds were placed in a pit. The bottom of the pit was covered with straw and then earth covered the valuable food. More straw was added as insulation and, hopefully, waterproofing it. However, the pit was often prone to attacks by rats in the cold winter months. Brian did his best to ensure there would be potatoes for dinner until the new spuds appeared in the late spring. He was given milk from the dairy in the big house as a concession, which was kind.

There was never enough money left over for 'extras' but the family never went hungry. Brian bought an ounce of Yachtsman plug tobacco every Friday and sometimes he walked to the village for a pint and a smoke of his pipe in Dillon's public house. He also enjoyed a chat with the locals. Lighting the pipe was an art in itself. First a suitable piece of tobacco was cut from the plug with the penknife. This was rubbed in the palm of the hand and rendered pliable and ready to enter the pipe.

The tobacco, now in the pipe, was pushed down firmly and then lit with a match. Getting it to light could take some time, with much sucking and puffing and relighting. Eventually, the tobacco burned slowly and only then could the smoker relax and enjoy the taste. Occasionally, it was required to spit out the excess fluid drawn into the mouth but this was part of the enjoyment. Brian invested in a lid for his pipe, which meant he could turn it upside down, which meant that frequent relighting was not required.

Margaret, who was known as Mags, would often go to a 'rambling' house in the evening to catch up with all the local gossip. The older women enjoyed a smoke and the 'dudeen' or clay pipe was the favourite. The chat would continue for several hours and sickness, death, weddings and juicy unconfirmed scandals were discussed. Widows were almost obliged to wear black clothes, cardigan, coat, skirt and shoes. On the head, they wore a black headscarf or veil and often, grey hair peeped out at the front. All women were obliged to wear a headscarf/veil or hat to church.

The Byrnes were religious, as many of their neighbours were. The Rosary was recited most evenings and the whole family attended Mass every Sunday. The Mass was in Latin, so usually the congregation said their own prayers, including the Rosary. The males sat on the right side of the church and the females on the left. Small children were exempted from this 'rule' and sat with their mothers. Holy Communion was only available at the first Mass, at 8.30am, as to receive one had to be 'fasting from midnight' and 'have the right intention.'

Brian and Mags were members of the 'Sodality'. One was for men and the other for women. The idea was to encourage men and women to go to confession and receive Holy Communion every month. There was a service on the first and second Friday evenings of the month, one for men and the next for women. Confession was on the Saturday and Communion on the Sunday.

The family was a happy one but Brian was a bit worried about his job. In 1920 the Irish War of Independence was in full swing and around 13.5 million acres of Irish land had already been re-allocated to tenant farmers by the Land Commission. Landlords were compensated. This reduced dramatically the large estates, which, anyway, were getting less and less economically viable. Many landlords were getting nervous about the political uncertainty in Ireland. Their class was facing an uncertain future in the troubled times and some simply took their fat cheques and returned to Britain. Their estates were promptly divided.

Brian and Mags had wanted to name their son Seamus Vincent but the parish priest in Rathangan, on being baptised there, insisted he must be named after a saint. Most Irish names – apart from Patrick, Michael, Bridget and, of course, Mary – were not acceptable. And so he was registered James Vincent Byrne.

Only three weeks after baby Seamus was born, fourteen civilians were shot dead in Croke Park during a Gaelic football match by British Forces. It was a reprisal for the execution of fourteen British intelligence agents by the IRA in Dublin that Sunday morning organised by Michael Collins. The tragic day was to become known as Bloody Sunday. The War of Independence was nearing its peak.

CHAPTER THREE

Unlucky Strike

*1912. Bill Byrne joins the DMP. While stationed in Dublin, he
meets Kathleen O'Connor.*

Brian was worried about his brother, Bill, who had joined the
Dublin Metropolitan Police (DMP) in 1912. He was now in the
Royal Irish Constabulary (RIC). He first considered joining the
British Army in the Curragh Camp but decided on the DMP, as
it sounded more Irish. He also wanted to experience what city
life had to offer.

His training lasted for six months and he was posted to Great
Brunswick Street Station in Dublin. He enjoyed his time being
shown the ropes on his beat. He loved to walk in St Stephen's
Green and Merrion Square on his day off and enjoy the trees
and the flowers. He also walked to Ringsend and sat watching
the ships come and go and breathed the sea air. He had never
seen the sea before he came to Dublin.

Bill missed the country living and the fresh air in County
Kildare but jobs were scarce in his hometown and the police
force was well paid. He shared a room with a colleague, Tom
Dempsey from Donegal and they both enjoyed canal walks and
the parks in the big city. They enjoyed fishing on the river and
canal banks.

At weekends the pair of them would go to a dance at the Ancient
Order of Hibernian's (AOH) hall in Parnell Square. Both men
were tall and slim and well built. The police training had done
them good, giving them muscular bodies. Bill was the more
handsome of the pair and both were very popular with the
girls, especially the country ones who, like them, were missing
home life.

Bill had his eye on Kathleen O'Connor from Kerry. She had sparkling blue eyes and long black hair and a figure that many of her friends envied. She was shorter than both boys, at five foot five: they were both over six feet. She gave each of them a dance but she fancied Bill the most. After three weeks, Bill plucked up the courage to ask her out. She hesitated at first but he was so relieved when she agreed to meet him in Sackville Street, opposite Nelson's Pillar, on Wednesday evening.

Bill put on his best white, collarless shirt and his 'Sunday' navy-blue, pinstriped suit. He fitted his clean collar, inserting the stud at the back of his neck and knotted his blue tie. He polished his best black brogues till he could almost see his reflection in them. He admired himself in the hall mirror, stroked his moustache and donned his flat cap. He was nervous about meeting Kathleen and hoped she would turn up as promised.

He walked down Great Brunswick Street passed his station and turned right at Trinity College, crossed O'Connell Bridge into Sackville Street (which was renamed O'Connell Street in 1924). He headed down to the Pillar. Many girls and boys assembled around the Pillar on this summer evening in May and Bill tried hard to spot his date among them.

As he peered into the crowd, he felt a tap on his shoulder and to his great relief, there stood Kathleen. She looked gorgeous in a lovely, tailored skirt with a white blouse and cardigan. Her hair was bobbed in the latest fashion. Her clothes were not new but they were well cared for, clean and pressed. She was a shop girl in Clery's department store and had access to all the latest styles in ladies' fashion.

They walked to a nearby tearoom and Bill ordered tea and scones with jam and cream. Kathleen thought he was so handsome and loved his well-groomed moustache. His eyes seemed to sparkle. They chatted about their backgrounds and how they felt homesick when they came to the big smoke. When he mentioned that he was a police constable, she appeared a little uncomfortable but he thought that it was just his imagination.

They went to see a film, silent of course, in the Ambassador Cinema on Sackville Street. They watched a short comedy film starring 'Fatty' Arbuckle called *A Noise from the Deep*. It also included the Keystone Cops on horseback. They thought it very funny. Afterwards, they walked together up the street. Bill offered Kathleen a cigarette (a Gold Flake) and they both enjoyed a smoke on O'Connell Bridge as they watched the Liffey flow gently by.

It was getting late and Kathleen said she must be back at her digs by nine-thirty. She shared a room with her sister, May, in Dame Street. Her brother, Pat, had a room further on along the street. He worked as a typesetter for the Irish Independent newspaper. They promised each other to meet again at the weekend at the AOH hall.

Bill and Kathleen dated for several weeks. They grew close and even had and kiss and a cuddle when they last met. Her kiss was wonderful; her lips were soft and warm. He knew he wanted her but he would have to wait. She didn't resist when he pulled her close; he was pleased about that.

Kathleen told her sister, May that Bill was a policeman but not her brother, Pat. The O'Connors were a strong nationalist family and the police were not very trusted. They viewed them as British and anti-Irish. County Kerry was known to be a very 'rebellious' county. She wondered what her parents would say but she put that to the back of her mind, for now.

The first trouble that Bill experienced was in August 1913, when a strike by tram crews led to a lockout by employers. The lockout was arranged by the redoubtable William Martin Murphy. Mr Murphy was an ex-MP for the Irish Parliamentary Party and owner of Clery's store, the Irish Independent newspaper, the Dublin Tram Company, among other enterprises. The employers objected to their employees joining James Connolly and Jim Larkin's Irish Transport and General Workers Union (ITGWU).

On 31 August 1913 Bill was on duty. There had been some rioting in Ringsend the night before. The DMP and the RIC were ordered to assemble in Sackville Street, near to O'Connell Bridge. There was a large crowd, mostly workers, in the street who were upset that the strike had failed to stop the tram service. Mr Murphy had replaced crews who had walked off the trams with inspectors and other employees, mainly office workers.

Things appeared to be getting out of hand and the police were given orders to break up the crowd. Bill could see the angry workers further down the street. Most assembled around Nelson's Pillar. Banners were already raised, denouncing the 'blacklegs' and supporting Jim Larkin and the ITGWU.

Police officers were ordered to form lines across the wide street. Batons were drawn and the order to advance was given. The workers seemed surprised at first to see the large force. Then the police charged, employing batons and boots liberally. There was panic as demonstrators tried to escape the charging force. Men were trampled underfoot. Some workers managed to organise themselves and, with sticks and debris, they counter attacked.

Bill was struck by a flying object that narrowly missed his left eye and hit the side of his head. Blood flowed down. He was not seriously injured. A man dived at him and tried to remove the baton from his hand. Bill hit him with his left fist, knocking the attacker off balance and releasing his grip on the baton. Bill then smacked him with the baton knocking him to the ground.

The riot continued for what felt like an age. Workers fell to the ground and were beaten by the police. Many officers were cornered and forced into side streets, where they were savagely beaten and had to be rescued by their colleagues. However, the police appeared to be over enthusiastic in controlling the crowd, leading to two men receiving fatal injuries. Approximately five hundred workers and police were injured.

When, eventually, Constable William Patrick Byrne of the DMP returned to the relative safety of his station, he was exhausted. His whole body ached and his head wound had to be stitched. He was a mess. Bill had been trained in crowd control but he never experienced such violence in all his life. He was horrified at the amount of injuries suffered by both civilians and police. He feared going back to his digs, as many knew he was a policeman and the day's events made this profession very unpopular with the public. He felt that he, perhaps, could not work in the city again.

Bill was helped by two colleagues to his digs in Barrow Street. He had removed his helmet and jacket. He flopped down on his bed and was soon fast asleep. His dreams soon developed into nightmares of the riots. The faces of the rioters seemed to mock and torment him. Several times he woke up sweating and once, he heard a deafening scream, which in fact was from his own mouth. He sat up in bed, trembling. So ended the original Bloody Sunday.

The strikes and the lockouts continued until January 1914, causing much suffering and even destitution for many families. The slums in Dublin were among the worst in the world. It was said they were on a par with Calcutta. Mr Murphy persuaded 400 employers to lock out workers who refused to withdraw their support and/or membership for/of the ITGWU, resulting in 15,000 workers having to depend on the TUC relief fund. However, Guinness' refused to lock their employees out. Further relief was given by the Society of St Vincent de Paul, whilst the Catholic and Protestant churches appeared to compete in the provision of soup kitchens. Dr William Walsh, Catholic Archbishop of Dublin and Dr Charles McHugh, Catholic Bishop of Derry, each contributed approximately £2000, a considerably large sum at that time (approximately £230,000 in 2020).

Chapter Four

The King's Shilling

1915. John Brennan joins the Leinster Regiment and is off to Aldershot, leaving behind a wife and two children.

In September 1915, John Brennan, with heavy heart, boarded the troop train to Kingstown (Dún Laoire)*, which would take him to the boat and to England. He was on his way to London to begin his military training with the Leinster Regiment. He had signed up for 'three years or to the end of the war' rather than the one-year option, which paid less. He said goodbye to his dear wife, Mary and his two children, Michael and Bridget, that morning. Many tears were shed. John and Mary had spent their last night holding on tightly to each other and slept little. They made love which was wonderful but tinged with a deep sadness and many tears. Mary was very upset, as were the children. She feared the worst for her dear husband and the thought of extra money was no consolation.

'Ah now Mary don't be so upset. Sure I'll be back home by Christmas; you wait and see. Ye know I love you. Look after yourselves now. God bless and keep ye.'

With that John was gone, disappearing over the bridge at Boland's Mills and Mary felt an emptiness in her breast, the children clung to her asking, 'When will Daddy be back, Ma?'

The family had suffered much over 1913/14 during the strike and the lockouts. Only for the relief agencies, the children might not have survived. The war had raised the cost of living and it was still difficult to make ends meet. During the war, a relief

---

* Originally known as Dunleary, the town was renamed Kingstown in 1821, in honour of the visit of King George IV that year. It returned to its former name in 1920 and is officially known today as Dún Laoghaire and more informally as Dún Laoire.

agency was set up with donations from the public to 'alleviate hardship caused by the absence of the breadwinner'. The Duke of Leinster donated one thousand pounds.

John boarded the ship, which was crowded. He had to search for a seat and eventually found one. He was pleased that it was near a porthole. Soon the mighty steam engines began to power up. He could hear and feel the propeller turning over and ship pulled away from the dock. He watched as the harbour lights faded from his view, which made him very sad.

The sea crossing was rough. The large vessel pushed through the waves and heaved from side to side. He had never been on a big ship before and he was seasick most of the way, as were many others. When at last the rocking eased, he got chatting to his fellow enlisters and it took his mind off his family, his loneliness and his fear of his future in the war. There were mostly men from Dublin and some from other counties, such as Kildare, Wicklow and Carlow. Some were in the Royal Dublin Fusiliers. Many were already in the British Army when the war started and others joined because they wanted adventure and relief from the humdrum of life in the early 20th century.

After arriving at Holyhead he boarded the steam train for London. He was tired and dozed a little but the sound of the train on the rails was noisy and the carriage rocked quite a lot. The clickity-clank sound of wheels on rails seemed to say, *You'll never come back; you'll never come back!*

He had a cigarette and offered some to his new friends. Again they chatted and the troubles brewing in Ireland was discussed. Most were disappointed that Home Rule was suspended but they hoped that what they were doing now would advance the cause and, after all, they were to fight for the freedom of small nations. They changed at Crewe and eventually arrived at Euston Station, London. From there, he boarded a train that took him to a military camp outside the city in Aldershot. His basic training would last about three months.

Military life was tough, at first, for John. The sergeant and the corporals were relentless in implementing the training regime and discipline was enforced with vigour. John was used to hard work and soon he was almost enjoying the routine. There was much marching through the countryside, wearing full kit, etc. Trenches were also dug in preparation for the Western Front. Some of his colleagues found it difficult to keep up, suffering with blisters on the feet from ill-fitting boots and on the shoulders from carrying heavy kit. They were struggling with life in an army barracks. The food wasn't bad but the sleeping quarters were often cold. At weekends the men enjoyed a few beers, games of cards and even music in the mess. There was a new-fangled phonograph and a few records. John liked the new release by John McCormack entitled *Keep the Home Fires Burning*.

There was one corporal who seemed to pick on John and try to break him, or so John believed. One day, in the parade ground on an inspection, Corporal Watson came up to John and stopped.

'Hey Paddy, why is your tie not straight?'

'My name is not Paddy; it is John, sir.'

'I asked you about your tie not your name, private.'

'You got my name wrong and I will straighten my tie, sir.'

John could see that the corporal didn't like him but he refused to get angry or be intimidated. Corporal Watson stared him in the face and swiftly moved on insulting another private down the line. Perhaps insulting the troops was part of the training programme.

He and his fellow recruits were now physically fit and had begun weapons training on the ranges. They were trained on the Lee-Enfield .303 rifle and some hand weapons. They attached bayonets to the rifles and stuck them into filled sacks. It was not the same as stabbing a real live man but it helped. They were given talks by experienced soldiers on leave from the war. They were not told the whole story about carnage on the front line but more about trench warfare and the mentality of the Germans.

Some of his Irish colleagues were also mocked and mimicked. One private even punched a sergeant for a racist remark and got solitary confinement. However the Irish regiments mostly had officers from the Anglo-Irish ascendancy class and they appreciated their fellow countrymen who, if treated fairly, were dependable, accepted discipline readily and were brave in battle.

John's regiment was told, in November 1915, that they would be off to France the following month to join the Royal Dublin Fusiliers at the Front. The men were a bit anxious but happy that their training would soon be over. Many wanted to put their training into action.

John wrote regularly to Mary, telling her of how the training was going and about the new friends he had met and what counties they came from. He asked about the children and friends and relatives at home. He always said he loved her and how much he missed her and the kids. Mary replied quickly, saying how they all missed him too and hoped the war would soon end and that he would be home again.

CHAPTER FIVE

Old Pastures

1913. In the after math of the Great Lockout and Bloody Sunday, Bill and Kathleen's relationship is under strain.

Constable Bill Byrne returned to work a few days after Bloody Sunday, 1913. He would have liked to have more time off but he wouldn't have been paid. He brought his uniform to the station in a separate bag, as he was advised to do. The city was still very sore after that terrible day and the lockouts still prevailed. Anyone who was associated with the DMP or the RIC were now enemies of the working class. Constables walked their beat in pairs and they were prone to be spat at and abused verbally. Some were even attacked by gangs and beaten up. Bill had almost immediately decided that he must get out of Dublin.

He had arranged a date with Kathleen O'Connor for Wednesday evening. They were to meet at the Pillar as usual and at the usual time. He was a bit worried about his stitches at the side of his head however, he spruced himself up and put on his best clothes and headed off. He waited at the Pillar for nearly an hour. Kathleen didn't show. He had a pint nearby and made his way back to Barrow Street.

He sent a note to Kathleen expressing his disappointment and wondered if she was in good health. It was the following week that he received her reply. She said it was not a good idea for her to be seen with a police constable at this time. The fact that he would be in civilian clothes didn't matter. Her brother was locked out of his job with the *Irish Independent*.

He wrote back to say he could meet her some place where they wouldn't be known. He said that he really enjoyed her company and that he was getting quite fond of her. She replied saying that she was afraid her brother would find out about his job, so she suggested that they wait until things quietened down and the lockouts ended. Maybe they could meet again, she unexpectedly added. In fact, Kathleen's sister, May had told her brother, Pat that Bill was in the 'force'. He hit the roof and went straight to Kathleen's flat, warning her never to see him again or he would have him beaten up or even worse.

Bill was very upset. He had liked Kathleen very much and he even thought he was falling in love with her. She seemed to have feelings for him too but, the events of that Sunday and the fact that he was party to the violence seemed to have muddied her mind. The 'Irish Question' was making headlines almost every day in the newspapers. Whilst the majority of the population in Dublin were behind the employers and somewhat anti-trade union, the people of the south and west of Ireland, in particular, supported the workers and anything that was pro-Home Rule and/or anti-British.

In September Bill made an appointment to see the station sergeant, John Daly. Sergeant Daly wasn't the most patient or understanding of men. Bill entered his office at 8am on a Monday morning towards the end of the month. Sergeant Daly was not in the best of form. He was off duty over the weekend and had a bit of a hangover. He lived in Drumcondra, on the north side of the city and few knew he was in the DMP, not to mention that he was a sergeant. He travelled into the city by tram, wearing civvies and he usually walked to his station from the Pillar.

'Ah, Constable Byrne. What do you want?'

'Good morning, Sergeant. I want to discuss something with you,' says he as he saluted.

'Yes, yes what is it constable? I am a very busy man,' says Sergeant Daly, lighting a cigarette and taking a swig from his glass of Jameson.

'I… I want a transfer to the RIC in County Kildare, sir.'

'A TRANSFER! A TRANSFER! You know we are very short of officers in this fucking station, what with that terrible performance the other Sunday and the lockouts. We need you here man.'

'Yes, I understand, sir but I need to be stationed nearby to Rathangan, as my parents are getting old and I need to be close at hand,' he half lied. His parents were in good form but yes, ageing.

'Well I can only see what I can do Constable. I will let you know but it you will have to stay here until these ugly lockouts and strikes end.'

'I understand, t'ank you Sergeant,' and Bill left.

Bill wrote to his brother, Brian in Rathangan, explaining that he asked for a transfer to Naas, Kildare or Newbridge. He told about the events in Dublin and how the police force was not very popular these days. He said he might come down to stay for a week, perhaps around Christmas if that was alright.

Bill continued with his duties, which were often difficult as the memory of Bloody Sunday was still quite fresh in the mind of the public and, of course, the lockouts continued. His duties often included guarding employers' premises that were picketed. Confrontation was common. Missiles were often thrown and there was never a shortage of verbal abuse – 'Get out! Out of the way you bastards and let us at those cunts inside' … and words to that effect.

Bill still thought about Kathleen. He admitted to himself that he was probably still in love with her. He didn't go to the AOH whilst he had the visible head wound, for fear of being recognised as a police constable. After a few weeks, he ventured there with his friend, Tom from the force. His hair had grown over the scar. He was disappointed that Kathleen wasn't there. He danced with a few girls and enjoyed the music. The girls were very chatty and were obviously attracted to him. Some of them were very attractive indeed but he couldn't get his first love out of his mind. He kept remembering their short time together and how she always managed to look so beautiful. It made him sad.

Tom and Bill were good friends and they went places together, including the pictures and their favourite dance hall, the AOH. One week in late November, they went to the AOH just for old times' sake. As usual, the girls were at one side of the hall and the boys at the opposite side. When the music started, the boys headed across the floor to ask for a dance. If one girl refused, it was not a good idea to ask her friend standing next to her. Instead, it was advisable to either go deeper into the crowd or move far up the line.

Bill approached an attractive girl who was wearing a lovely, bright-patterned dress and had jet-black, long hair. However, as he came closer, he noticed a familiar face behind her to the right. He couldn't believe his eyes: it was Kathleen O'Connor. He passed the awaiting beauty (to her disappointment) and went straight over to Kathleen.

'Hello Kathleen, how are you doing?'

'Ah Bill, I didn't see you coming,' she lied. 'How are you?'

'Oh fine. Would you like to dance?'

'Alright, if you want,' came the reply.

They danced a waltz, which they enjoyed as they could touch each other and have a chat. Kathleen looked as lovely as ever. They had another couple of dances together, including half sets, jigs and reels. She was asked to dance by other men, which made Bill a bit jealous so, he danced with other girls. At the end of the night, he made sure he got the last dance with her.

He asked if he could see her soon again, like next Wednesday evening. She told him that the lockouts were still making things awkward for her. Her brother didn't like her working in Clery's department store either but he would still be very upset if he knew she was dating a police constable. She didn't tell him that Pat already knew and forbade her to see him. Again, Bill was disappointed. Kathleen told him she was going home for Christmas and that she would write to him. That cheered him up a little.

Bill went to stay with his brother, Brian and his wife, Mags at Christmas. Kathleen went home to her parents' house in Castlemaine, in County Kerry.

Being back in Rathangan made Bill happy. The weather was cold but the sun shone. It brought back fond memories of his childhood in that village. He loved the open fields, the trees and the fresh air. He remembered happy Christmas days spent with his parents and siblings. The lovely dinners with a roast goose and potatoes and later, sitting around the fire singing and chatting. Brian and Mags were very hospitable. They were not long married and they were pleased to have family for Christmas dinner. Mag's brother and his wife and two children were also coming.

Christmas Day was as good as promised and all enjoyed themselves. The dinner was delicious. Brian asked Bill about his life as a DMP constable and living in the big city. He had never been to Dublin and Bill told him about the beautiful parks and the seaside places he visited. He didn't talk too much about the riots and the hostility he experienced but he did mention Kathleen. Brian and Mags were pleased he met someone and hoped there might be a 'day out' soon. In the afternoon, Brian borrowed Major O'Kelly's pony and trap and they went to visit their parents at the other end of the village across the canal bridge. William and Mary Byrne preferred to stay at home on Christmas Day. They went to first Mass and enjoyed a cooked breakfast. They looked forward to seeing their sons and Margaret in the afternoon. They all had a chat and a few bottles of porter and, of course, a chat about life in general. After the Rosary was said, the visitors returned home.

Bill and Brian looked forward to St Stephen's Day, 26 December, when the Kildare hunt assembled in the centre of the village, before heading off on a cross country fox hunt. The 'toffs', sometimes referred to as 'the quality', showed off their beautiful, well-groomed hunters and their spectacular jackets in green and red. Top hats and bonnets were worn together with expensive, black, English riding boots and tan breeches. They sipped their brandies and whiskeys from their hip flasks and chatted excitedly about the route the hunt would take. The women rode side-saddle and the younger riders often wore black hunt coats and some rode on ponies. Brian looked after Major O'Kelly's hunter mare. It was a magnificent animal and the Major was very proud of her. Brian ensured she was in tip top condition for the post-Christmas outing. The Master of the Hounds ensured the beagles were also in good condition and eager for the chase.

Soon the hunt was ready to leave the village. The horn was sounded, the beagles barked excitedly and the horses' hooves clattered their way out the Edenderry Road and on into the first field. Local farmers gave permission for the hunt to gallop across them. The day was frosty and the ground hard, which was better than the wet soggy ground they sometimes experienced. Bill and Brian waved them off. The local boys and girls ran with the riders to open the gates and hopefully be thrown a few pennies. When the hounds and horns faded into the distance, the brothers retired to Dillon's public house for a few jars. These they thoroughly enjoyed, sitting by the roaring turf fire. The cold frosty day added to the pleasure. Many of the men came to say hello to Bill and asked about life in the 'big smoke'.

Next day, Bill said goodbye to Mags and his brother, Brian brought him by pony and trap to the train station in Kildare Town. He felt sad leaving the countryside that he grew up in. He gazed at the plains of Kildare and the Hill of Allen and wondered why he ever left them.

Kathleen and May O'Connor had a long train journey to their home place in Castlemaine, County Kerry. They had to change trains at Mallow and continue on to Tralee. Brother Pat could not make it. He was still locked out of work and money was scarce. He often relied on his sisters to feed him. He also wanted to remain in Dublin, to see how things were developing. There was talk of the unions having to give in to the employers, thus revoking the lock outs. He was not happy about it but, frankly, he was fed up being out of work. Also, families were suffering much and he decided to help with the soup kitchens over the Christmas period.

Their father, Michael O'Connor, met the girls at the train station and was very pleased to see them again. They had a lot to catch up on at home. He embraced and kissed them both and loaded their luggage onto the 'family' ass and cart. He lit his pipe and off they went on their homeward journey. It was an eight-mile trek to the old, thatched cottage. The ass did well. The road to Castlemaine was rough and bumpy but they were pleased to be home again.

Their mother, Breda, was waiting at the half door of the old, thatched cottage when they pulled into the yard. Her tears of joy could not be held back as she rushed out to give her daughters a huge hug and a big kiss. The girls were also overcome, as they had not been home since the summer. Candles flickered as in greeting in the front windows and the fire in the hearth blazed, as if in excitement, as they entered the large front room.

Kathleen and May were very tired. They hugged their younger brother, Tim and went to their bedroom to change their clothes and have a quick wash and freshen up. Their mother had two basins ready for them and a large jug of hot water and soap. Soon they returned to the kitchen and were given hot cups of tea and homemade soda bread. Father had a glass of Irish whiskey. The family chatted until late. Life in Dublin was eagerly enquired about, especially the trouble with the unions and employers. When the girls began to doze after the Rosary was recited, all retired to bed.

On Christmas morning, the O'Connor family boarded the ass and cart and headed into the village for first Mass. Kathleen and May were warmly greeted by their neighbours and friends. All said how lovely they looked and admired their 'city' clothes.

Father and Tim attended to the chores of their little farm when they got home, having changed into their working, everyday duds. The cows had to be milked and the chickens, geese and ducks fed. The morning was damp but mild.

Breda cooked a delicious roast goose dinner with all the trimmings, which the whole family enjoyed. Afterwards, the girls and their mother went for a walk down the lane and they caught up with the local news, including weddings, courtships and funerals.

St Stephen's Day dawned with a hard frost. It was a relaxing day and, in the evening, the 'Wren' boys were expected. Kathleen and May, in particular, looked forward to this event. Also known as the 'Straw' boys, local and neighbouring boys, and some girls, dressed up in old clothing and often straw hats. They disguised their faces with mud and paint. They called from house to house playing music and dancing. They invited the younger occupants to join in the fun, which they usually did. They were given a few pennies, brown bread and cake and lemonade if it was available.

They recited or sang the following poem:

The wren the wren the king of all birds,
On St Stephen's Day it was caught in the furze.
Up with the kettle and down with the pan.
Give me a penny to bury the wren.

The O'Connor girls always joined in the fun and danced with the boys, trying desperately to identify who they were. It was really a good evening and they were all sad when the boys and girls moved on.

Kathleen wondered how Bill Byrne was enjoying the festive season. She really liked him and enjoyed his company very much – especially the dancing. She knew her mother and father would never accept a police constable into the family, which made her sad. After all, everyone was Irish but hatred of the law was endemic in the southwest of Ireland in particular.

The girls returned to Dublin on the train. There were the sad goodbyes and promises to come home again soon. They were sad to leave the dewy hills of Kerry once again and wondered if they would ever return to live in that part of Ireland.

In February 1914, Sergeant Daly called Bill into his office. He told him that his transfer request was successful and that they would be stationed in Naas, County Kildare. He was to report to the RIC police station there in two weeks. It was not very near Rathangan but Bill didn't mind. He was delighted and thanked the sergeant very much. Sergeant Daly even said that he was sad to lose such a good officer but he understood the reasons for his transfer.

Bill felt a bit sad to leave Dublin City as he enjoyed the parks, especially St Stephen's Green and the strand around Ringsend but he knew he had to go, as he still didn't feel safe there and then, he hadn't seen Kathleen for so long. He thought about writing to her again but decided to leave it for now.

Later in the week, Bill took a train to Naas. He went to the police station and met the sergeant in charge. Sergeant O'Brien welcomed him to the RIC and to the station. He was shown where he would live, which was a room in a family home. He was introduced to the lady of the house and he soon realised that police constables were welcome in the town – a bit different to Dublin. Many of the towns in County Kildare had RIC barracks and then there was the British Military camp in the Curragh. Most of the soldiers were from County Kildare and many also came from other parts of the country. Many families had fathers and sons in the army and some went back several generations. The British Army was the main employer for this part of the world and many families depended totally on it.

Bill was told to report to the barracks in ten days' time, when he would be shown the ropes and given familiarisation in the procedures of his new force, the Royal Irish Constabulary. He was also told that he would be trained in the handling of firearms, as the DMP were an unarmed force. Bill was pleased to find out that the RIC were paid more than the DMP.

The sergeant said things were quiet in County Kildare, which was more than could be said for many parts of the country. The RIC had a rule that officers were not allowed to serve in the county of their birth. However, Bill was born in Edenderry, County Offaly and lived there until he was fourteen. Later he moved with his family, less than ten miles away, to Rathangan in County Kildare. His father had got a job as a ploughman on an estate there.

CHAPTER SIX

War to End Wars

1915. John experiencing war in the trenches and worrying about his family back home

John Brennan joined his regiment in early December 1915 and travelled by train to London's Waterloo Station. The station was packed with servicemen returning from France and Belgium and others going in the opposite direction. The men who had been at the Front had a strange look on their dirty faces. Some of their uniforms still bore the mud of the trenches. He boarded a train for the coast. The carriages were actually horse trucks, which had been 'converted' to carry passengers. There was straw on the floors and the men were packed into them. The countryside, on the way down, was bleak and the weather was wet and miserable. John thought about what lay ahead: was he right in signing up at all?

In September that year, both the British and the French armies launched full-scale offensives against the German Lines in France. The Germans were prepared for them and the offensives, for the most part, failed. The British attack at Loos resulted in eight thousand men being killed and wounded. They had achieved very little at such a great cost.

In October, Sir John French, the Lord Lieutenant of Ireland, announced that 10,000 recruits from Ireland were needed at the Front the following month and a steady flow of eleven hundred per week after that. John's Leinster Regiment was included in the initial flow of Irish recruits.

The sea crossing was rough in the cold and windy December weather. On arriving at Boulogne, the regiment was transported to Ypres, close to the Western Front. The train stopped on several occasions for a 'shit/piss' stop. The men de-boarded and lined up to empty their bowels. When the whistle blew, they tidied themselves up as best they could and re-boarded.

John was a bit shocked at the state of the transport system. In Ypres, which was barely recognisable as a town, with bombed out streets, etc, British soldiers were 'resting' from battle. They were pleased to see replacements arriving. John noticed they looked noticeably tired and thin. They drank beer and frequented houses of 'ill repute' to try to have a good time and to forget the horrors of the trenches.

John and his companions were billeted in what remained of a hotel, where they rested after their journey from Aldershot. The men were given a 'communal' shower. It consisted of stripping off and lining up on duckboards. Cold water was simply poured over them. They often had difficulty relocating their uniforms, which were piled in a heap on the floor nearby. They made their way to the public houses and indulged in some liquid refreshment. Some actually availed of the services of the local ladies. John, however, did not and was happy to get some beer in and chat to his mates about what they expected to happen next. Some were eager to get stuck into the 'hun' whilst others preferred to get drunk and forget about tomorrow. Stories they heard from the battle-hardened troops in the town were horrific. Many of the new recruits chose to disbelieve them, thinking they were being spun yarns since most of them were Irish.

Next day the men of the Leinster Regiment were marched to the Front. They could hear the battle noises from far off. Shells burst and machine guns rattled. They entered the trenches and took cover. They awaited their orders. Some froze with fear; others were hyperactive and couldn't settle.

The days turned into weeks and John kept his head down. The winter grew colder and the rain fell steadily. Christmas approached and the thoughts of home, of Mary and the children never left his head. He missed them so much. He wrote a letter to Mary, not giving any information about the war, as was required by the censors. Some of his fellow soldiers had already been killed and many others injured. He told her how much he missed them all and hoped to see them in the New Year. Mary sent him presents of socks and tobacco, which he was very pleased to receive. Christmas Day was a lonely one. There wasn't much action. John managed to get to Mass, which was said by an Irish priest, Father John Murphy from Cork. He received Holy Communion, giving him some peace of mind. The officers gave the troops small pieces of chocolate, a bottle of beer and some French cigarettes. They wished them a happy Christmas and looked forward to a peaceful new year.

Mary also sent John a Christmas letter but it did not arrive till three days afterwards:

10 Barrow Street
Dublin

Christmas 1915

My dearest John,

This is to wish you a very happy Christmas and we all hope to see you in the New Year. Michael and Bridget, and especially myself, miss you very, very much. This is our first Christmas apart and the winter has been very cold and dark. The evenings are terrible without you around. Our bed is very lonely and cold and I wish you never signed up to go to the war. We get little news in the papers about what is happening out there. All we read about is how well the allies are advancing and pushing back the Germans. I hear of husbands and sons being wounded and some sadly killed. I pray every day that God will look after you and keep you safe. Please be careful and stay out of harm's way.

There is some good news, which I hope you are happy about: I am pregnant. It must have happened that last night we were together, as I am gone about three months. I am very happy to carry our third baby but, I very, very much long for you to be here when he or she arrives. I hope to God this terrible war ends soon; I really do.

Well, my love, I hope you are well and that the army is looking after you. It must be tough at times in that foreign land.

Michael and Bridget send their love, as do I. I managed to get them a few things, out of the army money, to put in their stockings for Christmas morning. They are really looking forward to Santy coming. We are going to Mammy and Daddy's for dinner, so that will be nice.

I really love you, John. Come home soon please, please.

Your darling wife,

Mary

xxxxx

John was shocked and immediately began to worry more about his little family back home in Dublin. What had he done? He thought he should never have decided to join up. They would have survived without the extra money from the army. He was sure of it.

The fighting continued into the New Year. The trenches became damper and some even flooded. Men were suffering from trench foot, from standing in mud and water for hours on end and also, frost bite. Mites, lice, bugs and rats were a constant annoyance for them and a huge health hazard. The lice infected their uniforms and the men often drew blood, scratching themselves. Soldiers were lost when they sank, often with their horses, in the mud and either suffocated or drowned. Many dead horses and mules lay rotting in the battle area. The stench was almost unbearable. Horses were the main means of transporting ammunition and general supplies to the troops. They weren't treated very well.

The trenches were mostly dug about two metres deep and a little less wide. Barbed wire was laid along the tops. Troops normally spent about eight days in the front-line trenches and then four days in the reserve trenches. Trenches were dug in threes, a front-line trench, a centre line trench and a reserve trench. The last was the safest, as it was usually out of the range of enemy fire. Communication trenches linked the three. Every four or five weeks or so, the troops were given 'leave' in a village/town several miles from the fighting. This was very much looked forward.

Because of the trench system, the Allies and the Germans were at a stalemate. In the early part of the year, British and French forces made numerous attempts at breaking through the German lines. A little was gained but casualties were heavy.

On 21 February 1916 the Battle of Verdun began. It would last until December, the longest battle of the war. It involved the German and French armies. The stalemate on the Western Front continued partly because German troops were moved to Verdun.

John Brennan was content with the situation. There was, of course, much shelling of the trenches and snipers succeeded in finding their targets on both sides. The noise of battle was deafening but there was a daily routine that could, be at times, be a little boring. The food was also boring and monotonous: mostly bully beef. One recipe that the cooks were to follow was to boil 5 cow heads – beef stew?

However, men were dying and being wounded every day. John witnessed indescribable horrors. One day, in the centre trench, John was taking a short break and was chatting to a comrade. When his comrade stood up to return to the front trench, he was hit in the head by a sniper's bullet. He died instantly. John was splattered with his blood. It was difficult for John to believe what now he got used to – seeing death on a daily basis. What did life and death mean anymore? He crawled back to alert his officer. The horror of war was dawning on the troops in this, the second year. There was little sense of adventure or excitement now.

The weather was improving as the spring approached. Some of the men hoped that this was a sign of better days to come and that the war would come to a close by the summer.

One spring morning Mary Brennan was sweeping the step of her house in Barrow Street. The morning was bright and clear. Michael was at school; young Bridget was inside, asleep in her cot. She noticed a telegram boy cycling up the street. She froze. Had he got one of those dreadful telegrams for her? She was so relieved when he passed by, she had to go inside and sit down. Her unborn baby kicked in her womb. She thought of John and wondered how things were in that dreadful war. The newspapers gave little information of what really went on at the Front. She just hoped he was safe and well. She said a little prayer to Saint Theresa, the Little Flower, in whom she trusted very much. A picture of the saint hung above her bed. Bridget awoke from her nap.

A few days later, there was a knock on the door. Mary again feared the worst but, to her surprise, it was her friend, Mrs Wilson from Grand Canal Street. Mrs Wilson was pale and looked terrible. Her hands shook.

'What's the matter, Mrs Wilson? Are you unwell?'

'Ah Mary, I've had some awful news.'

'What is it? What is it?'

'My dear son, Paddy was killed in France,' tears rolled down her face.

'Sit down Mrs Wilson. That's terrible. I'll make ye a cuppa tay.'

Mrs Wilson handed Mary the letter. Mary took it and it read:

B.E. Forces, France

4 April 1916

Dear Madam – it is with most sincere regret that I have to write and tell you that your son, No. 32856, Private P Wilson, of my Company, has been killed in action, about 3.30pm on 4 April 1916. My officers and men, one and all, join me in my desire to convey to you the great loss your son is to, not only his parents and relatives but his King and country and also, to my Company. He was a brave, reliable and smart soldier and a credit to the corps. I am arranging that his body be brought back from the trenches and that he will be interred in the cemetery by a Catholic priest, with full military honours. He will be greatly missed by both officers and men but it is gratifying to know that he died the death of a soldier, fighting for a great cause and no man can do more than give his life for his King and country. I may state that he was instantly killed by shell fire and it will be something to know that the end was sudden and painless. Please accept the most sincere sympathy of officers and men of the Company in your great bereavement.

Yours sincerely

T. Wilkinson (Captain)

O.C. 113 Company, France, 4 April 1916

Paddy Wilson was only twenty-two and had been in France for just three months. Mrs Wilson was devastated.

'Me poor Paddy, he was only a gossoon. I'll ne'er see him again. I t'ought they would bring him home to be buried in Irish soil, beside his Da.'

'Now Mrs Wilson, don't be upsettin' yerself. They'll bring him home when the war is over; I'm sure they will. Now there's your tay and I'll get you a little sup a whiskey in a minute.'

Mary thought the letter to be cold and impersonal. She dreaded getting something like that if anything happened to her husband. God forbid!

The fighting in the trenches grew fiercer. In early March, the Germans were pushing hard for a win. John's battalion had been about nine days in this pitched battle. Late in the afternoon, the Germans, while continuing to bombard the British positions, released a poisonous gas – a thick, yellow-greenish vapour – and then rattled the tops of the parapet with machine gun fire. The gas was terrible. Men were coughing and choking. The officers called along the trenches for men to dip their handkerchiefs and/or rags in water and place them over their mouths and noses.

The enemy could not advance because of their own gas, which gave the troops a chance to get out to the rear trenches and recover. John, however, was caught with a severe reaction and slumped in the centre trench. A comrade dragged him to the reserve one, where he was given first aid. In the meantime, the Germans advanced across no man's land but they were met with machine gun fire, as most of the soldiers had recovered from the attack and returned to the front trench.

There were many casualties. John was taken to the regimental aid post behind the lines. His breathing became worse and he struggled to remain conscious. Many wounded soldiers were being treated at the post. Some had been hit by shrapnel and others by bullets. Those affected by gas were in various stages of pain and discomfort. Those seriously affected were screaming in agony. One unfortunate soldier was even demanding to be shot, as his suffering was so unbearable. Others were blinded and totally confused.

CHAPTER SEVEN

Crisis and Opportunity

August 1914. Bill Byrne is now stationed in Naas. In Kildare, the outbreak of war is marked largely with celebrations.

Constable Bill Byrne enjoyed his new job in Naas. In the spring of 1914 things were quiet in the town and his job was routine but mostly trouble free. There was the occasional disturbance from the tinkers or travelling people and the local hooligans in the pubs. Also he had to sober up a drunk or two in the street but nothing very serious normally happened.

In the summer he got leave to visit his family in Rathangan. He stayed with both his brother and his wife and with his parents. Brian and Mags gave him the good news that she was expecting their first baby early the next year. They were very excited.

Again, he enjoyed the country life, the open fields, the haymaking and the gardening. He liked to walk along the canal and listen to the bird song. He heard a distant cuckoo and, in the meadows, a corncrake called unceasingly. He watched a heron snatch a tasty meal, in the form of a passing frog, from the still water.

He partook in a little fishing, with Brian, on the canal banks. The solitude was wonderful, especially when he remembered the noisy riots in Dublin. Bill's parents were very pleased to have him stay a few nights. They chatted about times gone by. He helped them with the gardening. They discussed the current political situation in Ireland. Would Home Rule be introduced? They hoped it would.

However, apart from the long-drawn-out issue of the Irish Question, another problem was coming to a head. The assassination of Archduke Ferdinand in Serbia on 28 June caused the many alliances of the main European countries to indicate that there might be trouble and even war. Some thought it would never come to this but others were worried.

All too soon Bill's holiday was over and he made his way back to Naas. It was the last week in July and he was told by his sergeant that it looked like a war would come. The Austria-Hungarian Empire declared war on Serbia on 28 July, followed by Germany declaring war on Russia and France on 1 August. This brought things to a head. When German troops entered Belgium, Britain declared war on Germany on 4 August. The outbreak of war was based on alliances only, threatening a member of one alliance drew the other members into the war. This didn't make sense.

There was great excitement in Naas when the news reached the town. Two days later, following the Mobilisation Order issued by the government, around three hundred reservists of the Royal Dublin Fusiliers were met at the depot by the local band of the Irish Volunteers. They were men of all ages. Some had been in the army maybe five-to-eight years earlier.

The *Kildare Observer* reported that:

> *When the hour for departure came, the gates of the barracks were surrounded by a large crowd of friends and relatives of the departing soldiers, which was considerably augmented when the band of the local Volunteer corps arrived, accompanied by a green banner with the inscriptions 'Nás na Ríogh' (Naas of the Kings) and 'Nás Abu'.*

> *The platform and bridges (of the railway station) were densely crowded with spectators, and as the train steamed out, amid the strains of 'Auld Lang Syne', played by the Volunteer Band and the explosion of fog signals, there was a remarkable demonstration on the part of the spectators, who cheered the men vociferously, hats, handkerchiefs and umbrellas being wildly waved.*

The cheers, needless to say, were heartily returned by the
departing soldiers, who, in a few minutes were beyond earshot,
and on their way to their destination.

Bill was on duty that day and witnessed the whole thing. When crowds cheered the departing troops and banners were waved, he found it hard to believe what was happening? He was sure this wouldn't have happened in Dublin. Most people in Kildare appeared to believe in what John Redmond was saying about going to war for the defence of small nations, which would result in freedom for Ireland. As stated before, many families, especially the poorer ones, relied heavily on the British Army for their livelihood. The Kildare County Council actually passed a resolution that was adopted. It "endorsed the action of Mr John Redmond, pledging the support of the National Volunteers to defend our shores against invasion..."

The *Kildare Observer* was a pro-British newspaper. Its rival, The *Leinster Leader*, had a pro-nationalist editor, Michael O'Kelly, whose staunch views were reflected in his newspaper. He was a strong supporter of the Irish Volunteers (Óglaigh na hÉireann). The true feelings of the people of Naas and indeed, the county of Kildare, were not reflected in the celebrations following the announcement that Britain was going to war.

Bill's surmise of these 'celebrations' not happening in Dublin was right. When the war began in earnest, in September 1914, a small group of committed republicans and socialists were meeting in the capital. They were determined that since 'England's difficulty was Ireland's opportunity', an Irish insurrection during this time had to be organised. They had different ideas about the freedom of Ireland than that of Mr Redmond.

When the excitement died down, Bill continued with his police duties. The county benefitted greatly from recruits passing through the camp at the Curragh and the barracks at Naas, which was the headquarters of the Royal Dublin Fusiliers. Local traders were very pleased.

When he was off at the weekend, he often attended a dance in Lawlor's ballroom. The girls were very friendly and he enjoyed dancing with them. However, he couldn't get Kathleen O'Connor out of his mind. He decided to write to her in Dublin. He hoped that she might agree to meet him some place where he wasn't well known. She wrote back to say she would meet him in Naas but she would bring her sister, May with her. He wasn't too pleased about her sister coming but at least he would see her again. They agreed a date and he looked forward to it very much. Kathleen was also looking forward to it. She had gone to dances in Dublin but none of the men she met were like Bill. All this war business changed things. Young men were volunteering and she often found that there were more girls than boys at these dances.

One morning in November Bill made his way to the railway station. He was excited that at last he would meet Kathleen again. He saw the plumes of smoke in the distance as the train approached. Soon, it was pulling into the station. Passengers began to alight. His eyes searched through the crowd and then he saw her. As usual she looked radiant. She wore a beautiful cream hat and a black, full-length coat with a fur collar. Her sister walked beside her in a less fashionable coat and hat but also looked very elegant. He rushed over to them and gave Kathleen a kiss and a hug. May simply offered her gloved hand, which he shook. They chatted as they left the station and made their way down the town. They had tea in a local cafe. Bill was a little annoyed that May was acting chaperone and he was unable to say what he wanted to Kathleen. *Never mind*, he thought, she came to see him and that gave him hope. It was a step in the right direction.

Bill had arranged a bed and breakfast house for the girls. They stayed for two nights, Friday and Saturday. Kathleen was still employed at Clery's department store. Things had settled down since the infamous 'lockouts'. This pleased her and, with the war breaking out, she thought she could be in a position to discuss her relationship with Bill (if it developed further) with her brother, Pat. Pat was employed again with the Irish Independent and seemed to have settled down. She hoped that meeting Bill again would mean that they could get to know each other and move forward.

On the Saturday, the three of them did some window shopping and Kathleen even bought some local bread and bacon to bring back to Dublin. May became more friendly and they enjoyed their day. In the evening, they went dancing at Lawlor's Ballroom. May got many dances and Bill and Kathleen got closer as they too danced. They had a wonderful evening.

On Sunday, they all went to Mass and had lunch in Lawlor's Hotel. The weather was cold and frosty but sunny. After lunch, they had a walk out of the town and passed the hospital. The fields were frost covered. The cattle munched their fodder, blowing out steam-like breath through their nostrils. Rabbits scurried into the warmth of the hedges, having searched in vain for food in the cold grass.

As the afternoon advanced, the sun sank slowly behind the bare trees and they made their way back to collect their bags and head to the station. Bill kissed both girls goodbye there and whispered to Kathleen, as they embraced, how he enjoyed her company and promised to write soon. She invited him to Dublin in the New Year. Yes, things were moving forward.

Bill returned to his digs in great form. Yes, he was in love and started to count the days to when he would meet his sweetheart again. He would again spend Christmas with Brian and Mags and also visit his parents in Rathangan. Kathleen and May were going home to Castlemaine again too.

CHAPTER EIGHT

Home Leave

John arrives home to a temporary respite – a changed man in a changed world.

Spring 1916: John Brennan continued to suffer from the after-effects of his gassing in the trench. He had been moved to the Casualty Clearing Station. He was in a ward where again, men were suffering badly from their injuries. Many had limbs amputated, either from severe damage and/or gangrene. Others were suffering from shell shock and wandered about the station, not knowing where they were or what was going on.

Some high-ranking officers took a dim view of this, so called, mental state and suspected that some soldiers were faking it. Men were even shot by firing squad for desertion when, in fact, they were suffering from shell shock. Others wandered from their trenches into no man's land and were shot either by the enemy or, sometimes their own comrades who believed them to be Germans.

One morning, when the doctors came around, he was given the good news that he was being sent home to Dublin for three weeks, to recover. John was extremely delighted. He would see Mary and the children soon again. He looked forward so much to leaving this hell hole and experience normal life once more. He couldn't wait to write to his wife and give her the great news. Their new baby would arrive in about three months. He was a bit disappointed that he wouldn't be there for the birth but, at least he would be with his beloved family once more.

John sailed from Boulogne to Dover, was taken by train to London and then, after a rest of a day there, he was put on a train to Holyhead. Life seemed to be a bit unreal to him. It seemed to be going on as near to normal as was possible. He was pleased with the comrades who accompanied him on the journey. They chatted about the horrors of war and how and where they received their injuries. Many could not really remember much. Some were badly wounded and had to be stretchered. Others were suffering from shellshock, with symptoms such as shaking, unable to speak and deep depression.

Irish servicemen were destined for the Royal Hospital in Kilmainham, Dublin to continue their recovery, if that was possible. There was little hope for many. At least John had all his limbs but his breathing was still giving him trouble. He had to give up smoking which he really enjoyed. The journey was tiring and tedious but the thought of meeting Mary and the children again kept him going.

Mary was overjoyed to get the letter from John. She could not contain her happiness. She dismissed the fact that he would only be home for a few weeks but to see him again would be heaven.

At last John's ship sailed towards Kingstown (Dún Laoire) Harbour. He had seen the east coast of Ireland from miles out. The Wicklow and Dublin Mountains looked so blue and welcoming. It gave him a feeling of peace and joy, which he had not experienced in a long, long time. As the ship drew closer to the harbour, he noticed a small crowd waiting on the quay. They waved excitedly and he searched their faces to see if Mary was among them. He was disappointed when he came ashore but Mary was not to be seen. Then he remembered her pregnancy and of course the children. He felt a bit silly to think that she would be in a position to meet him, of course not!

John Brennan boarded the train for his final journey home. He made his way up Great Brunswick Street, over the bridge at Boland's Mills, into Barrow Street and knocked on number ten. Mary opened the door and immediately hugged her husband. She wept with joy. His uniform smelled stale and rough but to hold him again was out of this world. The feeling was mutual except that Mary was so soft and feminine and smelled of pure woman. Her bump was now quite large and he didn't want to hug her very tightly even though he found it hard to resist. He was so pleased to be home. Inside he found his little daughter Bridget, now two years old, waiting in the kitchen. She was very shy and didn't recognise her father. Her mother came in, lifted her up and said, 'Don't you know your daddy?'

Her father had a little present for her, a bar of Fry's chocolate. He handed it to her, which she was reluctant to take but Mammy said, 'Take it, Darlin'. It's a present from Daddy.'

Mary put the kettle on and they both sat at the table while Bridget tucked into her present. Michael was at school. He was now nearly six. Mary noticed that John was coughing quite a lot and this worried her.

'John, have ye got a cold?'

'No Pet, it's the auld gas, don't worry about it, the doc said it will pass soon.'

'It's great to see ye, Darlin'. I was so worried when Mrs Wilson's son was killed.'

'Ah it'll take a lot to knock me off; the war isn't so bad really,' he lied.

As the day went on Mary noticed a change in her husband. He seemed to be very quiet at times. He had a wash, changed his clothes and the three of them made their way to the school, to collect Michael. The little boy saw his daddy immediately and rushed over to give him a massive hug. He was so pleased to see him that he too wept. John had the same present for his son, who held it to his chest. A whole bar of chocolate for himself! What a treat!

Mary suggested that John go to the pub after tea and have himself a pint but all John wanted to do was to stay at home with his beautiful wife, sit by the fire and enjoy being close to her once again. She asked about the war in France but he was reluctant to talk about it.

'Ah sure, life was a bit rough and ready and the grub was poor, but my comrades were very friendly. Sadly, I lost a few but such is life.'

He didn't elaborate any further and Mary got the message. She too was very pleased to sit by the fire and hold his hand. The baby moved in her womb and she dismissed the thought from her mind that John would, more than likely, not be at home for the birth but, they were together now and that was all that mattered.

The days passed and they enjoyed every minute of his leave. Mary was concerned, as John was having nightmares most nights. He told her not to worry, as the doctors had told him that it would pass. He had to go, several times, to the Royal Hospital to be checked by the medical team. He was told that his lungs were improving and that he should have a full recovery.

The weather was improving as spring arrived. It was now the end of March. They took a tram to Sandymount Strand and walked along the sea front, taking in the fresh sea air. Daffodils and snowdrops were appearing everywhere and the evenings were getting longer day by day. Yes, spring was here at last. John felt it was helping his breathing and his cough was not as frequent or rough as before. Sadly, he knew that he would soon be certified fit for duty, which meant that he would have to return to France and the Western Front. He immediately dismissed the thought. Life was for here and now.

One morning in early April the dreaded letter arrived. He was to report for duty in Ypres (which was miss-pronounced by the troops as 'Wipers') in four days' time. The goodbyes, this time, seemed even harder on John, Mary and the children. The night before he had felt his son or daughter move in his wife's womb. It was wonderful to feel new life, especially one containing his blood. He thought of all the loss of life he had witnessed in France in the previous months. There life was cheap. His comrades had sacrificed theirs and for what? More lives would be lost in the months and maybe even years to come. There was no end to the slaughter in sight. John pondered these things as he journeyed to the Western Front. Would he see his family again? Mary was thinking the same.

CHAPTER NINE

Romance Blossoms

Bill and Kathleen resume their relationship and begin to make plans for a future together.

Bill Byrne and Kathleen O'Connor communicated regularly by letter. In February 1915, they arranged to meet in Dublin. Bill got the train to Kingsbridge Station in the west of the city and took a tram to O'Connell Bridge, where he waited for Kathleen. She was late and he began to worry that she wouldn't show up. At last, he spotted her walking up Westmoreland Street.

As usual, she looked fantastic in her long winter black coat and matching leather boots. She wore a black bonnet and a grey scarf. They embraced and walked hand in hand down Sackville Street and had lunch near the Pillar. The day was cold and there was a promise of some showers but the lovers were only interested in each other.

They chatted over lunch and planned what they would do over the weekend. On Saturday, they did some shopping in Grafton Street and had a walk in St Stephen's Green. In the evening, they went to a dance in their old haunt, the AOH in Parnell Square. All too soon their weekend together was coming to an end.

On Sunday they went to visit Kathleen's sister, May and had lunch with her. May was pleased to see Bill again and thought they made a lovely couple. In the afternoon, they had a stroll along the banks of the Grand Canal. They discussed when they could meet again and both hoped it would be soon. Bill kissed Kathleen goodbye and said that he loved her. She was taken aback but gave him a long lingering kiss, which he took to mean that she loved him too. He boarded the tram to Kingsbridge station, waving goodbye as it trundled away. Kathleen did love him but was too shy to admit it.

From August 1914 to August 1915, approximately eighty thousand Irishmen enlisted in the British Army, peaking at the end of December, when the total was approaching forty-three thousand. The New Year saw a slight decline, which would continue rapidly through 1915. Reports of the wholesale slaughter of troops in the war, many of whom were Irish, resulted in this decline. Many RIC men had volunteered, both in Dublin and the rest of the country. The army was grateful for these men, as they were already trained in handling firearms and policing in general. However, this meant that there was a shortage of policemen, especially in the capital.

In the spring of 1915, Constable Bill Byrne received a letter from his superiors, to say that he was required to relocate to Dublin due to this shortage. He would return to his old barracks in Great Brunswick Street. Bill was pleased, as it would mean that he could see Kathleen every week. He wrote to her almost immediately.

Kathleen was delighted when she received the letter. She had been recently promoted in her job in Clery's. She was now a supervisor and her money had gone up considerably. She put some of it away in a post office savings account. If all went well in her relationship with Bill, maybe they could save for a deposit on a little house. Would he now ask her to marry her? She hoped that he would.

On a fine day in May, Bill arrived with his luggage at Kingsbridge. He was sad to leave Naas and his native county but he looked forward to living near his sweetheart again. He had managed to get a room again in Barrow Street. His old landlady, Mrs Kilduff, was pleased to see him. He settled into his familiar surroundings. He put his stuff away and left the house for a walk to Grand Canal Quay. He crossed the bridge to the banks of the Liffey. He saw the ships over at the North Wall discharging and loading cargo. He noticed several naval vessels anchored there, which reminded him that the war was still in progress. The May sunshine was very pleasant and he watched as the sun set behind the city. He had bittersweet memories of Dublin and he hoped that there would be no more trouble like that he experienced two years before.

He reported for duty the next day. Sergeant Daly was still in charge and was as grumpy as ever.

'Ah Constable Byrne, I thought I'd see you again. The super thought you were having too good a time down there in the sticks; so it's back to reality for you, me lad.'

'T'ank you Sergeant. Glad I was missed,' he replied sarcastically.

Later in the week, Bill was pleased to meet his old colleague and friend, Tom Dempsey. They promised to have a couple jars when they had a day off. Bill looked forward to it.

The next weekend, Bill and Kathleen met at the Pillar. They went to a film and on Sunday night, they went dancing at the AOH. They were both happy at how their relationship was progressing. Kathleen said that her brother was still not enamoured with the fact that Bill was in the RIC but was willing to overlook it, as long as she was happy but, 'if he mistreats you,' he warned 'I will have him.'

They had a wonderful summer together. Things were fine in the city and Bill enjoyed his job there. Kathleen was happy with her job in Clery's too.

Kathleen went home to Kerry for two weeks in August, as usual. Her parents and family were delighted to see her. The weather was lovely with only a couple of days of rain. She helped bring in the hay and help with farming in general. She got blisters on her hands, not being used to the manual work. Also, after such work, her whole body ached but she slept very well.

Her father kept sheep on which the family greatly depended to simply exist. Life was hard but her father and brother managed to put food on the table. Her mother also helped. Kathleen saved up some money, which she donated to the family purse. Her parents were grateful.

Some evenings, she went with her mother to 'rambling' houses, where all the news and local gossip was discussed. Fewer men from that part of the country enlisted in the British Army, so the existence of the 'Great War' was not topical. Some of the local RIC men did join up but, as mentioned before, policemen were viewed with suspicion. She also enjoyed nights of music and dancing in these houses, which often went on into the early hours.

On the second Sunday, Kathleen went on a day trip to Dingle with three of her old school friends. She enjoyed the day very much. The scenery was spectacular. The cool, clear Atlantic air was so refreshing. Alas, however, the holiday came to an end. She told the family about Bill but left out his profession – she wanted to tell them but was afraid of possible adverse reaction.

Bill met his friend, Tom for a drink in Merrion Square. Bill was surprised at how many RIC officers had enlisted in the army and were away fighting in France. He was equally surprised at how many had already been killed and injured there.

'Remember Peter McDonagh, who was on our shift, Bill?'

'Yeah, Tom. He was a good friend. He joined around the same time as me.'

'Got shot on the Western Front in March; lived for a few days but never recovered.'

'That's very sad. Did they bring his body back home?'

'No, it seems the policy is to bury them near where they died. I hope his grave is marked.'

Tom said that many men in Dublin enlisted when the war began but the numbers had declined during 1915. Like the Brennans, many families were benefiting from the 'separation money' that they received. He didn't fancy joining up, as he heard the reports of the horrific casualties and deaths, which appeared to be increasing day by day. He said that he heard, from undercover detectives, that there were rumours of some kind of an insurrection being planned by the IRB (Irish Republican Brotherhood). He told Bill to 'keep it under his hat'. He didn't think anything would come of it.

The pair met regularly for a few pints and a chat. They both liked to have a 'flutter' on the horses and several times, they went to the races at Baldoyle and Punchestown. They never won much but they enjoyed the atmosphere and the craic.

Bill saw Kathleen regularly too and their relationship got better and better. He brought her to the All-Ireland football final on 7 November. Kerry played Wexford at Croke Park. Sadly for Kathleen and Bill, Kerry lost by three points. However they enjoyed the game, even though it was a cold day. She consoled herself in remembering Kerry had beaten the same team the year before – in a replay.

On Christmas Eve they met once again at the Pillar. They went to the pictures and enjoyed the short films. Afterwards they had a drink in the Batchelor's Inn on the quays. There was music playing and the craic was great. The pub was packed so they couldn't talk very much. Bill had something to say and was a bit worried she wouldn't be able to hear him. However, in the interval, when it was quieter, Bill turned to Kathleen.

'Kathleen, I love you so much.'

'I love you too Bill.'

'Will you marry me?'

'Oh my God! Of course I will, Bill.'

From his waistcoat pocket, he produced a ring, which he had saved up for over many months. It was a small gold ring with an even smaller diamond. She loved it and was totally overwhelmed and kissed him firmly on the lips. People at the bar turned around and cheered. It was a wonderful moment. Bill bought drinks all around. It was a wonderful night.

On Christmas Day they had dinner with May in her flat. May was delighted for them. Their brother, Pat called later and congratulated them both. He could not hide the fact that he was not that friendly towards Bill but he knew that Kathleen loved him, so he put the fact that he was an RIC man to the back of his mind, at least for the present.

Bill and Kathleen discussed their wedding plans. They decided to have it in May 1916, in the Sacred Heart Church in Milltown near Castlemaine but Bill had to write to her father, asking his permission first. Kathleen was very excited. They would write to the parish priest as soon as her father agreed.

The wedding breakfast would take place in her home, as was the tradition. She started to make a list of guests and, of course, all their aunts and uncles would have to be included. Bill thought his parents would not be able to attend, as it would be too far for them. He doubted that many of his aunts or uncles would come either. His brother and his wife would most certainly come; at least, he hoped so. They looked forward to being man and wife so much.

CHAPTER TEN

Death and Resurrection

Once again, John is witnessing the horrors of war. Back in Ireland, a terrible beauty is being born.

In the middle of April 1916 John Brennan joined the Leinster Regiment in Ypres. As he approached the town, he could hear again the sounds of battle and his blood ran cold. The scene in Ypres was depressing. Men were taking a break from the trenches; many looked tired and emotional. There was a lot of drinking going on and some were availing of the services provided by the local 'ladies of the night'.

John had a couple of beers with a few lads of the Royal Dublin Fusiliers. One actual Dubliner, Mick O'Connell, asked how his home city was and told John how much he wanted to be there again.

'Were ye down at the Pillar at all, John?'

'Bedad, I was Mick. It's still there and Nelson is even still at the top, looking down at everyone.'

'Ah, what I'd give to be there now, enjoying a pint in Mulligan's.'

'Sure you'll be there sooner than ye t'ink Mick, dis auld war must be nearly over.'

'Ah I don't know about dat, John; the Germans are giving as much as they get. Sometimes, I t'ink I'll never see auld Dublin again.'

Next day John marched to the Front. Shells were exploding all around. The noise was something else. His ears rang. Bullets screamed past, ricocheting off stones, posts, etc. Yes, he was back at war alright. He kept his head down in the front trench. Bodies lay decomposing in no man's land and the stench was unbearable. Day turned to night and back today. However, the weather was improving: it didn't rain so much anymore. After a few days, the fighting became almost routine. Men died and men were wounded. The troops went back to the reserve trenches to rest. Reinforcements arrived to replace the dead. Less and less Irish Volunteers came.

John's breathing was getting worse with the smell of cordite, dead bodies, smoke and even traces of that dreaded toxic gas. Because of this, he was relieved of trench duty and was given the task of helping with the big guns, some distance behind them. He was given training in setting up the guns and determining the required range to set in order to avoid 'friendly' casualties.

He wondered why he had been certified fit for duty. He thought, perhaps that because the army was getting so short of 'cannon fodder', the medical people were being pressured into cutting corners.

He wondered how Mary was getting on with her pregnancy and how she managed to look after the children. He worried about them all.

Mary was, indeed, struggling with her condition. Her neighbours were a great help. If she was unwell, one of the local mothers brought Michael and Bridget to school. She was finding it hard to do some of the housework due to her large bump. She wished her husband could come home; she missed him very much. There were a lot of stories going around about husbands and sons being killed and injured in the war. The disastrous campaign in Gallipoli, which ended in January, was responsible for many deaths. Irish troops suffered badly. She still dreaded that telegram or letter.

News came through in the late afternoon of Easter Monday, 24 April, that there was trouble in the city. There were reports of much shooting and that the GPO had been taken over by rebels. Military men, policemen and rebels were reported to have been killed. Mary found it hard to believe but she spoke to eyewitnesses who confirmed the goings on. A young lad came running down Barrow Street screaming. There were men with guns in Boland's Mill and they were shooting at the RIC officers. The men who took over Boland's Mill were under the command of Éamon de Valera, the future Taoiseach and President of Ireland.

Had the war come to Dublin? Mary thought, maybe the Germans had arrived at Dublin Port and were taking over the city. What would now happen to herself and her children? She was frightened. Later, Mrs Wilson called to give her further news. She said that the IRB and the Irish Volunteers were staging a rebellion against British Rule.

'Did ya hear the latest, Mary?'

'No, Mrs Wilson. What's goin' on?'

'A bunch of lunies have taken over the GPO. They say that Ireland is now a republic.'

'Ah go on! A republic – what does that mean?'

'I don't really know, Mary. I hope we will still get the separation money.'

'I hope so too; it's a handy few bob.'

On 1 March 1915, the Soldiers' Separation Allowances increased for a private's wife and two children to 21 shillings a week. Mrs Wilson's allowance was ten shillings, as her son had been killed. Had he lived, she would have received 17 shillings and 6 pence per week. She didn't deserve to have her money cut, since her son gave his life for 'his king and country.'

Constable Bill Byrne was off duty that weekend and had met his fiancée Kathleen at the Pillar, on Easter Sunday evening. They went to the AOH for a dance. Lent was now over and dances were at last permitted by the Archbishop of Dublin. They enjoyed the evening very much. Afterwards, they went to a Lyons tea house and enjoyed a chat and a smoke. They were in love.

He walked her home to her flat in Dame Street. She invited him in for more 'tea' but they had to sneak in, to avoid the landlady discovering the violation of her rule: 'No boyfriends in the rooms'. They did have tea and a cigarette. They embraced, which led to passionate kissing. They cuddled each other as they kissed but Kathleen drew the line when Bill's hand wandered a bit too low. However, she permitted him to caress her beautiful breasts for a short period but then suggested that he go home, as both of them were getting a bit too excited.

He agreed and said he very much looked forward to their wedding day, on 10 May, less than three weeks away. She said she looked forward to it too and that she loved him very much. He said that he loved her too and slipped away, quietly down the stairs, closing the front door gently behind him. It would be the last time he would ever see her alive.

Bill heard a knock on the door at half past midday on that Easter Monday. He had not long finished his breakfast, having had a lovely long lie-in. He had sweet dreams of his fiancée. There was an RIC constable at the door. He was told to dress quickly and report for duty at the station. There were some disturbances in Dublin Castle and Sackville Street. Reinforcements were urgently required.

Bill put on his uniform and headed down to the station. It was a warm, sunny afternoon. Officers were arriving, others milling about, changing into uniforms, donning helmets and selecting and checking their firearms. Bill wondered what was happening in the city centre. After all, it was a beautiful bank holiday Monday. Why would there be a disturbance?

His unit assembled on O'Connell Bridge. There was some commotion going on at the GPO down Sackville Street. Passengers on the upper decks of trams, at the terminus by Nelson's Pillar, noticed a man in military uniform standing outside the GPO, reading a proclamation and wondered what was going on.

A band of volunteers marched from Liberty Hall, up Abbey Street and into Sackville Street. The shoppers looked on in bemusement and some even jeered. The band then charged the GPO and smashed the windows. Shots were fired from it and returned by the military and the policemen. There were soldiers reinforcing the DMP and RIC officers. A DMP policeman, James O'Brien, had already been killed at Dublin Castle – the first policeman to die on that day.

Barricades were erected by the rebels in Abbey Street. A tram was overturned. A bicycle shop was broken into, to provide material for the barricades. This resulted in civilians looting it and other shops. Another two policemen were killed and the order was for the DMP and RIC men to be withdrawn. Bill Byrne was included in this withdrawal.

A contingent of British Lancers moved down Sackville Street, towards the Pillar and were fired on from the GPO. Several of them and their horses were killed. The first fire in Sackville Street started at 9.30 pm, in a looted shoe shop. By the end of the day, 15 civilians, including 9 children, 11 rebels, 28 military and 3 policemen had been fatally wounded. Some of the children were killed searching for food.*

On Tuesday, the 25th, the Rising continued. There was some confusion as to what was happening. The only newspaper published was *The Irish Times* but the rebels were disappointed that there wasn't much mention of the insurrection.

Bill was again on duty, mostly dealing with shop looting. Many civilians were arrested. The rebel leaders, Patrick Pearse and James Connolly, were worried about the looting. Pearse issued a message, saying that looting was being done by 'hangers-on of the British Army' and that 'Ireland must keep her new honour unsmirched.'

He had already issued a 'Manifesto to the Citizens of Dublin' via printed handbills as follows: 'The country is rising in answer to Dublin's call and the final achievement of Ireland's freedom is now, with God's help, only a matter of days.'

---

* For more on this aspect, see *Children of the Rising: The untold story of the young lives lost during Easter 1916* by Joe Duffy (Hachette Books Ireland, 2015)

Kathleen went to work in Clery's, as usual that morning and was surprised to see what was happening. Her department store had not been affected by the looting so far. She noticed that there was a large presence of British troops in the centre of the city. It was estimated that as many as seven thousand were now in place there. Martial law had been proclaimed. Barricades were being erected at almost every street corner. She wondered where Bill was and that if he was safe.

The beginning of the repression of the 'Rising' was assisted by the fact that many 'Irish' soldiers were home on leave or on recruitment duties in Dublin from the war and were drafted into the army. Reinforcements were also drafted in from the British Army Camp at the Curragh.

Kathleen watched from the second-floor window of her women's clothing department. Some customers had come in to shop; others came in because they were frightened. Kathleen helped her colleagues to make tea for them, as few were interested in making any purchases. Gunfire could be heard from what seemed to be every part of the city. A battle was taking place at Amiens Street railway station, where rebels were attempting to prevent British reinforcements from making their way to the city centre. After lunch, it was decided, by the management, that the store would close.

Fighting in and around the GPO intensified and the safety of Clery's employees could not be guaranteed. British snipers had positioned themselves on the roof and at windows of Trinity College and were firing towards the GPO.

Kathleen left the building and walked towards O'Connell Bridge. Many of her fellow civilians made it as far as the bridge and immediately turned left down Custom House Quay. Kathleen was just about to turn when she was hit by a sniper's bullet, which had ricocheted off the bridge wall and went straight through her neck, severing an artery. She collapsed on the pavement hitting her head on it. Her dear friend, Mary McKenna tried to revive her but she was already dead. Mary whispered an act of contrition in her ear. A priest was requested by one of the bystanders.

Kathleen O'Connor, aged twenty-three, was one of the 21 civilians, including 5 children, to die on that day.

CHAPTER ELEVEN

Destruction and Despair

*The events of Easter 1916 cast a long shadow and for some,
take a heavy, personal toll.*

Next day, 26 April, the Irish Citizen Army, formed after the
1913 Lockout, hoisted its flag over the Clery's/Imperial Hotel
building, which was owned by the employers' leader, William
Martin Murphy.

Constable Bill Byrne had worked almost seventeen hours
the day before. He was exhausted. He awoke to the sound of
gunfire. He dressed and had breakfast and made his way to the
barracks. He had to take another route, due to the occupation
of Boland's Mill.

A British gunboat on the Liffey, the *Helga*, destroyed the empty
Liberty Hall at 8am. Bill was sent to O'Connell Bridge. He had
to retreat, as the military were persistently machine-gunning
the GPO from there. Later in the day, the military began to shell
the same building from D'Olier Street. It was around that time
when a telegram was handed to Bill. He felt weak at the knees
and wondered what had happened. Was there a family death?
He opened it and read:

> Constable William Byrne No. 650 RIC Dublin
>
> *Regret to inform you STOP that your fiancée Kathleen
> O'Connor STOP was fatally wounded in Sackville Street
> STOP at 2.30pm on April 25th, 1916 RIP STOP*
>
> Chief Constable Anthony McCluskey STOP

Bill staggered and had to be supported by a colleague. At first,
he thought it was a mistake, that they had got it wrong. He had
to sit on a wall near Trinity College. The British Army was now

in full swing, shelling the rebels. Many buildings in Sackville Street were now ablaze. The noise was deafening.

A fellow officer called his sergeant, who read the telegram. Bill was relieved of his duties and sent back to the station. The city he grew to love was disintegrating around him and his personal world had collapsed completely. He was unable to return to his flat, due to the escalation of the fighting. The Battle of Mount Street Bridge was taking place. Two British battalions coming from Kingstown (Dún Laoire) were held down by thirteen rebels. There were over two hundred British casualties. So Bill just sat in the canteen and stared out the window, not noticing the smoke rising from beyond the streets. He had to see his beloved Kathleen once more, he had to find out where her body lay.

Kathleen's body was removed to the Mater Hospital, having been given the Last Rites by a passing priest. The nurses, most of whom were nuns, were horrified to see such a young pretty woman being brought in. This was their first day receiving the wounded and the dead from the Rising. People were realising that this was not just a token protest against British Rule – the rebels meant business. Bread, milk and basic food was beginning to become scarce and many families were going hungry, especially in the city centre.

At last, Bill made contact with Kathleen's sister, May. She told him that the body had been removed to the Mater. He made haste to the hospital, avoiding the troubled areas, which meant that it took quite a long time. He was shown to the mortuary and when he saw her lifeless body, he collapsed in tears. Never was he so distraught in all his life. The beautiful life they planned together was lost forever. How could he go on without her now? May came into the mortuary and threw her arms around him. They both sobbed uncontrollably.

Mary Brennan was worried about her two children and her unborn baby. Food was in short supply. Mrs Wilson came to see her and gave what rations she could spare.

'How are ye doin', Mary?'

'Janey, Mrs Wilson, I am very worried for the children: there is not much food for dem to ate.'

'Here's are few little bits dat may help, Mary but I heard there was flour to be got free at Boland's Mill.'

'T'anks. You're very good. I'll get young Johnny, next door, to see if he can get me some flour.'

'Ye know, Mary, maybe the rebels are right. Look what happened to my dear Paddy; what did he die for? If the British weren't in Ireland, he would still be alive.'

'It's hard to know, Mrs Wilson. I'm very worried about my dear John. I wish he were here with me and dat he never joined up.'

Everyone in Barrow Street were now wondering what was going to happen. Many widows and spouses depended very much on the 'separation money' from the British Army. Since the GPO was by now practically destroyed, there was no way they would get their money that week. The schools were closed on Tuesday, the 25th and for the rest of the week. Mary saw the British gunboat pass upriver along the Liffey. Later in the week, the smoke was very visible from Barrow Street and at night, the sky appeared to be on fire.

John Brennan heard about the rebellion in Dublin during the week after Easter. He was at the Front, where the fighting was growing fiercer. That week, over 500 Irish soldiers lost their lives in the Great War. He was told by a Dublin Fusilier, when he was in the reserve trench on a break that much trouble was going on in the centre of the city. John couldn't believe it. He thought of Mary and the children. Would they be affected? He had to find out but the fighting continued and information about the Rising came in dribs and drabs.

John's unit were due a week's rest at Ypres. The men were relieved to get a break from the trenches. The weather was still improving. They were sad that many of their comrades were no longer with them. Many were dead and others badly wounded. The horrors went on. Many of the troops tried to forget them by indulging in alcohol and having the craic with their mates. John also went to the bars, to take his mind off his troubles. However, with the news from Dublin, some of their British comrades tended not to be very friendly. Remarks were made and some members of the Irish regiments were even jeered at.

'What are you paddies up to?'

'Go home, you fucking traitors.'

'Can't trust you lot, can we?'

'Bastards!'

It was difficult for the Irish lads. They were having mixed feelings about the war in general. They wondered what and for whom were they fighting. John could not get Mary, Michael and Bridget out of his mind ... and, of course, the unborn baby.

Kathleen O'Connor's funeral took place in St Francis Xavier Church, Gardiner Street in Dublin. The troubles were still going on in the city. Her body was removed to the church on the Wednesday evening. The funeral was shared with three other families, as deaths of civilians were increasing. One was a young boy aged only eight.

There was a large crowd gathered in Gardiner Street. The bell tolled loudly. Bill's friend, Tom Dempsey, accompanied him to the church. May and Pat O'Connor were also comforting each other as the coffins were carried in. Kathleen's parents were unable to make the journey. They were distraught, as was her brother, Tim, who could not come either. After the service, Bill, May and Pat greeted each other and Bill introduced Tom. They went for a drink in Dorset Street and tried their best to drown their sorrows.

Next day, after ten o'clock Mass, Kathleen's body was taken, together with the other victims, to Glasnevin Cemetery, where she was laid to rest. The four hearses had to have permission to pass through the cordon set up by the British Army to contain the rebellion. The continuous shelling and gunfire could be heard as they moved towards the cemetery. Smoke could be seen in the distance. Bill, with the help of May, Pat and Tom, was just about able to compose himself at the graveside. Flashes of his happy time with Kathleen went through his mind: her lovely face, her smile, her kind nature, her voice, her laugh – he recalled it all. Life looked so bleak now; how could he go on without her? Tears ran down his face.

Thursday, 27 April 1916, following the intensive shelling by the military, the Imperial Hotel/Clery's building collapsed.

> *And Nelson on his pillar**
> *Watching his world collapse*
> – Louis MacNeice, *DUBLIN*

---

* Opened in 1809, celebrating the Battle of Trafalgar, Nelson's Pillar survived the 1916 Easter Rising. It lasted another 50 years when the IRA blew it up, in March 1966.

Chapter Twelve
Change and Sacrifice

*The rebels surrender but soon, executions and imprisonments
alter the public perception in Ireland.*

Mary Brennan and her neighbours were almost prisoners in their streets while Boland's Mill was occupied by the rebels. Some civilians were killed and injured in the skirmishes around the mill. It was dangerous to go too near to that area. Some rations were getting through but Mary still worried about her children. However, on the afternoon of Saturday, 29 April, Patrick Pearse surrendered to the military, mostly to prevent any further civilian loss of life.

The following morning, the rebels in other areas, including Boland's mill, also surrendered. The prisoners were marched from the Rotunda Hospital grounds, where some had been kept overnight, to Richmond Barracks. Some of the crowd who lined the route jeered and others even spat at them. The centre of the city was practically destroyed and people were hungry and very tired of it all.

However, the mood of the population of Dublin and the rest of Ireland changed dramatically in May, when the rebels were executed in Kilmainham Gaol. Between 3-12 May, fifteen rebel leaders were shot, including the seven signatories of the Proclamation. The first executions took place only two days after the last rebel surrendered. The last to be shot was James Connolly, tied to a chair. It was a huge mistake by the British Military Governor, General Sir John Maxwell, who seemingly misread the situation. Maxwell had been appointed 'supreme military governor' and given carte blanche to deal with the situation.

After the Rising, over three thousand men and women were arrested in Dublin and the rest of Ireland. Many of them were sent to prisons in England and Wales, where they were interred without trial. Quite a few of the prisoners were transported by cattle boat. The guards were issued with life belts, in case they were torpedoed by the Germans but the prisoners were not. This infuriated the population at large and anti-British feeling increased throughout the country.

On 21 May, Maxwell visited Maynooth College, to reprimand the president for giving his blessing to the men from the town who marched to Dublin to join the rebellion. He was told, in no uncertain terms, that his interference was not acceptable.

Mary was pleased that the trouble appeared to be finally over. Bread and milk slowly became more available. She received a welcome letter from John, saying that he was in good form and that he hoped the rebellion had not affected her too much. As the month of May progressed, she felt that baby would soon be arriving. The weather improved and life was gradually becoming close to normal again. The centre of the city remained a mess. She managed to get her separation money paid once again from another post office.

Bill Byrne was still in a state of shock following Kathleen's untimely death. He struggled with life. Tom Dempsey persuaded him to return to work – which, eventually, he did. The two men sensed that the situation had very much changed in the city. The anti-British feelings were obvious. They didn't feel safe anymore. The case of the internees in British jails was reported widely in the newspapers.

Bill was reminded of Kathleen everywhere he went. The Pillar still stood in a devastated Sackville Street, which was a poignant reminder of the happy times they had after meeting there. The AOH dance hall had been spared in the shelling. It was getting unbearable, so he asked, once again, to be transferred to Naas.

Sergeant Daly was a bit more sympathetic this time and said he would have a word with the Chief Constable. He realised that Constable Byrne was suffering with his loss and he felt that, perhaps, he could no longer be relied on to perform his duties to the best of his abilities. A change from the city would be for the best. The sergeant explained this to Chief Constable McCluskey, who reluctantly agreed to the transfer. Bill was pleased and wrote to his brother in Rathangan, saying that he hoped to be back in Naas soon.

The Rising did not affect the Byrne family in Rathangan very much. Unlike Dublin, where families almost starved that week, country families had fresh vegetables, homemade bread and milk available in good supply. Poorer city families often relied on bread and tea and milk if they could afford it. When supplies were disrupted, there was almost a full famine.

Brian and Mags were shocked when they got Bill's telegram, to say Kathleen had been killed. They sent one back, sending their condolences and inviting him to spend some time with them. Their son, little Joseph, was now a year old and enjoying the spring weather. Mags was pregnant again and they looked forward to the new arrival towards the end of the year.

Major O'Kelly's son, John was already at the Western Front with the Dublin Fusiliers. The Major was very worried about him, as he saw the reports of the massive casualties in Flanders and only hoped that God would spare him.

The farm had been going well since the war began. There was much demand for vegetables and meat and prices had gone up. One of his labourers had also joined the 'Dublins' and was also at the Front.

His second son, George was still at college and decided not to enlist. The Major was pleased. There was some talk about conscription coming to Ireland but there was much opposition to it. The truth was that the British Army was running short of replacements.

Brian was busy on the farm. They were one workman short when Mick Sullivan joined up, in 1915. The *Leinster Leader* reported casualties, including two men from Rathangan. The families were devastated and it brought home the seriousness of the Great War. Many had lost their lives in areas such as Naas and Newbridge and, of course, the Curragh. Brian was pleased that his brother, Bill didn't enlist.

The news of the Rising came as a surprise to Brian and Mags. His friends in Dillon's pub had mixed feelings about it. Some still nurtured a traditional loyalty to the Crown, as it provided a living for many in the county. Others were delighted that, at last, there was a rebellion against it and hoped for Ireland to be free from foreign rule once and for all.

The Irish Volunteers had stirred up much nationalist feeling in the county just before the war broke out. Companies were formed in the towns of Maynooth, Celbridge and Newbridge. There was a lot of arguments as the porter flowed.

Many local families were getting the separation money and were worried that it would stop, when and if Ireland broke away from Britain. People looked forward to the weekly county newspapers, to see how events in Dublin were progressing. There was much sadness and anger when reports of the executions came through.

Later, the *Leinster Leader* reported that prisoners from Kildare, who were arrested after the Rising, were still being held in an English detention barracks without trial. However, the British, under pressure of bad publicity and a change of public opinion, decided to declare an amnesty on 21 December 1916. Most internees were then released for Christmas but, not all prisoners were released at that time and some would have to wait six months.

Bill tried his best to settle down to just being a policeman in Naas. He felt that the respect he was given, in his previous time in the town, was not now shown. He had spent some time with Brian and Mags, which took his mind off recent events. Again he enjoyed the summer weather, helping out on the farm. It was so different from the hell that Dublin had become. Over a dozen policemen were killed during the week of the Rising. This worried Bill. However, he kept his head down and carried on with his shift duties.

There was, of course, still British Army personnel in the town. The celebrations of 1914 seemed far behind now. As the war went on, many families lost loved ones and some had their loved ones return maimed and crippled. The mood was definitely changing.

Bill was often very lonely so, on his days off, he would often go to a pub, as far as possible from the town and indulge in a few drinks. He did not make friends with any of his colleagues in the barracks and kept himself to himself. The pub he chose would be within a reasonable cycling distance and he would be careful not to have too many drinks. This was fine in the summer months but, when winter set in, it was sometimes a bit more difficult to cycle back to his digs.

He was careful not to be recognised as an RIC man, so he never frequented the same pub two evenings in a row. He went to different places but always sat on his own, in a corner, away from the local clientele. Sometimes, fellow drinkers would try to get Bill involved in a conversation but when they got too friendly or inquisitive, he left. They thought him a strange customer and some suspected him to be a British spy.

A very pretty young lady once sat beside him and tried to chat him up. He simply answered any question with a yes, no or a silent 'No comment'. Finally he gave her the distinct impression that he was just not interested. She gave up and moved away.

In the spring of 1917, Bill cycled to a pub in the village of Kill, named the Dew Drop Inn, which was about four miles away. It was a lovely evening. The birds sang as he cycled along the winding road. The trees were beginning to dress in their summer attire and the setting sun slowly sank behind the far-off hills. The evenings were getting longer and this put him in a good mood.

He fancied a couple of pints of the best ale. The RIC barracks was situated directly opposite the pub. He chained up his bike and entered through the back door. He made himself comfortable on a barstool close to the door. He ordered a pint of his favourite ale. He lit a cigarette and began to read the *Leinster Observer*.

As he read the sports page, two men entered the backdoor. One stood and looked at him, he lowered his face to Bill's ear and said, 'Good evenin', Constable. How are ye t'day?'

Bill froze. *Who could this be?* he thought.

'Do I know you?' he asked.

'I'm sure ye do, auld friend. Remember the courthouse in Naas two weeks ago?'

Bill thought hard. Yes, he was a witness in a trial concerning an Irish Volunteer, who was later sent down for stealing a shotgun from a farmhouse.

'No, I don't remember,' he lied.

'Ye fucken lying, little bastard,' roared the stranger. 'You got me brother sent down for five years, so ye did.'

With that the man grabbed Bill around the neck and flung him to the floor. He kicked and punched him as he fell. Bill kicked him between the legs and the man fell backwards. The second man then jumped on Bill, throttling him. Bill hit him on the side of the head but he didn't budge. The first man was up again and laid into him, kicking and punching him. Men at the bar stood back as the two men got stuck into their victim.

Suddenly, two RIC officers appeared with batons drawn. They whacked the two assailants across the head and back with their batons and then, one of them fired a shot into the ceiling. There was silence. A third policeman arrived and they dragged the two men off Bill, who lay unconscious on the floor. One of them recognised him, telling the others that he was one of them.

The assailants were arrested and taken to the barracks. Bill was given first aid by the landlady. He came to. The third officer stayed with him. When Bill had sufficiently recovered, he too was escorted to the barracks. He was questioned by the sergeant and asked to make a statement. He was later taken back to his digs by taxi.

CHAPTER THIRTEEN

Presumed Dead

Battle of the Somme. Mary Brennan gives birth to a son but soon fears that she may have lost a husband.

On 4 June 1916 Mary gave birth to a baby boy. She decided to name him John, after his father but to lessen any confusion, she would call him Sean, the Irish version of John. Her mother and father looked after little Michael and Bridget. Her labour was long and painful but the midwife, Josie Smith, helped enormously. Again, she wished her husband were with her. Mrs Wilson came to see her and brought the usual kind little gifts for herself and the children.

'T'anks, Mrs Wilson. You're very good. I don't know what I'd do without ye.'

'Not a bother, Mary. Sure we have to look after each other in these hard times.'

Michael and Bridget were so delighted to see their new baby brother. They wanted to pick him up and kiss and cuddle him but their mother told them that they could do that later, when he got a bit bigger.

John got the news, the following week, that he was a father again. He was delighted but again wished that he were there. He was worried about the developments in the war. The stalemate situation at the Western Front continued. Casualties continued to occur on a larger and larger scale. The French were teetering on the brink of defeat at Verdun. The British reluctantly agreed to join in a huge Anglo-French offensive somewhere along the opposing lines, which would relieve pressure at Verdun and hopefully break through the German lines.

John and his comrades realised that there was something afoot but, of course, they were told nothing. He managed to send a short note to his wife, saying that he was very pleased about the arrival of their son and that all was well. He promised to write again very soon.

The British high Command, under General Sir Douglas Haig, wanted to begin the offensive in the Belgian region of Flanders but it was decided, as early as December 1915, to move further south to the Somme area. Because the French were under pressure in Verdun, the date of the attack on the German lines was brought forward to 1 July. The British were not happy with this, as they needed more time to prepare but the promise of the French cooperation and their predicament in Verdun compelled them to agree.

Haig was of the view that, although his army hadn't sufficient heavy artillery, the employment of many troops would eventually ensure a breakthrough. In fact, the British only had 34 pieces of heavy artillery of 9.2 inches or larger, whilst the French had twice as much. The French had less of the front to attack than the British. The French had also more experienced 'big gunner' personnel than their allies. General Haig didn't appear to realise or care that thousands of men would be killed and/or wounded.

The plan was to bombard the German lines for the best part of a week and then make a 'surprise' early morning attack. The British command convinced themselves that most of the German troops would have been killed in the bombardment and any survivors could simply be bayoneted or shot, clearing the way to victory.

They did find out, through reconnaissance that the enemy had dug themselves very deep trenches, some 30 to 40 feet deep, reinforced with concrete, steel and timber. They managed to pack quite a few of them with high explosives and set them to explode just before the planned attack. Afterwards, it was suggested that many of the Germans merely sat in their 'comfortable' trenches, drank coffee, played cards and smoked while the British bombarded their position. However the truth was that many of them were killed and many more were severely injured. Quite a few of their trenches were destroyed but, there was enough of them left to man the machine guns and get ready for the Allied attack across no man's land, on 1 July.

John was fighting near Ypres, which meant his battalion would have to make their way south, to the River Somme area and miss the opening attack. As they marched, they could hear the bombardment in the distance. John wondered what lay ahead. His thoughts were of his family at home and wishing he were there with them. He wondered, as most of his comrades did, if he would ever see them again.

Just before the attack was launched, the British commanders were optimistic that their plan had worked. The infantry was to advance in long waves, followed by more waves at one-minute intervals. The officers believed that the unrelenting bombardment had weakened the enemy to such an extent that the troops would have a safe passage across no man's land. However, almost as soon as the barrage had ceased, the German artillery counterattack swept away most of the first wave of British troops. Included in the first of the casualties was Captain John O'Kelly from Rathangan, son of Major George O'Kelly. Within minutes of going over the top, he was mowed down by machine gun fire. He didn't stand a chance.

The soldiers were required to carry around 70 pounds of equipment, which included ammunition, food and gear (spades and/or shovels, etc) to enable them to establish a stronghold on the acquired enemy line. They were to walk upright at a reasonable pace and it was expected that any barbed wire would already be sufficiently cut to allow uninhibited access to the German trenches. The first day would see almost 60,000 British casualties, including nearly 20,000 fatalities. 4000 'Irish troops' lost their lives, most of whom were from the 36th (Ulster) Division – 'Carson's UVF in Khaki'.

The German counter-barrage attack severed telephone lines to the British command headquarters and it was assumed that all was going well. Further waves of men were ordered to follow their comrades into absolute slaughter. Many were killed before they even left their trench. Some managed to get across but were caught up in barbed wire and were simply picked off by the enemy. One German soldier reported that they were very surprised to see lines and lines of men appearing across no man's land. All they had to do was fire into them – no aiming was required.

The carnage continued for days. John's battalion soon came on the scene. They saw the dead and the wounded and the general horrors of war but were ordered to get involved in the intense fighting. Gains had been made by the British and John was among troops taking the village of Ginchy, forcing the Germans to retreat. His unit fought for days to hold on to their prize.

All around, territory was being gained and lost by both sides. Many of John's comrades were wounded and killed and things looked very bleak indeed. They held on to their now almost destroyed village as long as they could, until they were gradually forced back by the enemy. Men fell as they retreated but John remained upright.

Mary Brennan was finding it difficult to look after three children, mostly on her own. Michael was four, Bridget two and the four-week-old baby, Sean. Her neighbours were very helpful, which was a gift. Sometimes, her parents also gave her a hand. She was pleased that July had come and that the summer was here. The school was on holiday, which was another bonus but she still had to feed the baby in the night, which meant that she was permanently tired.

Mary had not heard from John for some time. There were reports in the newspapers of a major battle in France, along the River Somme. Of course, there were casualties but the reports told of advances by the British and French armies. She tried not to read any newspaper articles and reports on the war. As the month progressed, she became more and more worried. She usually got a letter from John every two or three weeks but now, it was now over a month. She prayed that he was safe. Her worries made sleeping more difficult and she often asked Mrs Wilson to come and look after the children. Mrs Wilson always obliged.

Mary received a letter from the British Expeditionary Force in France. Her heart sank when it came through the door. Was it that dreaded news that many of her fellow army wives had already received? She sent a neighbour's young boy to ask for Mrs Wilson to come quickly. Mrs Wilson soon arrived. Mary was sitting by the fireplace holding the letter in her hand and weeping.

'Ah Mrs Wilson, t'anks for comin'. I got this letter from the army and I'm afraid to open it.'

'Let me have a look, Mary; it may not be as bad as ye t'ink.'

Mary handed her the letter and Mrs Wilson opened and read it.

'What does it say, what does it say,' Mary cried. 'Please tell me.'

Mrs Wilson sat down opposite Mary and began, 'It's from the army as ye say. It says that John is missing in action and...... presumed dead.'

Mary fainted in her chair and Mrs Wilson rushed over to catch her before she fell to the floor. They both wept uncontrollably. Mary held her friend tightly.

'Me poor John!' she sobbed. 'Me poor John. What will happen to us now and the children without a daddy? What can I tell them?'

Mrs Wilson calmed her down a little and put the kettle on.

'It doesn't say he is actually dead, does it? It says he is only presumed so. We can only hope and pray that he is still alive and may yet turn up.'

This was little consolation for Mary. Her world had collapsed and she couldn't imagine a life without her husband. Life was hard enough in Dublin after the rebellion but she always believed that John would return again.

CHAPTER FOURTEEN

Telegram

War continues to take its toll, wreaking sadness upon families and playing havoc with best laid plans.

As already mentioned, the county of Kildare was doing quite well since the war began. Farmers were producing food, which included cattle and sheep. The stud farms provided many horses for the army. Much of the foodstuff was being exported to England. The shopkeepers and traders were making money from the large British Army camp in the Curragh and from the various barracks around the county. Troops were coming and going – all good for trade.

Major George O'Kelly was doing well also. A lot of his land was now being used to produce vegetables instead of grazing cattle. There was extra money for the farm labourers including Brian Byrne. Conscription had been introduced in early 1916 in Britain but there was fierce opposition to it in Ireland. This meant that farm labourers in Britain were becoming scarce, which made further demands on Ireland to produce more food.

Life had little changed for Brian and Mags since the Rising. There was plenty to do. Mags, unfortunately, lost her baby in early 1915. Her baby daughter was still born. She gave birth to her son Joseph on 1 March. She was still not quite able to carry out any heavy work, but she helped out where she could. She weeded the vegetables, thinned turnips, etc. She had her baby son to look after.

Bill had come for a short holiday before he took up his job in Naas. He was a changed man since Kathleen was killed. He was moping about the house and was often very depressed. They worried about him.

Major O'Kelly sat in his study reading *The Irish Times*. He read about the great offensive that the British and French allies had launched against the German lines on the Western Front. He had just returned from his morning walk through his grounds. It was a beautiful summer's morning but he could not help thinking about his son in the battlefield. He had a premonition that something was wrong.

He then spied the lone telegram boy cycling up the avenue. He knew the worst had happened and slowly walked into the hall to answer the door. He read the telegram with shaking hands. It was dated 15 July 1916 and said that the Commander regretted that his son, Captain John O'Kelly, was fatally wounded on 1 July 1916. There was the usual nonsense about how brave and courageous his son had been, how everyone was very fond of him and how he served his king and country, etc.

He was numb. Gone was his first-born son and heir. What a price he had to pay for this senseless war. Maybe he could have done something to get John a position where he didn't have to go to the Front. His wife, Elizabeth, appeared at his side, looked in his eyes and saw the despair there and knew that the news was the worst. They held each other and cried. They wondered how they could tell their daughter, Martina and their second son, George junior.

The Major glanced around the large entrance hall and his eyes rested on the photograph of his son graduating from Sandhurst. How handsome he looked in his uniform. Both his mother and himself were so proud of him. Now, it was all gone. John was only twenty-five. He had all his life in front of him. He would have inherited this estate and, perhaps, married into one of the great landowning families.

The Major walked to the garden. The plants and flowers were in full summer bloom. He loved the rose garden. He adored the scent of the different varieties and their beautiful shades of pinks and reds and yellows. He remembered bringing his first-born little boy here. How he used to run around the lawns, hiding behind the scrubs and laughing as he ran from place to place. Yes, he loved his other children dearly but his first son would always be special. The first child always is. Now he had to come to terms with the fact that he would never come home. No more would he greet him with a hug as he arrived in the house. No more would he go horse riding with him and enjoy a chat in the drawing room later, over a glass of fine old whiskey. They used to discuss army life and the ways and ills of the world. He wondered how he could go on.

He walked down the avenue, not really knowing where he was going. The trees were in full bloom but he failed to notice them. His mind was numb.

'Good mornin' Major,' came a voice from the lodge house. It was Brian Byrne. 'How is t'ings this mornin', sir?'

The Major couldn't find the words to answer his employee. He stood up straight, adjusted his stiff upper lip, 'Ah Byrne, I was miles away. How are things on the farm?'

'Fine sir, yeah everything is fine.'

'Glad to hear it, I'm afraid we got some bad news, Byrne.'

'Really sir, what is it?'

'Sadly, Captain John was wounded fatally in France.'

'Really sir, I am very, very sorry to hear it. Master John was such a lovely young fellow; we all loved him very much.'

'Yes, thanks Byrne. We are so very sorry too but these things happen in war. War is so terrible; I have to admit.'

'Yeah, it is Major. What about Mick Sullivan? He bought it in Gallipoli last year. His family was devastated.'

'Yes, I agree, Byrne. It is devastating indeed.'

The Major went on his way down the road, not knowing where he was going or what he should be doing. Life was changed forever. He wandered in a daze for about an hour, until he met a fellow landowner, Sir Reginald Williams, driving in his new Model T Ford.

'Good morning, Major. Enjoying a morning stroll? Beautiful day, isn't it?'

The Major told him about the death of his son. Sir Reginald was deeply sorry and asked him to pass on his condolences to his wife and family. The Major accepted a lift with his friend and alighted at his own gates.

When the days and weeks passed, he came to terms with the situation to a degree. He still thought about his son, day and night. The Major realised that his country was changing fast. The old order that existed up to 1914 and the outbreak of war was slowly evaporating. As already stated, anti-British feelings had increased since the executions in Dublin. The rebellion had been very badly handled by the British government. General Maxwell should never have been given carte blanche to deal with the aftermath.

In fact, the British government was, all but in name, a military government. Prime Minister H.H. Asquith had lost control over events when he agreed to allow a cabinet committee to direct the war, with the exclusion of himself. David Lloyd George had made the suggestion. Asquith resigned in December 1916 and was succeeded by Lloyd George.

The participants in the Rising and others who were suspected of being collaborators in the rebellion, had been imprisoned, mostly in British camps/prisons but it was a mistake to house them in the same detention establishments. Radicalisation took place in these places and, when the prisoners were released, the seeds of the War of Independence had already been sown and were some were now bearing fruit.

CHAPTER FIFTEEN

Behind the Wire

Don't mention the war! John bears witness to yet another aspect of war as he becomes a prisoner of it.

John Brennan was struggling to defend the village of Ginchy. His comrades were falling fast around him. He thought his time would soon be up and he said a silent prayer to St Therese. A shell exploded quite close and he was bowled over by the blast.

John came to, smelled the cordite and heard the noise of the battle as it continued. He opened his eyes to see two German soldiers staring down at him. Their guns were trained on him. He could feel no pain. Where was he, he wondered? Was this a dream, a nightmare?

'Hallo englisch schweine,' said one of the enemy soldiers.

He could not speak; he was in shock.

'Get up! Get up!' the soldier ordered in perfect English.

John managed to sit up. One of the rifles poked him in the chest.

'GET UP, I SAID, GET UP!' the soldier shouted.

John struggled to his feet, feeling weak and a bit dazed. He raised his hands.

'Turn around; keep your hands up.'

John obeyed.

'Now walk. WALK!'

The German soldiers marched their prisoner back to their resting area. John saw several British and French soldiers there. Their hands were tied behind their backs. Some were wounded and were unable to stand. They had been given First Aid. Some wore bandages on arms, others on legs and a few around their heads. John recognised a few of them. They nodded to him.

He was brought to a medical centre, where he waited for a considerable time before he was examined by a doctor. He was told to strip and was given a full examination. The doctor told the 'Unteroffizer' (corporal) that Private John Brennan was fit for manual labour.

The corporal escorted John to a prisoner holding area, consisting of a barn-type wooden building. Most of the barn was built by the British and French prisoners themselves. He was given a meal of black coffee and black bread. He was allowed to associate with the other prisoners. There were some men from the Dublin Fusiliers among them. They chatted about how they were taken prisoner and how they were being treated. There were stories of men being beaten and abused by the German soldiers. They told John that some of their comrades had already been sent to the Eastern Front, to do forced labour in retaliation for Britain and France forcing German prisoners to work at their lines at the Western Front. Not many survived at the Eastern Front, due to cold, exposure, starvation and disease.

It was estimated that eight to nine million prisoners were taken during the Great War. The figures include both sides. Stories of maltreatment were rife, both in the German army and the Franco/British forces. Some, of course, were true. In 1916 the German prisoner of war camps experienced outbreaks of typhus and other diseases, mainly in Russia but also at the Western Front. It was legal, under international law at the time, to use prisoners of war for forced labour. However, only non-officer ranks were included under this law. Officers were normally held at different locations and not required to work.

Next day John was marched back with nine other men to the German lines. There, he was required to carry out forced labour, including carrying supplies and even ammunition to the German soldiers on the firing line. It was highly dangerous work and even on the first day, one of his comrades was killed. Other jobs included burying the dead and repairing damaged trenches.

The prisoners were often beaten if the guards thought they were slacking. They were given little food and expected to work long hours. In the evenings they were marched back to the camps. They got no cigarettes or reading material. John found it difficult to cope with his situation and was in constant fear of being beaten. Some nights, he slept in the open, as the summer was hot. The days were also hot, which made his work more difficult. Some prisoners were tied to posts and beaten, which apparently, was also a punishment for German troops who misbehaved.

The days ran into weeks and John was getting weaker from working long hours and not getting enough food. Dinner often consisted of items like horse beans, greased by margarine and a herring and black bread for supper. However, more food was usually provided, when working in the trenches, if there was enough left over from feeding the German soldiers. John also found it hard to sleep. His mind was on how his young family were coping, especially baby John.

One day in September, as the Battle of the Somme raged on and on, seemingly never ending, John was carrying ammunition to the front line. As he ducked through the back trenches with a heavy box of grenades, he was hit in the left arm by a sniper from the British line. The bullet went straight through his upper arm, fracturing his humerus. He dropped the box and fell to the ground. A German soldier dragged him to the rear trench. He was bleeding heavily and the soldier applied a tourniquet, which managed to stop it. John was able to sit up but was very dazed and shocked. He was given a drink and asked if he needed help to return to the safer area. John said he could make his way himself and off he went.

The loss of blood made him feel dizzy and he had to rest a few times. The pain was extreme. Eventually, he reached the prisoner camp, where he was given medical assistance. The doctor dressed and bandaged his wound and his arm was put in a splint. He was sent to his bunk and told to rest. He found it very difficult to rest, never mind sleep. There were no painkillers available.

Next day, John was brought to the medical centre and again, his wound was cleaned and dressed. Some ligaments had been damaged in his arm, which meant that he had difficulty moving it and also, his hand. He was deemed unfit for further manual labour.

After two weeks, he was sent to a prisoner of war camp at Limburg an Der Lahn in Germany. It was over 600 miles from the front. They were loaded into cattle trucks. The train took nearly 24 hours, stopping at many stations along the way. The trucks were very uncomfortable and cramped. Some found it hard to breath. Others just slumped on the floor and endured the journey as best they could.

Food was in short supply and as tasteless as ever. At some stations, the local people jeered at them, shouting obscenities and making gestures. The guards also joined in and several men were assaulted and generally abused. Propaganda and rumour led civilians and troops to believe that German soldiers were being brutally treated by the British, and now was their chance for retaliation. It was a long and tiresome journey for John and his comrades and they were pleased when at last they arrived at the camp.

The prisoners were taken to blocks where many men were already being housed. The conditions in these camps were unhygienic and lacking in any sort of comfort. Due to overcrowding, some men had to sleep on straw. There was one water pump per building, where men could obtain a drink and also have a sort of wash.

The guards sorted the new arrivals into those who appeared to be fit for manual labour and those who were wounded. They were medically checked at a later stage and, those who were fit were sent to work. Some were taken to farms and others to mines and building projects. The work was hard and the diet poor. However, the population of Germany, on the whole, were suffering from lack of nutrition from similarly poor diets.

Some prisoners would later die due to hard work, poor living conditions and malnutrition. Those who objected to working were forced to do so at the end of a bayonet. Occasionally, the camp was inspected by the Red Cross and by American diplomats but the Germans knew in advance and made sure that the camp looked well maintained, with safety equipment in place and that the prisoners were being well treated. Extra water facilities would be installed for the visits and extra bedding and blankets provided. However, when the inspections were over much, if not all, of these extras were removed.

John was monitored by the medical staff and his ability to work was assessed frequently. He was always hungry. His arm continued to be painful. It was now October and the weather grew colder and wetter. As the winter approached, many men suffered from cold and exposure. Some of the wounded died due to gangrene and other wound-related infections and diseases.

John was lucky. He was strong and kept himself focused. He liked to chat with his fellow prisoners, especially the Irishmen. They talked of home and their life before this terrible war. He reminded himself, from time to time, of the terror of the trenches. This made him feel somewhat grateful for being away from it all. He didn't miss the horrendous injuries and deaths that he witnessed and the deafening, relentless noise of war. It was very boring at times. Again, there was nothing to read and cigarettes were very scarce.

As Christmas approached, the men were delighted to be told that they could send a letter home. There were stipulations, however. They were required to report that they were well treated and well fed. Also, they were not to give any details of the war and if any return letters mentioned it, they would not receive them. John was over the moon. He could now write to dear Mary.

Limburg
Military Prison Camp
Germany

December 10th, 1916

My Dearest Mary,

I suppose you must be wondering why you haven't heard from me since the summer. I am well and I am being held in the above camp. I don't know what you have been told about my whereabouts. Don't worry, we are all being well treated and the food is good. I am in good health. I was wounded in July but I was unable to write to you till now. My arm is getting better day by day. Please send me some cigarettes (you know I prefer Woodbines) and some books. We have nothing to read here, only German books which I don't understand. I would love some Boland's bread and some Irish butter if you can manage it. A bit of Irish cheese would be lovely too. If you can fit in a jumper and socks, I'll be very grateful. You can send a parcel up to 10 pounds free of charge, don't put any stamps on it.

All I can say is that I miss you all very much. How is baby Sean? I'd love to see him. He must be getting big. Give my love and kisses to dear Bridget, Michael and baby Sean.

Love you lots and lots.

Your loving husband,

John

PS: Don't ask about the war.

Christmas Day in the camp was the same as any other. The men got an extra sausage for dinner. The black coffee and the black bread were as disgusting as ever.

In the New Year, parcels began to arrive from England and Ireland. There was food, cigarettes and clothing enclosed in these so-very-welcome packages. Some had special little gifts enclosed; photos of children and loved ones, chocolate, mementos of all kinds. It was a dream come true for men who were losing hope of ever hearing from their families again. The food supplemented the awful diet and was a lifeline for many. The cigarettes gave the prisoners a little relief from the hardship of prison life. Clothing gave them some protecting from the cold of a harsh winter.

On 9 January 1917, the usual consignment of parcels arrived. Some were from the Red Cross organisations in Britain and Ireland. There was also a few from Switzerland. They contained much welcome clothing and equally welcome food. One parcel was addressed to:

Pte John Brennan, Leinster Regiment

℅ Limburg Military Prison Camp, Germany.

John was overwhelmed. *A parcel from home for me*, he thought, *really!* He picked it up. He recognised Mary's handwriting. *Was it really her writing?* he thought. *Yes, it was!*

He held it for a while and thought of his little family back in Dublin. Then, he peeled off the brown paper. First there was a beautiful hand knitted woollen jumper in brown, within it were four pairs of grey socks, a box of Woodbines and some Fry's dark chocolate. Then, he saw the white Boland's bread. He couldn't resist tearing a piece of it away and gulping it down. What joy he felt. Also enclosed was some Irish cheddar, a half-pound of Irish butter and a several of books, including his favourite *Boys Own* publications. John was so pleased to get these beautiful presents that tears ran down his face. There was also a note from Mary which he held to his lips and kissed.

Mary Brennan had struggled to accept that John was dead. Since receiving the letter telling her that he was 'missing presumed dead', Mary could not come to terms with his death or to admit to herself that she was now a widow.

Mrs Wilson called to see her regularly, which was a blessing. The summer days were lovely, bright with the occasional shower. She often took her children for walks along the Liffey bank and sat by the strand at Ringsend. Soon, however, autumn arrived and the evenings shortened almost daily it seemed. Michael was back at school. Little Bridget and baby Sean needed her attention but she was pleased she had her children to love and take her mind off her troubles.

Mary dreaded the coming of winter and Christmas. Another Christmas without John was almost unbearable. As time went on, the realisation that he would probably never come home began to sink in. The children didn't ask about their father much now and she worried that they might be forgetting him. Of course, baby Sean had never seen him and was too young anyway. What was she going to do? She never told Michael or Bridget that he might be dead, or that they may never see him again. She just said that he should be home soon and that he was alright. She tried to convince herself as well but in reality, she couldn't.

Two days before Christmas, a letter appeared under her door. Mary picked it up and gasped. She recognised John's writing. She wondered if this was a letter he sent before he became officially 'missing' and delayed in transit or, did it mean that he was still alive? She tore open the envelope and snatched out the letter. It was from John and he was alive. She had to sit down. She read it a hundred times, it seemed and at last, she accepted the truth: her husband was not dead.

She ran next door to her neighbour and one of her neighbour's boys was sent to Mrs Wilson with the good news. Mary could not think of a better Christmas present. She was on cloud nine. She told Michael and Bridget that daddy was well and that she hoped he would be home in the New Year.

The cost of living in Dublin had risen quite a lot since the war began. Households were spending most of their meagre incomes on food, fuel and rent. There was seldom much left over. Much of the clothes that they wore were second hand or hand-me-downs but Mary made sure that a parcel for John would contain the best that she could afford. The woollen jumper was the most expensive but she was willing to sacrifice clothes for herself to buy it. When the parcel was packed and weighed – just under ten pounds – she enclosed her note.

My dearest husband John,

What a wonderful Christmas present was your very welcome letter. I was told you were missing and presumed dead. What a shock that was but I somehow believed, all along, that you were alive. I prayed night and day that you were and that you would return to us. Now I thank God that He has answered my prayers. All I need now is for you to be safe and return to us soon. Michael, Bridget and baby Sean send their love.

I love you so much.

Your loving wife

Mary xxxx

CHAPTER SIXTEEN

Occupational Hazards

An RIC raid, to recover arms, results in Bill's cover being blown.

Constable Bill Byrne was somewhat traumatised by the events in the Dew Drop Inn. The sergeant suggested that he spend some time in the office at the barracks when he returned to work. This he did. He was not yet fit for patrol duties.

By June 1917, Bill felt that he was ready for full duties. He always went on patrol with another officer. Naas had changed quite a lot. People seemed less friendly towards the police than in previous years. However, there were still the traders who did much business with the British Army. Many families still depended on the army for their livelihood. Most suffered losses in the war. Husbands, fathers and sons would never return. Some young men would never be the same again because of severe injuries, including losses of limbs. Others suffered from shellshock and mental problems and would never be themselves again.

Life had changed in Ireland, in general. The political situation changed. The population were no longer content with Home Rule but were now pressing for a country completely free of British rule. Bill knew that the Irish Volunteers were reorganising in Kildare. Joseph McGuinness was elected a Sinn Féin MP for South Longford in the May by-election, even though he was in jail in Lewes. He only won by thirty-seven votes. Sinn Féin's slogan was, 'Put him in to get him out'. Sinn Féin MPs did not take up their seats in Westminster anyway.

In August, Bill was selected, by the RIC, to take part in a surprise operation in County Kildare, under the supervision of County Inspector Kerry Supple. A convoy of cars raided several houses, starting at midnight. They were searching for Irish

Volunteer arms, which were suspected to be held in different districts, including Rathangan. Bill was not told which districts he would be raiding. He wondered if anyone might recognise him. Anyway, he thought that he would be alright because it was a dark night and it was raining quite heavily.

The car, a Vauxhall D-Type, British Army issue headed for Monasterevin first. His fellow officers were also a bit tense and nervous. They all carried firearms. The road was dark and wet and the driver had to drive quite slowly. Potholes were everywhere. They passed several cyclists returning from pubs, etc. They were difficult to see and one was just avoided by the unmarked car. The driver, who was the sergeant, told the officers where they were headed. Bill was pleased. Naas was over twenty miles from Monasterevin. It took them a long time to get to their first house. It was just outside the town.

The medium-sized farmhouse was in darkness. The RIC men alighted from the car, which was parked just outside the gate. They made their way across the yard to the big oaken door. The sergeant banged on it and shouted, 'Police! Open up!'

There was no response. He again thumped the door, giving it a couple of kicks at the same time. They heard the owner coming down the stairs shouting, 'Alright! Alright! I'm coming. Hould yer whisht.'

The two farm dogs went mental in the hayshed and came to see what was going on. The large farmer released the bolts and opened the heavy door. The police rushed in, pushing him aside. However Constable Bill was nipped in the rear end by one of the dogs. His flesh was not broken, due to the thickness of his police trousers but it hurt like hell.

'What the fuck is going on?' cried the farmer as they pushed past.

'We're searching your house; stand aside,' came the reply.

The four policemen emptied drawers, opened cupboards in the kitchen and reception room spilling their contents on the floor and, finding nothing, dashed upstairs. Wardrobes were flung open. Nora O'Neill leapt out of bed screeching, 'What do you want, you bastards?'

Dinney O'Neill dashed up to the bedroom shouting, 'Get out of my house you fuckin' cunts.'

He was ignored.

One constable lifted the double bed and found a gun case. It contained a double-barrelled shotgun.

'That's me farm gun; I am entitled to have it!' shouted farmer O'Neill.

'Over here, Sergeant,' yelled Constable Fleming.

The constable produced a .303 Lee Enfield rifle from the inside of the wardrobe.

'Is this your farm gun too, Mister O'Neill?'

Farmer O'Neill had no answer; he was holding the gun for the Irish Volunteers. A further search recovered ammunition for the same gun.

'We are removing these items, Mister O'Neill and you will be charged with possession of illegal arms without a license. Goodnight, sir.'

With that, the policemen left the house and continued to their next destination. Bill was anxious but it was his job after all. This is what he signed up to do. The men got into the car and the sergeant started the engine.

'We're off to Rathangan next,' he told the officers.

Bill stifled a gasp. This was his home village. He will certainly be recognised there. *What can he do?* he thought. It was only about seven miles away. He had to think fast.

'Sergeant, a dog bit me in the arse as we entered that house. Can I stay in the car this time sir?'

'No you fuckin' well can't, Constable Byrne,' came the answer. 'Are you some kind of sissy or something?'

Bill shut up and hoped for the best.

The next point of call was Ryan's shop in the Main Street, Rathangan. The owners of the drapery shop lived above it. Again the sergeant banged on the door. The local dogs immediately responded and howled in unison. Again, there was no response from the shop. The sergeant lifted the letter box lid and shouted, 'Open up! Police!'

Jack Ryan opened the window above the door and peered down, wiping his sleepy eyes.

'What do you want?' he called.

'Open the door now!' he was told.

Jack struggled down the stairs, still bleary eyed and unlocked the door. The police rushed in, pushing him aside. Bill kept his head down. Again the officers ransacked the upper rooms where the family lived. Jack was swearing at them but they took no notice. His wife rushed to the bedroom where her two children were screaming. After thirty minutes, no arms were found. The sergeant told Jack to open the shop door.

'There's nothing there, Sergeant, only material and garments. No arms.'

'We'll have a look anyway, sir.'

'Bastards,' said Jack under his breath.

Again, Constable Fleming discovered two revolvers hidden in the back of a drawer.

'Got something, Sergeant!'

'Well done Constable Fleming, you'll be a sergeant very soon.'

With that Jack Ryan recognised Bill.

'Ah, I know you. You're one of the Byrnes, up the road.'

'You must be mistaken, sir. My name is Joe Duffy,' Bill lied.

'No you're not. Ye all get the fuck out of my shop.'

'Before you call the police, Mister Ryan,' replied the sergeant, sarcastically, 'I'm charging you, John Ryan, with possession of illegal firearms. You will receive the Charge Notice in the post. Goodnight, sir.'

The children were still upset, as was their mother, Bernie. The place was a mess.

Bill was mortified. He thought about his brother, Brian and his family and of course, his parents. *What will happen to them now?* he thought. The four policemen piled back into the car. Neighbours were watching from the 'squinting' windows. The dogs still howled. The sergeant didn't say anything on their way back to Naas. He was pleased with his night's work and the arms haul. He looked forward to getting a commendation from the inspector.

Later in the week, the sergeant called Bill into his office. He was pleased with the raid and passed on the inspector's congratulations on the recovery of the illegal firearms. Bill mentioned that he had been recognised by Jack Ryan in Rathangan. The sergeant said he discussed this with the inspector and also the events in Kill. They agreed that it was best for Bill's security that he be transferred to North Kildare. Bill was happy with this. He was told that he would be transferred to Kilcock as soon as it was possible.

This raid by the RIC did nothing for their popularity in Kildare, never mind the whole of Ireland. The population became more and more dissatisfied with the security services and their style of policing. They were very much looking to Sinn Féin to help achieve an Ireland completely free of any British interference. As said before, Home Rule was now no longer an option.

The lot of the RIC officer got worse when forty republican prisoners, who were rearrested following the General Amnesty following the Rising, went on hunger strike in September, in Mountjoy prison. They demanded to be considered political prisoners or prisoners of war. One of them, Commandant Thomas Ashe, who took part in the Rising, consequently died later that month, whilst being force fed. He was arrested in Dublin in August and was taken to the RIC barracks at Newbridge. Bill was selected to accompany him to the Curragh Camp later, where he was court marshalled. This was Bill's last assignment before he was transferred to Kilcock.

Ashe's funeral was organised by the IRB. Thirty thousand attended it. Michael Collins stepped forward after a volley of shots were fired and announced, 'Nothing additional needs to be said. The volley which we just heard is the only speech which is proper to make over the grave of a dead Fenian.'

Bill was pleased not to be stationed in Dublin that September but even in his new village, tensions were rising. He was reconsidering his career and what else he could do whilst settling in but, decided to delay any decision until Christmas at the latest.

In October 1917, Éamon de Valera became president of the Sinn Féin political party, succeeding Arthur Griffith. The latter had set up the party in the early part of the century, to pursue an Irish Republic by peaceful means. It was mistakenly blamed by the British for the Easter Rising. The party was getting much support by the electorate and de Valera was the man to build on this. He had won the by-election in East Clare in July, taking the seat left vacant by Willie Redmond, the brother of John Redmond MP, who was killed in Flanders.

CHAPTER SEVENTEEN

Hardship and Turmoil

John is still in prison and winter is harsh but, there is light on the horizon.

The winter in Germany seemed to go on forever. The jumper and socks that Mary sent John were wonderful. He was given an overcoat from a Red Cross parcel, which was a godsend. He enjoyed reading the books and he swapped them with his fellow prisoners. Still, the days were long and sometimes, the nights even longer. As usual, he hoped the war would end soon and that he could return home and be with his family again.

His arm had improved but it was still painful in the cold and damp weather. He had regained some use of it and his hand but, he feared it would never be the same again. He was given light jobs by the guards and was not required to go to the mines or farms.

One morning, John saw a truck arrive with more prisoners. He watched them alighting. They looked startled, weary and underfed. John recognised one young man. It was his old friend and fellow Dubliner, Mick O'Connell. He was delighted to see someone from home. He didn't approach Mick as he was supposed to be cleaning the yard. Later, John and Mick met in the mess. They shook hands and embraced each other.

'Ah John, great to see ye. How is t'ings?'

'Not bad, Mick. How are ye keepin'?'

'We were captured when me and two of the lads wandered into a wood and got lost; we were lucky the Gerrys didn't shoot us.'

The two men exchanged stories of their war experiences. Mick considered himself very lucky to have survived this length of time. The spring of 1918 had at last arrived. Many of his friends and comrades had been killed and injured. He had just managed to keep sane and he made sure he kept his head down whenever he could. He had trouble with his hearing and was very deaf in his right ear. He lost a toe through frostbite and/or trench foot. He had not been home for over three years and he missed Ireland very much.

Mick told John of the disastrous offensives made by the French army the year before. On one of them, there were 200,000 casualties, including 30,000 fatalities. The result was that the French soldiers mutinied and refused to take part in any further offensives. They were only willing to defend their own lines. Approximately forty men were shot for this subordination and many more were sent to prison. The British high command only heard about it weeks later and the Germans never found out.

This put much pressure on the Allied forces but luckily, the Americans had entered the war in the spring of 1917. Mick was captured when the Germans made an all-out attack at the end of March, on a large section of the British line, forcing them to retreat. Many British and Irish soldiers lost their lives in a massive bombardment by the Germans, before sending in their troops. They hoped to break through and win the war but failed, mostly due to the appearance of the American reinforcements.

Mick had a similar journey to the prison, at Limburg, that John experienced. It was slow and uncomfortable and he also suffered abuse from the guards and some civilians. He was commanded to appear before the camp Commandant. Next day, he was examined by the medics, passed fit for manual labour and sent to a mine several miles away. John wondered if he would ever see him again.

He was surprised about Mick's stories from the Front, especially that of the continuing stalemate there. The prisoners of war were fed German propaganda by the guards and that printed in a newspaper they received called *The Continental Times*, which was printed in the English language in Berlin. It told of German victories and trenches being captured, all with very little casualties on the German side. There were also stories of London being bombed by Zeppelins, leaving very little standing. This was not widely believed but it was a worry for the men just the same.

Unknown to John and the Irish prisoners, politics in Ireland were rapidly changing. Sinn Féin were now the dominant party. In the spring of 1918 the British were running short of reinforcements, due to the vast amount of casualties caused by the German offensives. Conscription had been in force in Britain since 1916 but, the government were now planning to introduce it in Ireland. This met massive opposition in Ireland, from all political parties and the Catholic Church. The political parties were united in opposing it.

The Military Service Bill was passed in the House of Commons in April. The Irish Parliamentary Party, led by John Dillon (John Redmond had died in March, from a heart attack), left the House and returned to Ireland in protest. Later that month, a pledge against conscription was signed by almost the whole of nationalist Ireland. A one-day general strike was held on 25 April. The entire country closed down, with the exception of Belfast. The next month, the government launched a crackdown on Sinn Féin and leaders were arrested in the name of the 'German Plot'. This was named after the failed attempt to land German arms on Banna Strand, near Tralee in County Kerry, by Sir Roger Casement. Republican activities increased, as did arrests by the RIC.

In May, Private John Brennan was very surprised and happy to receive the news that he and other 'unfit' prisoners were being released and returned to their homeland. The Germans were unable to provide food, etc for prisoners who could not work and made the decision to send them home. Their food supplies were getting very low and the number of prisoners was getting larger. Some prisoners were already suffering from malnutrition and several would not be able to travel. John could not believe his luck.

CHAPTER EIGHTEEN

Outcast

Life goes on for Bill, as he tries to make the best of what he has, even if he can no longer go home.

Brian Byrne cycled to Dillon's pub for his usual Friday pint. The autumn weather was fine for a change. He had heard about the police raids in the county in August. Many locals in Rathangan were very upset about it. The feeling in County Kildare was beginning to match that of nationalist Ireland as a whole. Many families, of course, had men fighting in the war but RIC activities were souring their loyalty to Britain.

Brian ordered three pints of porter: one for himself and one for each of his friends, Chris and Andy. They lit their pipes and settled down at a table, intending to right the ills of the world. Andy produced a pack of cards and dealt them out for a game of twenty-five. They placed a halfpenny each in the pot.

'How is t'ings up in the big house, Brian?' asked Andy, puffing on his pipe and spitting into the 'spittoon' on the floor.

'Ah not bad, Andy. The Major hasn't been himself since the son was killed last year, but the farm is doing well with supplying vegetables and meat to the army at the Curragh.'

'I don't know whether ye heard or not, Brian, but there is a rumour that your brother, Bill was with the police which raided Ryan's shop last month,' inquired Chris.

'Jaysus! Where did you hear that, Chris?'

'Well, it's around the village that Jack Ryan recognised him. Some of the neighbours t'ought they knew him too.'

'Really! No one said anyt'ing to me.'

Brian was taken aback. He knew that Bill was having a tough time in his job – what with been beaten up, etc – but he never told him about the raid. He changed the subject.

'I hear de Valera may be top man in Sinn Féin soon. Did ye hear dat, lads?'

They said they did and hoped he would do something about the state of the country.

When Brian returned home, he told Mags about what he heard. She didn't hear about it either. She told him there was no mention of it the last time she visited a rambling house.

'Maybe they're keepin' it from us,' Brian said.

The Major was certainly not himself since his son John was killed. He seemed to have a lot on his mind. He was pleasant enough to Brian and Mags. He was not happy with the continuing slaughter of young men in France especially. The news of the war was usually bad but the 'spin doctors' tried to maintain that the Allies were on the verge of victory. Few believed it, the carnage had gone on far too long. On the first of July, the anniversary of John's death, he never appeared at the farm nor was he seen outside the house. His wife, Elizabeth sat in the garden alone. Martina, their daughter, had gone to London to visit her brother, George. It was a very sad day.

One afternoon, the Major called Brian to the yard at the back of the farm buildings. Brian put down his fork and came in.

'There was a letter addressed to you, put through my door early this morning,' said the Major. 'I didn't see who brought it.'

He handed Brian the letter. He opened it and it read:

Mister Byrne this is to inform you that your traitor brother, RIC Constable Bill Byrne, is advised not to show his face in Rathangan again. If he does, he must face the consequences.

Signed the Commandant of the Irish Volunteers, South Kildare. September 1917

There was no name of the commandant given.

Brian was shocked! The Major saw it in his face and asked what the matter was. Brian handed him the note.

'We must show this to the police, Byrne,' advised the Major.

'No way, sir,' replied Brian. 'Dat would endanger the whole family; even me parents would suffer.'

The Major thought for a few moments and then agreed, it would be dangerous. He promised Brian that he would discreetly find out who sent it.

'Don't worry, Byrne, no one will know; I will be very discreet. I have friends in high places.'

Brian wasn't too sure what 'discreet' meant but he trusted his employer.

When Brian told his wife, Mags, she too was shocked. Their son, Joseph was one year old and Mags was expecting a baby in the New Year. Brian wrote a letter to Bill in Kilcock, telling not to dare come home as his life was in danger. He decided not to tell his parents, as it would worry them too much. He thought about slipping into the RIC barracks in the Main Street but quickly decided against it, as surely it was being watched.

Bill was settling into his new post in Kilcock. It was a pleasant little town, situated in north Kildare on the Royal Canal. The railway line from Dublin to Sligo ran alongside it. Like in Rathangan, he enjoyed walking along the canal and trying his luck at fishing there. He lived in the barracks at first. It was a temporary arrangement until he found digs elsewhere. He was advised not to stay in the town. He considered the village of Summerhill, which was about seven miles away but a better option might be the town of Maynooth, which was less than four miles from Kilcock.

His work was less stressful than he experienced in Naas. There were the usual drunks to be straightened up and guided home after closing time. There might be a report to be completed for a stolen bicycle or an investigation into a report that a stray cow was wandering along a road unattended. His duties included cycling along a pre-determined route through the countryside. He enjoyed this very much and often he had to invent something to put in his report. However, he was aware of the changing political climate in the area, which was mirrored throughout nationalist Ireland.

Bill received his brother's letter. He was disappointed with the news that he could not visit Brian and Mags, or his parents for the foreseeable future but he wasn't surprised. He knew of fellow RIC constables who had been intimidated by the Volunteers and Sinn Féin and had resigned as a result. Threats were made against RIC officers and also their families. Bill worried mostly for his elderly parents, who lived outside Rathangan village and had no close neighbours. They were very isolated. He was also very annoyed and sad that he would not be in a position to visit any of his family at Christmas, which was only a few months away. Again, he was considering resigning before Christmas but even if he did, it would still be dangerous for him to visit them. He thought, perhaps he could meet them in another town. He decided to write to Brian and see if this could be arranged. This made him feel a little better.

Bill cycled to Maynooth on a day off to see if there was a room available in the town itself. He didn't fancy staying too far out, as he believed that he may be more vulnerable in a lonely townland. On arrival, he visited the Leinster Arms hotel in the Main Street. He was pleased to see that it was busy. It was close to the railway station and also St Patrick's Seminary. The college was where future priests were trained and finally ordained for every diocese in Ireland, with the exception of Dublin. Ironically, Maynooth was in the Dublin diocese. St Patrick's College, together with Carton House, the residence of the Duke of Leinster, boosted trade for the shopkeepers and merchants in the village. Bill decided to find lodgings there, as he considered that there was less risk of him being recognised as a police officer. He could blend in with the many visitors.

He enquired at the hotel and was given an address in the Main Street at Mrs Mooney's. The good lady did have a room available and accepted Bill as a paying guest. The rate was quite high compared with that charged in Naas but, he liked the house and the fact that Mrs Mooney also had a restaurant downstairs. The RIC gave him a generous allowance towards his lodgings, so that helped.

Bill settled into Maynooth very well. He called to the barracks to introduce himself. The sergeant said that visiting the pubs was not advised at the moment except, perhaps, when they were full and a stranger could not be easily noticed. He told him that on the first day of the Rising, thirteen men from the town marched to Dublin, along the canal, to join it. The men were led by Domhnall Ua Buachalla, a local shopkeeper, who would be elected Sinn Féin MP for North Kildare in December 1918. Ua Buachalla was ordered by the police to remove his name in Irish from his shop front and replace it with 'Daniel Buckley'. He refused and was fined. The sergeant suggested that Bill could cycle along the Dublin Road to 'The Jockey' Walsh's pub. It was less than two miles away. Bill thanked him for his advice. Later, he would walk along the Royal Canal and enjoy the peace and tranquillity of the countryside, only to be interrupted by the sound of a passing train. He often sat by the canal beside Pikes Bridge and watched the little 'pinkeens' pass peacefully by. He envied their world; their only worry was to avoid being snapped up by a hungry heron or a large, equally hungry, pike.

One day, Bill boarded the train to Dublin. He walked along the quays from Amiens Street Station*. He walked past the Customs House and along the quay of the same name. He wondered what he would find in the centre of the city. He arrived at O'Connell Bridge and realised it was the very spot where Kathleen was

---

* Opened in 1844, as Dublin Station, it was renamed Amiens Street Station ten years later, after the street on which it is located. In 1966, on the occasion of 50th anniversary of the Easter Rising, the station was renamed Connolly Station, after James Connolly, one of the leaders of the rising.

killed. His heart sank. Turning the corner quickly into Sackville Street, straight ahead, silhouetted against the bright sky, Nelson's Pillar loomed menacingly. His heart skipped a beat. It made him feel very sad. His eyes filled. He remembered the wonderful times he had with his fiancée in the city. The Pillar was where they met for their first date. Sackville Street was still practically in ruins. Clery's department building, where she worked, was gone, nothing left. He went into the Bachelor Inn but left almost immediately; he could not stay. This was where Kathleen accepted his proposal for marriage only two years before.

He walked over to the Liffey wall and stared at the dirty river slowly passing below. He likened it to his life and how it was passing so quickly. A passing stranger put his hand on his shoulder and asked if he was alright. He said he was and thanked him and turning, he realised that the stranger was, in fact, a young priest. 'Thank you, Father,' he shouted.'

Once Bill was a happy young man joining the DMP and looking forward to a bright future. Now, his country was changing faster than he could keep pace with. He could no longer look forward to holidays in the village in which he grew up.

Bill had written to his old friend, Tom Dempsey, before his trip to Dublin. Tom never replied so Bill made his way down Great Brunswick Street to his old station. The desk sergeant didn't recognise him but on producing his identification card, he was told that Tom no longer was in the force. He had resigned a few months before. It was believed that he was threatened and intimidated by the Volunteers and thought it best to leave. He went to Tom's lodgings, to see if he was still around. The landlady told him he had returned to Donegal but she didn't have his forwarding address.

Brian wrote to Bill and said that he would meet him around Christmas in Dublin, if that was convenient. He said that their parents would not travel this time as it was winter and anyway, it might not be a good idea for too many of the family to travel together, in case they were being followed. Bill was pleased and wrote back to say they could meet in the St Stephen's Green area of Dublin, a few days before Christmas. He said there was a good bed a breakfast hotel that he knew there.

CHAPTER NINETEEN

Homecoming

John makes the long, winding journey home. Mary is there to greet him once more. A lot has happened in the meantime.

At long last John received a date for when he would be released. He didn't mention that he would be set free in his letters to Mary. He worried that it would build her hopes up and maybe the Germans might change their minds. His letters to Mary were very similar to each other. He told of his little job in the camp and about meeting Mick O'Connell. The war was never mentioned but he always said he was being treated well and that he hoped to see them all soon. Mary's letters were somewhat similar. She told him about how the children were doing and that baby, Sean was so handsome and growing fast. He looked like his father. She always told him that he was missed and hoped he would be home soon.

The day that John looked forward to so much dawned, at last, on 10 July. He and his fellow inmates were loaded on to cattle trucks. They were taken by the train to Luxembourg and eventually on to the Dutch port of Rotterdam. The journey was long, tedious and uncomfortable but John and his companions were pleased to suffer the inconveniences as long as they reached their homeland. At Rotterdam they overnighted in an empty warehouse before setting sail in the early morning bound for Harwich. The sea was rough and the north wind was cold but none of the prisoners complained.

John, with five of the prisoners including two fellow Irishmen, were taken by train to London. The men were met by an army officer and brought to Charing Cross Hospital to be examined. The medical team recommended that they be kept there for about three nights. Some were suffering from malnutrition and others had infections and/or sores. The doctor was not pleased with the state of John's arm, as it didn't set properly. He said there was not much he could do about it. They were given a hot meal and a hot bath, which was absolute heaven. John never had a hot bath and had not washed properly in over two years.

He sent a letter to Mary from London giving her the great news. He was surprised that the city was largely intact, given the German propaganda that they received during their time in prison. He half expected to see Zeppelins flying over the vast metropolis and German soldiers patrolling the streets.

The weather was fine and sunny. He and his comrades enjoyed sitting in the hospital grounds, taking in their surroundings of lovely flowers, well-trimmed lawns and beautiful green trees. They had missed all this for so long that for a time, they thought it was just a beautiful dream. The years spent on the Western Front and in the miserable camp in Limburg would continue to haunt them for the rest of their lives. Sleep would be always difficult for them. John, in particular, had nightmares almost every night. He hoped they would recur less often when he got home to his wife and family. He looked forward so much to seeing them again.

John was certified fit to travel and he boarded the train for Holyhead at Euston Station. The train was so much more comfortable than the cattle trucks he experienced in Europe. He soon settled down in his carriage and gazed at the wonderful scenery as it passed the English countryside. He read in the papers that the war still continued on the Western Front, where he had spent so much time. In July, whilst John was still in London, the Germans made their final offensive at the Front. However, the Allies counterattacked and seized the initiative. He tried to blank out the horrible scenes he had witnessed but he found it difficult. The flashbacks he experienced were becoming more constant and he wondered how he could cope when he got to Dublin.

John boarded the mail boat at Holyhead. There were several soldiers who had been wounded and were being sent home on board. Some were severely injured, missing limbs and scarred for life. He spoke to them but some were unable to engage in conversation. Others were clearly shell shocked. One was dumb another had uncontrollable shakes. He did manage to communicate with a few. They did not want to discuss the war. He pitied them and again, wondered what the war had achieved, if anything.

At last the ship made its way, very slowly in John's view, into Kingstown (Dún Laoire) Harbour. He had been standing at the rail for over an hour and as forward on deck as he could manage. Again, the blue mountains of Wicklow and Dublin seemed to welcome the ship and her passengers home to the arms of Mother Ireland. The morning was bright and beautiful. There was a gentle fresh westerly breeze caressing the faces of the returning sons and daughters. John was elated. He was so pleased to set his feet on Irish soil again. He swore to himself that he would never again leave it.

He searched once more the awaiting faces to see if could spot Mary and the children. Again, he remembered that little Sean was only a toddler. Suddenly there she was: his beloved Mary smiling broadly in the crowd. He could hardly believe his eyes. She looked so lovely in a light blue summer coat, auburn long flowing hair, sparkling blue eyes and cherry red lips. They ran together, embraced tightly and kissed. They both dreamed of this day for so long, tears flowed. They walked hand in hand to the train station, stopping occasionally for yet another kiss.

On the journey into town they chatted and chatted. Mary told him of the hard times they endured during the Rising. She told of her great friend, Mrs Wilson and how she helped her when the chips were down. How Michael and Bridget were getting on at school and how little Sean was growing fast. John told her how he missed them all and how much he looked forward to seeing his youngest son for the first time. Mary asked him about his experiences in the war but he was reluctant to tell her any detail of what he saw and/or endured, either at the Front or in the camp. She knew it was painful for him so she didn't enquire any further.

Soon they were making their way down Great Brunswick Street (Pearse Street) and home to Barrow Street. Mrs Wilson was at the door, having looked after the children. Michael and Bridget hardly recognised their father and stood back very shyly. Sean hid behind the table. Their mother took the hands of the older children, brought them over and introduced them to Daddy.

'Don't ye not know your daddy, children?'

Michael and Bridget came over hesitantly and John hunkered down and embraced them both. Michael remembered him, as he was three when he first left but Bridget was still not sure. Mary retrieved Sean from behind the table and took him in her arms.

'Sean, this is your daddy. Say hello.'

He buried his head in her neck; he was very shy.

Later they all had dinner together and the children were warming to this new man in their lives. He brought them little presents from London, which endeared him even more. There was chocolate for everyone, a tin car for Michael and a dolly for Bridget.

Mary was so happy that their little family was together at long last. She never wanted them to be parted ever again. John was also very happy. It had been two years since he was last with them. Mary looked so lovely, she glowed in the long summer's evening. He regretted ever leaving her to cope on her own but he had to put all that behind him. Putting his memories of the horrors of war behind him was going to be a difficult challenge. He secretly prayed and hoped that he could manage it, for all their sakes and his own. He promised himself that he would take every day as it came.

John slept well that night. Having Mary in his arms was wonderful. He relished her softness, her warmth and her feminine scent. It was heaven. Mary too was so pleased not to have to sleep alone anymore. Having a man again in her life was, for her too, a heavenly feeling, especially when it was John. They cuddled for ages before they fell asleep, still holding each other tight.

CHAPTER TWENTY

Christmas Visitations

Christmas 1918. Bill and brother, Brian meet up in Dublin.
Brian fills him in on all that has been happening.

Bill Byrne made his way to meet his brother at St Stephen's Green in Dublin. It was 21 December, the Saturday before Christmas 1918. He came on the early morning train from Kilcock to Amiens Street Station. The day was frosty and cold but the sky was cloudless. He crossed Butt Bridge purposely to avoid O'Connell Bridge and all its dark history. Grafton Street looked lovely in all its festive attire.

Brian was already waiting for him at the gates to the Green. They were both pleased to see each other. They shook hands and made their way to a coffee house in Grafton Street. They chatted together over the coffee. The shop was crowded with Christmas shoppers. Brian told him of the cold shoulders he experienced around Rathangan. He knew that people were talking about the family. Sinn Féin were doing very well in County Kildare following the recent elections. Now that the war was at last over, the British Army was less busy and less popular in the county. Many families still depended on the army for their livelihood. Trade in the towns had fallen off as well.

Brian told Bill of an incident in Naas some time ago, where British soldiers attacked Irish Volunteers from the Kill Company, who were leaving the town. The volunteers pulled down a Union Jack from a telegraph pole and were attacked by the soldiers, many of whom were locals, home on leave. Their wives and girlfriends also joined in. Bill had heard of such incidents and also knew of few celebrations in the towns when the war ended. Several shops did display pro-British regalia and flags but it wasn't popular any longer, in the changing times.

Brian said that Major O'Kelly was worried about the changing Ireland. His class was becoming a target for anti-British sentiment. Since the beginning of the war, the 'old order' steadily disappeared not only in Britain but, perhaps, more so in Europe. By 1918 the Kaiser in Germany and the Tzar in Russia were removed and the Austro-Hungarian and Ottoman empires ceased to exist. Now cracks began to appear in the walls of the once mighty British Empire. Ireland was challenging its very existence and other nations within the Empire were taking notice.

Already the 'big houses' were legitimate targets for the IRB and the Volunteers. As mentioned before, quite a few landlords, including those living in Britain, had sold their estates and returned to their homeland. Some of the once magnificent country houses now lay empty and were slowly falling into disrepair. Those landlords who remained found the estates becoming more and more difficult to maintain. Labour was still much in demand and had become more expensive. However, some landowners did not have immediate family in Britain and many had long roots in Ireland, going back several generations. They considered themselves 'Anglo-Irish' and were referred to as the 'Ascendancy'.

Major O'Kelly's family was actually Irish. It was one of the few Catholic landowner families who survived the Penal Laws and who managed to hang on to their faith and land. Elizabeth O'Kelly was from a Protestant family and she converted to Catholicism when she married George. Her family were not entirely happy with the marriage but accepted it because of George's rank in the British Army and the fact that he inherited an estate.

The Major never really got over the death of his first-born son, John. His interest in the estate was waning as time went on. Brian noticed this. The place began to show signs of neglect. The gardens were no longer kept as beautiful as they were in years gone by. Elizabeth was losing interest too. She was the one who managed the gardens. She had allowed them to decline.

Brian did his best to maintain them but he was always busy in the farm. Their daughter, Martina, had moved to Dublin to live and work. Their son, George junior, remained in London and had married an English girl. They had a son, whom they also named George. He returned home occasionally but he too was worried about the political situation. His father advised him to stay in London until the future of Ireland was decided. He knew that the country would, more than likely, be partitioned and he feared that this would bring about more unrest and even violence.

The Major spent his days reading *The Irish Times* and the *Kildare Observer* and followed the developing situation. The rise of Sinn Féin worried him. He learned of a visit by the Irish Republican Army (IRA, who were not the renamed IRB but the name adopted by the Volunteers) to his friend, Sir Reginald Williams, at his country house. They arrived late one evening and demanded he hand over his firearms. Sir Reginald said he only had a shotgun but the IRA officer and his men forced their way in and, producing a revolver, the officer forced him to take him to the cellar, where he knew other guns were kept. Two rifles and a revolver were stored in a cabinet there and Sir Reginald handed them over. The Williams family were traumatised by this visit but were reluctant to report the incident to the RIC for fear of reprisals.

Sir Reginald called to see Major O'Kelly the next day. He asked him to keep the visit a secret but warned him that he may get one soon. The Major was shocked and implemented extra security measures to his house and the estate. He made sure the large gates were locked at six o'clock each evening. Extra barbed wire was erected where possible. This would not entirely prevent a raid by the IRA but, perhaps, hinder and delay one.

Brian and Bill went for a stroll in St Stephen's Green in the afternoon. Time passed quickly. Later they checked into their bed and breakfast hotel in Aungier Street. They had dinner in Dame Street in the early evening. Bill was painfully reminded that Kathleen once had a room on that street. However, they went to a public house after dinner and had a long chat over several pints of porter. They reminisced about their childhood in Rathangan, remembering the friends and neighbours there and the characters they both knew. They remembered their parents and the love and care that they lavished on their children. They had very little materially but they gave their children what they had an abundance of – love. Those days were now long gone.

Bill asked Brian about his new son, Thomas, who was nearly six months old. It was his first Christmas. Brian said he was a wonderful baby and thanked God for this wonderful gift to Mags and himself. Bill looked forward to seeing him as soon as he could. They both remarked on how vulnerable they were now. Brian asked Bill about his situation in the RIC and said he was worried about him in these uncertain times. Bill said he was considering perhaps leaving the force but, he said he would wait to see what would happen in the New Year.

Next morning, Sunday, they both attended Mass at the White Friar Street church. The church was packed with worshipers, all looking forward to Christmas. A crib was set up at the side altar, awaiting the arrival of the infant Jesus. Bill and Brian were both reminded of the happy days when they were young and how much they used to look forward to the joy of being at midnight Mass on Christmas Eve with all the family. How different things were now was their shared thought.

Brian said his goodbyes and wished Bill a very happy Christmas and hoped they would meet again in the New Year. Bill said likewise and made his way to his station. He felt sad that he would be on his own for the first time at Christmas in many years.

CHAPTER TWENTY-ONE

Flashbacks and Nightmares

*John is glad to be home again, in the bosom of his family but
also struggles to put the nightmares of war behind him.*

John Brennan awoke early after his first night at home in Dublin.
He didn't know where he was for a time but then he felt the
warmth of dear Mary beside him. He was so pleased to be safe
from that terrible war. She was already awake and staring into
his sleepy eyes. She kissed his lips and they embraced.

'Oh John, I am so pleased you are home and safe again, here
in me arms. I really missed ye and I worried every day about
your safety. When I got that message that ye were missin' and
presumed... Oh! I can't say the word... I cried for days and
days.'

'Dear Mary, I too worried about how ye felt when I didn't write.
I didn't t'ink they'd say I was dead. I can't believe that I'm home,
safe and sound.'

However, John wasn't sound: his sleep was interrupted with
flashbacks and nightmares.

'Did I wake ye in the night, Mary? Did I shout out?'

'Yeah, you did John. Did ye have nightmares?'

He was annoyed that Mary heard him scream and shout in the
night.

'Maybe I'd better sleep downstairs tonight, Pet?'

'Ah no, love; it was probably because it was the first night.'

However, John struggled with sleeping. He had good nights
and bad. Mary was worried about him. Some nights he woke
the children on others, he went downstairs to give them all a
break. He became irritable during the day and sometimes he

just sat on a chair and said nothing; he just stared through the window.

John also had trouble with his sex life. He was unable to have an erection. Mary was a bit worried about it as they had not made love since he came home. They kissed and cuddled, which was lovely but she wanted more, as did John. She did not want to ask him about it. However one evening he said to her.

'I suppose, Mary, you are wonderin' why I haven't asked for a bit since I came home?'

'Ah sure, John, I did t'ink about it but sure, it doesn't matter as long you're here with me every day,' she lied.

'Well, Pet, my little mickey won't stand to attention for me anymore.'

'Is that it, John? I'm sure he will obey you if I give you a hand,' she said with a laugh. 'Anyway it's not that little, is it?'

That broke the ice as it were. They went to bed that night and she helped him as best she could and they had some success. It took nearly a week of 'trial and error' before they finally resolved the issues and made mad, passionate love. All was well again. They were both very pleased. It was that night their fourth child was conceived.

After a few days Mary managed to coax him out the house. They made their way to the river and walked along the bank with little Sean in the pram. The summer weather was fine and sunny most days and John began to feel better. The horrors of the past were fading a little and he managed to push them to the back of his mind. Mary was a great help. Some weekends, John, Mary and the three children would take a tram to Sandymount Strand. They always had a wonderful time walking along the sea front and taking in the sea air. John really enjoyed the fresh air. It cleared his head and seemed to ease his mind. Michael and Bridget loved to paddle in the cool water, they loved to splash and run about. John even rolled up his trousers and joined them. Mary was happy to see him laugh and play with the children. She hoped it would cure his disturbed sleeping and restless days.

John enjoyed being at home with his wife and children. They gave him a lift and the fine August weather cheered his heart. He was still getting paid by the British Army but it was reduced, as he was no longer away from home.

In August the Battle of Amiens took place, which was the opening phase of the Allied 'hundred days' offensive' that would eventually lead to the end of the war in November. John decided to look for a job. He realised that if the war were to end soon, as it appeared it would, there would be lots of men returning home and seeking work. There was no heroes' welcome for returning 'British' soldiers, either in Ireland or, indeed, in many areas of Great Britain at that time. The rise of Sinn Féin did no favours for the Irish soldiers who had served the king. Many firms refused even to interview them.

John's arm would never be completely functional and this was a liability in finding a suitable job. However, he managed to hide it well. He went to the docks at Ringsend to enquire about a job. When asked where he had been over the last three years, John reluctantly told them about his time in the army.

'Nothin' goin' here at the moment, Mister Brennan. Leave your address and we'll get back to you.'

He waited for days but no letters came.

John went to the pub on a Friday evening. Mary had encouraged him to go as she thought it may help him to overcome his problems. The pub was crowded with workers having an after-work drink before the weekend. He looked around but didn't recognise anyone. He ordered a pint of porter. The barman was friendly enough.

'Hiyah John. How're ye doin'?' came a voice from behind.

John turned around and there he saw Johnny 'the Hopper' Treacy, dressed up in a fine suit, shining shoes and a cigarette in hand.

'Great to see ye, Johnny. How is t'ings?'

'Oh wonderful, John. Got a job in the bookies in Townsend Street. They look after me very well; don't have to work too hard.'

'Really, Johnny? That is great. Don't suppose there is a job for me there.'

'Well, ye never know. I can enquire for ye.'

'Please do. Here, I'll buy you a pint.'

John ordered another pint for his old friend and joined 'the Hopper' at a table by the window. The evening sun shone in. John opened the window as the smoke was affecting his delicate lungs. That noxious gas in the trenches had definitely damaged them. The warm breeze eased his breathing.

They talked of what happened since they last had a chat, three years earlier, in 1915. Shortly afterwards John had decided to join up. The Hopper said he tried to join up too but, because of his short leg, he was considered unfit. John didn't really believe that he had even gone to the recruitment office. However, the Hopper said he was pleased that he was rejected, when he learned of the carnage at the Front and the fathers, brothers and sons who never returned.

John reluctantly related some of the stories of the horrors that he witnessed in the war. He didn't go into too much detail but the Hopper was fascinated. He wanted to hear more but John drew the line and swiftly changed the subject. He enjoyed the drink and the chat with his friend. The porter made him feel a bit better and talking about his experiences seemed to free him from their grip on his soul.

John heard no more about a job in the bookie's office. He got the impression from his friend that he was only telling half the truth. The Hopper, he thought, was into something dodgy with the gangsters of the city. It was best that he didn't get mixed up in that sort of business.

A few days later John walked to Sackville Street to see how the rebuilding of the city was progressing. The Imperial Hotel/ Clery's site was being rebuilt and other damaged buildings being repaired. The GPO, which was gutted, showed signs of restoration to its former glory. The street was busy with shoppers and he was pleased that business was getting back to its previous level. He stopped at the Clery's rebuild and was impressed with how the work was advancing. He spoke to a worker who was having a break and a smoke near the street. The man told him that they were short of labourers and if John wanted a job, he was sure there might be one available. The worker told him he was from Donegal and he used to be a DMP Constable in the city.

'My name is Tom, Tom Dempsey. Pleased to meet ye.'

'Hello Tom. I'm John Brennan. I was in the war.'

Tom introduced him to his foreman, Mick McGahey. Mick asked John about his experience and where he last worked, etc. John told him the truth of how he fought in France and was then taken prisoner.

'Ah sure, John, I can give you a start but I wouldn't broadcast the fact that you were in the British Army. Tell them to mind their own business; that's what I would do.'

John thanked Mick and said he would show up for work on Monday morning. He hurried back to Barrow Street to tell Mary. She was delighted. The pension money they were receiving barely met their outgoings and sometimes it didn't even do that. She had run up a few bills in the shops and now she hoped she could clear them. Things looked good at last.

CHAPTER TWENTY-TWO

Another Dance

For Bill, the prospect of getting his life back on track beckons.

Christmas Eve in Kilcock was relatively quiet. The weather was wet. Constable Bill Byrne was on late duty. The pubs were filling up and there were a few 'travelling' families knocking about, which was a bit of a worry. He knew that some of the regular drunks would make their way to midnight Mass later and, perhaps, create a disturbance. His colleague was a bit anxious, as he had less experience than Bill. He assured him that all would be well and suggested that they stay close together, in case there was any trouble.

As it happened there were no disturbances. They had to check a few men who had overindulged and send them home. Others, they removed from the pubs when asked to do so by the licensees. Bill managed to get to the church and attend Mass, which he was pleased to do. After his shift finished, he cycled back to his lodgings in Maynooth.

Christmas Day 1918 was the same as other Christmases for most people but for Bill, it was one of the loneliest he had ever experienced. Maynooth was quiet; everyone appeared to be having a family dinner. Mrs Mooney invited him to her family dinner, which was very kind of her. He accepted and he was pleased to have some company. There was only Mrs Mooney and her son and daughter. Her husband had passed away some years before. She cooked a lovely roast turkey dinner, with roast potatoes, carrots and cabbage.

Her son and daughter were in their twenties. They both worked and lived in Dublin. She was a nurse and he worked on the trams. They were very friendly to Bill and he felt less lonely as the afternoon went on. They even shared a bottle of very tasty

French wine. He hadn't tasted wine in a long time and he felt the glow in his face after the second glass.

The public houses were all closed, by law, on Christmas Day but they all knew that they would be full of clandestine drinkers. Bill fancied a couple of pints but couldn't run the risk of been identified as a lawman in one of these premises. However, he had a lovely day and thanked Mrs Mooney and her children for allowing him to share their family day, before retiring to bed.

St Stephen's Day dawned bright with a clear sky and some frost on the ground. In the square, the local hunt assembled at ten o'clock. There was much excitement. The children loved to play amongst the horses, to the annoyance of the huntsmen and women. The hounds howled with excitement and the horses became edgy and nervous. There was the clang of iron on stone. It was all part of the hunt day. Bill came to have a look at the horses. He remembered Major O'Kelly's beautiful hunters and the joyful hunt days he himself enjoyed in Rathangan, when he was growing up.

In the evening, Bill decided to go to a dance in the local parish hall. He hadn't been to a dance since Kathleen died. His friend and fellow RIC man, Joe Delaney had encouraged him to go as he said that there were often lovely girls there and the music was usually good. The two men had a couple of pints in Pitt's pub and headed to the ballroom. They joined the queue.

Yes, there were some very pretty girls entering the hall. In the queue there were also several young lads a bit the worst for drink. Some were refused entry by an off-duty RIC constable, who was acting as an unofficial bouncer. The two men paid their money and proceeded to the dance hall. As in the AOH, the men were assembled on one side and the girls on the other. The band was tuning up and first impressions were good.

Bill and Joe made their way to the mineral/tea bar. There were two couples drinking lemonade and sharing a plate of biscuits at the bar. They chatted away to each other and were already enjoying the evening. The men ordered two glasses of ginger beer and lit a cigarette each. Soon the music started and after a couple of songs, they realised that the band – the Naramore Céilí band – was, in fact, very good. They made their way to the dance floor once they had finished their drinks and their cigarettes.

They studied the form on the opposite side of the hall and agreed to ask two girls for a dance. The girls accepted and all parties enjoyed it. The men danced with several other women and they really enjoyed the evening. Bill was particularly happy for he had not enjoyed an evening out in many years.

One girl whom he danced with was Marie Callaghan from Kilcloon. She was tall and slim, very pretty and wore a beautiful cotton dress. He noticed his friend, Joe also fancied her. He wanted to ask her for a date. He foolishly missed the chance to ask her. He hesitated as he was too shy and a bit insecure. He went to ask her for another dance but a young man just beat him to it. Anyway that was the last dance. He felt a bit disappointed.

Joe and Bill agreed to come to a dance together soon. They would check their rosters and see when the next dance was scheduled. They both looked forward to it very much.

In 1918, there was concern in Ireland about the health of returning British Army soldiers from Europe and, especially from France. Venereal disease, in particular syphilis and gonorrhoea, was considered to be in danger of infecting 'pure' young Irish girls. Sinn Féin issued a 'Public Health Circular No.1', suggesting that all soldiers returning from the Great War should be blood tested for a sexually transmitted disease. It suggested that the cost of such a scheme should not be borne by county councils but put on 'proper shoulders'. It was never to be adopted by the government of the day and many looked on it as an expression of a nationalist/republican ill feeling towards these returning men who fought for the 'Empire'. However it was true that many young serviceman had frequented 'dens of iniquity' in France and other countries a bit too often.

When waiting to be examined, John heard a fellow soldier say, 'I think I am a goner.'

John said to him, 'Don't be silly. What are ye on about?'

The soldier went in and as he passed John on the way out, he whispered, 'I am a goner 'ere' and laughed loudly.

John was pleased that he never availed of the services of women of ill repute although, he was often tempted.

However, troops also brought back another deadly disease – Spanish flu. The flu apparently originated in the USA and not Spain, as the name suggested. It was called 'Spanish' when the King of Spain, Alfonso XIII, died from it. Censorship, mostly because of the war, meant that news of the spread of the pandemic was not widely reported. Spain had a free press hence the name. American forces reportedly brought it to France towards the end of the war, where it rapidly spread. It is estimated that approximately 23,000 people died of Spanish 'flu in Ireland.

Later in January, Bill and Joe found that they were both off duty on a particular Sunday night. The *Leinster Leader* carried an advert for a dance again in the town hall in Maynooth. They met in Pitt's public house us usual and enjoyed a few pints of porter. The bar was full so the risk of being recognised as RIC men was low. However, they didn't stay too long there and moved next door to Joe Caulfield's bar. Again, it was almost full and they ordered another two pints.

Having topped up their Dutch courage, the two men headed for the dance hall. It was nearly ten o'clock, so many of the dancers had already gone in. They peeped into the hall on their way to the mineral bar. They were pleased to see many girls dancing and some more sitting in the 'girls' side of the hall. Bill tried to spot Marie Callaghan but had no success. Anyway, they ordered two bottles of ginger beer and smoked a cigarette each. The band was already playing and sounded reasonably good. They made their appearance in the dancehall. They scanned the talent and, like before, they selected two girls and went and asked them for a dance. They enjoyed dancing with different girls and the feelings were mutual.

Bill was dancing with a friendly, blonde, young lady when he noticed Marie Callaghan arriving in the hall. To his disappointment she had a young man with her. He tried to avoid looking at her as she walked to the other end of the hall but failed. His partner saw the change in him, made an excuse and left him on the floor.

Bill watched the couple as they entered the mineral bar. He looked around to see what Joe was getting up to. He was busy chatting up a pretty girl and appeared to be making progress. Bill decided to take a peek into the mineral bar. Marie and the young man were chatting together and enjoying glasses of lemonade.

He returned to the hall and asked a girl for a dance. She obliged. After that dance the band had a break. Raffle tickets were being sold. He bought two. He chatted to a couple of men about the racing in Baldoyle the day before. One said that he had three winners but Bill wasn't inclined to believe him. Soon the band started up again. To his surprise, he noticed Marie on her own, talking to some girlfriends. He dashed over and asked her to dance. He thought that she was hesitating but then she said yes. They chatted as they danced a waltz.

She was beautiful and interesting. She was five foot five and had curves in all the right places. He saw the young man she came in with dancing with another girl. She waved at him. He asked who he was.

'Ah, that's me younger brother, Mick. He came to the dance with me to act as a chaperone. Me mammy gets worried about me and wouldn't let me come to Maynooth without him.'

Bill was so pleased and when the set ended. He asked her to accompany him for 'a mineral'. To his delight and surprise, she agreed. Marie thought Bill to be very handsome. She liked tall men and she admired his moustache and fine serge blue suit.

They drank lemonade and Bill offered Marie a cigarette. She said she didn't smoke but she didn't mind him having one. They chatted away.

She lived with her family in Kilcloon and she worked in a shop in Maynooth. Her father had a job as a farm labourer, not far from their rented cottage. Bill hesitated in telling Marie that he was a policeman but, when he did, he told her that he was soon leaving the force because of the political situation. She was pleased that he was but wondered what else he could do. That was a difficult question.

They returned to the dance floor and continued to swop their experiences of life. Bill didn't mention Kathleen, although he knew that Marie was interested in knowing about past relationships. He just dodged the question; however, she said that she had a previous boyfriend but they broke up. She didn't say why. They made a date to see each other again.

CHAPTER TWENTY-THREE

War is Over

It's all about 'one day at a time' for John Brennan. Ireland's
political landscape is changing fast.

The general election in December 1918 saw Sinn Féin win 73
seats. They put forward a candidate in every constituency, with
the exception of Trinity College. Of course, none of them would
take their seats in Westminster. It is interesting to note that, for
this election, the Irish electoral system was revised, which meant
that women over thirty were allowed to vote for the first time.
This increased the electorate by one and a half times. Also, the
Labour Party agreed not to put up a candidate in constituencies
where Sinn Féin had already put forward one. It appears that
some voters then voted for the latter as a protest vote.

On 21 January 1919 these elected MPs assembled in the Mansion
House in Dublin to form the first Dáil Éireann. They decided to
call themselves Teachtaí Dála (TDs) – representatives or deputies
of the Dáil. They set up an Irish parliament to run parallel and
in opposition to the British administration at Dublin Castle.

John Brennan turned up for work in Sackville Street on a
Monday morning in October 1918. He was to help mix mortar
and take it to the bricklayers in buckets. At first, his left arm
hurt like hell but he successfully hid the pain and used his right
one as much as possible. He kept himself to himself as he didn't
want anyone to know that he served with the British Army.
He was pleased when, a few days later, he met up with Tom
Dempsey. They became friends and they had a couple of pints
together on Friday evenings.

'I'm sure you had a tough time in the war, John?' Tom asked

'I certainly did, Tom,' John replied. 'It was a bitch. It certainly wasn't what I had expected. I saw some awful t'ings happen. Many of my friends and comrades were killed or seriously wounded.'

He didn't go into any further detail and added, 'But I t'ink you had a bad time in the DMP, didn't ye, Tom?'

'Ah that was rough too, John. After the Rising we were grouped with the British soldiers and treated with pure contempt. I t'ink we were considered even lower than the soldiers. Many of me colleagues were injured and some even killed. It was horrible.'

Tom told him about his friend, Bill Byrne, who lost his fiancée that Easter week. He told him of Bill's request to get a transfer out of Dublin, which was successful. Tom also applied for a transfer but he was refused. He continued to work on into 1917. It was when he was attacked whilst on patrol one evening and suffered a severe beating that he resigned from the force. It was the last straw, as he had been subject to much verbal and some physical abuse up to then.

Tom reluctantly decided to leave the city he enjoyed living in and went home to Donegal. There was not much employment in that part of Ireland at that time, or any time really. Young people simply grew up and emigrated. He stayed with his parents for nearly six months and then returned to Dublin. He got this job almost immediately as much labour was required to rebuild the city. Like John, he kept the fact that he was once a DMP constable to himself.

John and Mary were happy. She was pleased that he found himself a friend – someone to talk to other than herself. They could talk about manly things. The new job kept the wolf from the door. John still suffered with nightmares and periods of depression. When this happened Mary left him to himself. She was a bit worried when he sometimes 'took to the drink' and came home drunk on quite a few occasions but usually the depression would pass and he would return to nearly his old self. She knew that his experiences of the war would probably never leave him and she had to accept it. He was never angry with her, nor was he ever violent.

She was told by a neighbour that, when she was putting out her milk bottles one evening, she saw John approaching, rather unsteadily, down Barrow Street. She said to him, 'Hello John. How are you doin'? Are ye alright?'

He replied with a loud, 'WHO GOES THERE?'

'Ah John, it's only me, Missus Farrelly, what's up?'

With that a truck came trundling down the street, making a loud revving engine noise. John turned around swiftly and saluted it.

'The last of the Crossley Tenders,' he exclaimed and with that he proceeded on his way home.

Mary was very annoyed with Josie Farrelly but kept her mouth shut. She just wanted to spread gossip. *Cheeky bitch,* she thought.

When the war at last ended in November 1918, around 100,000 Irish veterans returned home. Somewhere in the region of 30,000 Irishmen had been killed. Many of the veterans were unable to work due to physical and mental injuries but more were fit enough and sought employment. They faced discrimination due to the changes in Irish politics. John was pleased that he had a job and pitied these men. There was certainly very little heroes' welcome for them in their own country.

John was still worried about his behaviour and especially his drinking. He didn't want to upset his wife and children. He loved them very much. He discussed it with his friend, Tom, over a pint one Friday. Tom told him that he knew of men who returned from the war who were simply unable to adjust to civilian life. They were discharged for various reasons: mainly for serious injuries and/or bad health, physically or mentally. Many took to the drink and became alcoholics and others just couldn't cope with life in general. Many marriages were ruined and families split up. Suicides were not unknown. Tom said that he knew of policemen who suffered a similar fate. The number of RIC officers who were resigning grew rapidly. Now that the war was finally over, many more cases of wrecked lives were expected and this was a worry.

John realised then that he was not the only one and this made him feel a little better. He thought it was just himself. He made a promise not to drink too much and to, maybe, discuss his feelings and problems with Mary. It was difficult for a man in the early twentieth century to reveal his feelings to a woman, even if it was the woman he loved. He thought it would make him look weak and less manly. He resolved to try and bring himself to discuss it with her. After all, she was pregnant with their fourth child and she needed him as much as he needed her.

John only had the two pints that evening. Tom understood. On his way home John went over and over in his head what he would say to Mary. She was surprised but pleased when he arrived home early. She made two cups of strong tea and joined him by the fire.

CHAPTER TWENTY-FOUR

Career Change

Bill is realising that there is a price to be paid for the life that one chooses.

Bill and Marie met again, as arranged, outside the post office opposite the town hall in Maynooth on Sunday night, 26 January 1919. On his day off he had called into Dawson's shop where she worked. She was a bit shy and maybe a little embarrassed but they had a nice chat. When he left her colleague teased her about this handsome young man. She said he was lovely; she loved his moustache and the fact that he was tall. Marie agreed with her on all points but said that it was not serious. Secretly she hoped it might become so in the near future.

The couple walked slowly down Main Street as they chatted till they came to Carton Avenue and then walked back to the town hall. Marie was dressed in a dark winter coat and wore a headscarf. Bill thought she looked so beautiful even in the dark January night. They chatted as they walked and, when they entered the hall, he suggested that they have a mineral. When she handed in her coat to the cloakroom, Bill could not but be very impressed with the beautiful cotton, blue dress that she was wearing.

'Ah! That's a lovely dress you're wearing, Marie. You look wonderful.'

'Ah go on, Bill. Sure I have this dress for donkey's years.'

'It still looks very nice.'

'T'anks.'

She said that her brother, Mick, had escorted her to the town and, when he saw her meet Bill, he headed over to Pitt's pub for a drink with his friends. The band had already started playing and soon they were dancing together.

'Can I escort you home tonight, Marie?' Bill asked hesitantly when the evening was coming to an end.

'Maybe not tonight, Bill, as Mick said he'll do it as Mam requested.'

'Ah that's alright. Can I see you in the week? I'm off Wednesday if you're free.'

'Alright Bill. Wednesday is me half-day off, so we can meet and maybe have a walk along Carton Avenue.'

'Great.'

Bill returned to his lodgings at Mrs Mooney's feeling wonderful. He hadn't felt like that for a very long time. Marie was really a lovely girl. Was he falling in love again? He thought he might be.

Bill cycled to work next morning in a good mood, still thinking of Marie. However, he was a bit worried about how things were developing in the New Year.

On the day that Dáil Éireann was formed, five days before his last dance with Marie, two RIC officers were shot dead by volunteers at Soloheadbeg, County Tipperary. They were local policemen who were merely guarding explosives being ferried to a quarry. There was no connection between the two events. Many believed the shots were the first to be fired in what became known as the War of Independence or the Anglo-Irish War. Dan Breen and Sean Treacy, hardline nationalists/republicans, became impatient with the progress of events and took the initiative to start the war.

Bill and his fellow officers at the police station in Kilcock were getting very nervous. There were only four constables and a sergeant at the barracks. Two constables were normally on duty on the day shift. The sergeant lived there and one constable was usually on the night shift. The night shift was usually a 'rest' shift, with the constable having a sleep in the day room. The fourth man was on a rest day. The shifts could be decreased or increased when circumstances required. This suited Bill very much as he could swap a shift if he wanted to be off duty, such as going to a dance. The sergeant decided that, from that Monday, the two-day shift constables were to be sent out together on patrol.

The New Year saw the role of the RIC change completely. Their job, up to then, was upholding the law and keeping the peace. Now they were busy conducting searches for arms and looking for persons wanted for nationalist and republican activities. It appeared that since the formation of the Dáil, officers were occasionally subjected to verbal abuse and intimidation. Police rather than military were becoming targets for the Volunteers. Merchants were refusing to serve police officers and their families were shunned. Bill had flashbacks of his days in Dublin and it sent shudders down his spine.

On Wednesday Bill waited near Dawson's shop for Marie to finish work. He had a lot on his mind. His day off had been cancelled and changed to the night duty due to tensions in the county. Marie noticed he was not the happy man she met on the Sunday before.

'What's the matter, Bill? Ye don't appear pleased to see me?'

'Ah Marie, yeah I'm very, very pleased to see ye. It's just that t'ings are changing rapidly in the country: two of our lads were murdered last week in Tipperary.'

'Yeah, I saw that in the paper. Very sad for their families.'

'I'm not sure if I can stay in the force now.'

'Yeah, it's a big worry alright, Bill.'

The killings of the two policemen shocked some of the less extreme members of Sinn Féin. They didn't see this as the way forward.

The couple walked down Carton Avenue hand in hand. The day was cold following a heavy frost. The sun shone low in the sky and they both looked forward to spring, as the winter appeared to go on forever. The first day of February would soon arrive, which was 'Lá Fhéile Bríde' (St Brigid's Day), traditionally the first day of spring in most of Ireland, especially County Kildare. However, they both knew that the weather would not improve very much on that day.

They sat on a seat at the east end of the Avenue, had a cuddle and even shared a kiss. Marie asked him if there were something else that he could work at. He said that he had much experience of farm labouring and perhaps he could enquire around the town and see if anything was going. He asked her if she knew of any vacancies. She said no but that she would keep an ear out.

Marie noticed the ornate west gate to the estate and residence of the Duke of Leinster, Carton House. It was the gate through which the Duke's carriage passed on its way to the Protestant Church at the end of Main Street, close to the college gates, on Sunday mornings. She suggested that he enquire there. She believed that being an RIC constable would stand in his favour, considering how politics were developing in the country. Bill agreed and promised her that he would make enquiries. This cheered him up a bit and they resumed their walk back a different and longer route to the town. They had a cup of tea in Mooney's restaurant and said their goodbyes. They made a date to see each other again.

Missus Mooney was pleased to see that Bill had a friend and told him so. However, he couldn't help noticing that her attitude to him had somewhat changed, not for the better, he thought. Were the events of early 1919 changing her view of the legitimate Irish police force? He thought it might. The time to change his profession was near at hand.

On 3 February Éamon de Valera escaped from Lincoln Prison. He had been sent there in May of the previous year, when seventy-two Irish nationalists were arrested for being involved in the 'German' plot. The escape was masterminded by Michael Collins and Harry Boland. De Valera had copied the chaplain's key when he was saying Mass and had the details sent out via a Christmas card. The copy of the key was returned to him via a cake and the escape was executed. Later, in the early summer, he went to the USA to fund raise, not returning until Christmas 1920.

On 10 April 1919 the Dáil called for a boycott of the Royal Irish Constabulary. At first, it was an idea that appealed to members such as de Valera and Griffith, in an effort to support a 'peaceful' boycott rather than encourage full scale violence against the police force. However, it did nothing for the morale of men like Bill Byrne. The RIC was unofficially being boycotted anyway. He made up his mind to resign soon and try to obtain employment elsewhere. This would not be a very difficult thing for a single man to do but for his colleagues, who were married and who had young families to support, this could mean much hardship, so they mostly had no option but to stay on.

Incidentally, in 1914, the majority of RIC men were Catholics – 81 per cent. A later statistic states that 70 per cent of the constables were Catholics whereas 60 per cent of higher ranks were Protestants.

CHAPTER TWENTY-FIVE

Armistice

The Major receives an unexpected and unwelcome visit.

'Ah Byrne, have you got a minute?' asked Major O'Kelly as he entered the yard.

'Of course, sir,' replied Brian.

'I think we should be tightening up security on the estate, what with Sir William's recent visit from a terrorist organisation.'

'You mean the IRA, sir?'

'Yes, of course, Byrne. I want you to ensure the main gates and the side gate are locked every evening from six o'clock. Can I rely on you to do this?'

'Yes, of course, Major.'

Brian and Mags Byrne, with their two boys, got on with their lives as normal as they could. Brian heard about Sir Reginald William's encounter with the IRA. He knew that Major O'Kelly was increasingly worried about getting such a visit. As mentioned before, he instituted other security measures around the estate after the event. This included extra barbed wire, high fences and hedges cut tightly to prevent break-ins.

It was furthermore worrying for the Major and other landowners when the Military Service Bill was passed in April 1918. This meant that conscription in Ireland would be legally enforced, giving rise to much agitation. The arrests of prominent Sinn Féin members in the summer was fuel for the fire. It gave Sinn Féin much welcomed publicity and boosted their membership considerably.

On an evening in October, Brian and Mags had just finished their tea. Mags was about to give baby Thomas his bottle when she heard a noise outside. Brian heard it too and raced to the window. There was a group of men at the main gate. The light was fading but he could see that they wore dark clothes and caps but their faces weren't covered. They were attempting to open the gate but seeing it was locked, one of them tried the side one. It was locked too. Then they shouted, 'Open up! Open up!' as they rattled the main gate violently. Young Joseph became frightened and began to cry. Brian went outside to see what the racket was all about.

'We are the Irish Volunteers,' announced the leader. 'Let us in as we need to speak to the Major.'

'I t'ink the Major is away lads; can I give him a message?' Brian lied.

'Don't give us that shite, Mister Byrne. We know he is there, so let us in or your wife and family will suffer the consequences.'

Brian went and got the key and let them through. One of the men said on departing, 'Remember, we know who you are. Leave the gate open for our return. And you never saw our faces, understand mister Byrne? By the way, how is that brother of yours?'

'Yeah, yeah sure, sure. Whatever you say. He's fine t'anks.'

They mounted their bicycles and headed up the avenue.

With that, Brian re-entered the house. Mags was crying and hugging her baby and her young son. Brian tried hard to comfort her and two-year-old Joseph, who was clinging to his mother and still crying.

'What's goin' to happen to us, Brian?' she asked between sobs.

'Ah don't worry dear they won't harm us; they will leave us alone.'

He was worried, however. What if they attack his employer and maybe set fire to the big house? He needed this job to support the family and he was also very fond of the Major.

Major O'Kelly and his wife, Elizabeth were finishing their evening meal. The servant was taking away the dishes and the Major lit a cigar. He heard footsteps on the gravel outside the front door. He wasn't expecting visitors. *Who could it be*, he thought? With that, the doorbell rang.

'Can you get that, Wilson?' he called to his butler/servant.

Michael Wilson went to the door. As he opened the door, it was rudely pushed in knocking him aside.

'What the…?'

'Move back, man. We need to see the Major.'

Four men, wearing balaclavas, rushed into the hall.

'Who is it, Wilson?'

With that the dining room door flung open and the men entered, one had a revolver drawn. Elizabeth O'Kelly fainted, slumping in her chair.

'Get out! Get out of my house at once,' ordered the Major, raising his hands.

'Hands over your head,' was the counter order.

'I must attend to my wife.'

'Quickly, quickly.'

The Major cradled Elizabeth in his arms and gave her some water to drink. Eventually she came to.

'Liz, Liz are you alright?'

'What's … what's happening, George?

'Hurry up, Major! You have two minutes to sort your wife out.'

George helped her to the chaise longue.

'It's alright, my darling. I am just going to have a word with our guests. Wilson, can you stay with my wife whilst I step out of the room?'

'Certainly, sir.'

The Major left the room with the volunteers.

'What do mean by bursting into my house and disrupting our dinner and upsetting my wife like this?'

'Hand over your head or else,' was the reply.

The Major explained that he only had a shotgun but the leader demanded that he hand over his hunting rifle as well. He knew he had them and if he didn't hand them over immediately, he would ransack the house and further upset his wife. The Major was wondering how they knew about his firearms but he did have a service revolver stashed away separately that was not mentioned.

'Ok, ok. I'll get them.'

'And one of my men will come with you,' said the leader.

The Major went to the kitchen and retrieved the weapons. The revolver was hidden upstairs. The man snatched them from him and demanded the ammunition. The Major said he only had a few bullets for the rifle and searched in the drawer for them. He found a small box and handed them over.

'Hurry up! Hurry up! We haven't got all night,' shouted the leader.

With that the four intruders headed for the door. One of them was surprised to see a crucifix hanging over it, as he believed all big houses were owned by Protestants. They slammed the door behind them, mounted their bikes and raced down the avenue.

Major George rushed into the dining room to see how his wife was doing. She was still lying on the chaise longue sipping a glass of brandy that Wilson had given her.

'What are we going to do, George?'

'It's a'right, darling. It was just a bunch of bandits looking for arms. They won't be back,' he hoped.

He intended to have a word with Brian Byrne in the morning to ask why he let the raiders in but he suspected he was forced to do so. He also suspected that the men had guessed that he had a shotgun but the existence of his rifle appeared to be known – how?

Eventually, Major George and Elizabeth O'Kelly settled back into life as best they could. They knew that the Great War was drawing to a close and that was good news. They had regular letters from their children, George and Martina. They were keeping well, as was his grandson, little George. There was some hope that, with the end of the war in sight, that the trouble which arose because of the conscription bill would cease and peace would return to Ireland. However, the Major was concerned about the way that politics in Ireland was developing. He wondered how the general election in December would go and what effect the results would have.

When the war eventually ended on 11 November, there were some celebrations in the country. This could not be compared with the celebrations – especially in Naas and Newbridge in County Kildare, as the Major read in the *Kildare Observer* – with those in 1914. Several shops and businesses displayed British flags and the Union Jack was hoisted over the Courthouse in Naas. The above newspaper reported soon after the armistice that:

>...*there was a general feeling of relief, if there was little outward manifestation of jubilation. Towards evening, there was some flag waving by the military, who later indulged in pranks and demonstrations to show their joy at the termination of the war.*

CHAPTER TWENTY-SIX

Nightmares Persist

John vows to mend his ways and tries to forget the past.

As John and Mary supped their tea, John just stared into the fire and lit a cigarette. Mary didn't like him to smoke on account of his lung damage but she knew his nerves weren't the best. He said nothing for some time, then Mary asked, 'Is everything alright John? Ye seem a little quiet.'

'Yeah, I'm alright Mary. Tom and me were just talkin' about t'ings.'

'What t'ings?' She sounded a bit anxious.

'Well Pet, ye know I love ye very much and I'm worried about me behaviour of late. I say silly t'ings when I have a bit too much to drink and then I have those horrible nightmares and I know they disturb you and the children. I know ye must be t'inking, I'm going mad.'

Mary looked at him very seriously and John froze a little.

'Ah Darlin', what are ye on about? You're not going mad. I know that the auld war has done your head in a bit. What do ye dream about anyhow?'

John told her of a particular nightmare where he sees a cloud of gas crossing no man's land and, as it approaches, it turns into a massive green monster and grabs him by the throat and he can't breathe. Another is where he is talking to his comrade in a trench and when he turns to look at him, his comrade has no head and blood oozes from his neck but he continues to talk. He tells Mary about a man slipping into the mud from a duckboard and begins to disappear but suddenly, he is that man and......

'Stop, stop John! I don't want to hear anymore, t'ank you. Those are terrible nightmares but ye know I love you very much too.

Just drink a little less and I'm sure your bad dreams will go in time. Come here and give me a hug and a kiss.'

They embraced, kissed and hugged each other. John felt relieved and a tear came to his eye.

'T'anks Pet. I'll mend me ways from now on. I'll cut down on the jar. I never mean to drink too much but it tends to help me forget the horrors of the war and gives me a bit of a break from them. But you are my rock, ye know that and being with you gives me so much peace and happiness.'

The New Year of 1919 was quite eventful. John was becoming a bit worried about his job in Sackville Street, with all these soldiers demobilising in the city. As already mentioned, some were not fit for work but others were young and very fit, especially those who had not spent a long time in the war. However, the changing political situation, with the setting up of the Dáil and the murder of the RIC men in Tipperary, made ex-British servicemen less popular and less likely to be employed by many. Nevertheless, the centre of Dublin still needed much restoration and John felt less insecure. There was also the fact that policemen were being targeted more than military personnel.

He met his friend, Tom every Friday evening for a drink after work. They enjoyed a chat and each put forward solutions for putting the world to right. He made sure he didn't consume too much porter although he was often very tempted. Mary was due to deliver their baby in a few months, so he also made sure not to stay out too late.

One day at work, John was approached by a shop steward of the ITGWU. 'If ye want to keep working here, I'd advise you to join the union.'

John thought for a moment. The steward noticed his hesitation and added, 'You fought for king and country and I'm sure you wouldn't want that publicised now, would you?'

'No problem, me boy. I wanted to join the union anyway. Sure, I spent most of the war in a German prison camp and I only joined up for the extra few bob.'

'Exactly, you took the *king's shillin'*, didn't ye? Don't worry; I'll keep me mouth shut.'

John was surprised that word was going around that he was in the army. Since he came back from Germany, he was mostly concerned with himself and his family. Even in the building site, the sound of a man shouting or loud noises made him nervous and gave him flashbacks. He had not really considered how Ireland was changing fast. The British had incorrectly labelled Patrick Pearse and the other leaders of the Rising as 'Sinn Féiners' or 'Shinners' and now Sinn Féin were gaining momentum.

John believed that joining up in 1915 was a big mistake. He had seen so many of his friends and colleagues killed or wounded and some even being severely mutilated. He knew he was lucky to come home relatively unscathed. He was lucky to have Mary and the children, to have a job and also a house to live in. He considered the war to have been a complete disaster. Four years of fighting and for what?

He believed that the call for men to fight for the freedom of small nations was pure propaganda. Britain had no intention of honouring it in the case of Irish politics. Many Irishmen joined because of this and about 30,000 never returned. Home Rule was not now acceptable by either Britain or Ireland and much of the population of Ireland wanted nothing less than a full republic. Sinn Féin were now pushing for this.

John also believed that an Ireland free of British rule was probably now the best option. He felt duped by politicians in the past and also hoped for a new beginning. He wasn't in favour of an armed struggle as he had more than enough of war and death. Maybe a negotiable agreement might be a peaceful option.

Chapter Twenty-Seven

Job Hunting

Bill discovers another side to life and a world that he never knew existed.

Bill Byrne continued with his career in the RIC for a few more months into the summer of 1919. His relationship with Marie Callaghan had progressed very well. He met her regularly, either in Maynooth or Kilcloon. He cycled towards Kilcloon from his lodgings and she cycled from her house to meet halfway. The evenings were getting longer and brighter and they often cycled together around the ancient walls of Carton estate.

One weekend she brought him to her home to meet her parents. They appeared to be happy that their daughter was seeing this tall handsome man. Privately, they were a bit concerned about the dangers RIC men were facing. However, the county of Kildare was relatively safe due to the large number of British soldiers stationed in the Curragh and towns such as Newbridge and Kildare. The Volunteers/IRA were finding it more difficult to continue their policy of rendering Ireland ungovernable by the British on account of this military presence. However, there was still much intimidation, etc of the police force taking place, following the Dáil's decision to boycott the RIC. The new Irish government of the Dáil was never going to be recognised by the British government, which led to confusion as to who exactly was in charge.

Bill considered seeking alternative employment in the St Patrick's College in Maynooth. He thought he could apply to do security duties there or work on the almost self-sufficient, large farm. He made enquiries locally and he was told, in a message sent to Missus Mooney, to attend for an interview with the bursar.

On the day of the interview he arrived at the gate lodge early and was told to follow the path straight under the archway ahead. He would find the bursar's office at the far end of the large square at the other side. Bill was amazed at the size of the college. As he passed through the archway he noticed the spire looming large above the outstanding Gothic buildings, designed by the architect, Pugin, who, incidentally, designed part of the houses of parliament in London.

The foliage and shrubs in the formal gardens of the square where amazing. The June day was bright, warm and sunny, which brought out the best of all the plants on display. Climbing plants jostled for position on the dormitory walls surrounding the square and were now displaying beautiful shades of green. The climbers appeared to peep into several of the many windows as they made their way to the roof. What did they see? The air was filled with the scent of summer flowers and bees busily gathered nectar as they buzzed from plant to plant. Gardeners were equally busy as they attended the masterpiece.

Several students were gathered at one corner of the square, close to the magnificent church. They were dressed in their obligatory black soutanes. One glanced at Bill as he approached the large central door. The door was beautifully finished in carved oak. He rang the bell and, while he waited, he wondered as to what world was this in which he now found himself. He had never seen such opulence in his whole life.

A middle-aged servant opened the door, asked Bill his name and told him to follow him. He led him, along a long corridor, to a side room near the bursar's office. The inside of the college was as magnificent as the outside. Bishops and cardinals, in all their finery, peered down at him from paintings as they walked to the room. Through the windows he noticed a smaller square with a pond and small shrubs. The base of the massive spire was also visible.

The reverend bursar's secretary appeared from the office and invited Bill in. The bursar, a considerably overweight priest with a friendly, if a little red, face sat behind a huge desk and motioned to him to take a seat. Bill was asked the usual questions about where he was born, where he attended school, etc and about his career to date. The good priest was a little taken aback when the RIC was mentioned. He told Bill that he would let him know if there was a vacancy available that would suit them both. He thanked him and left. Bill thought that this was a 'don't contact us; we'll contact you' situation but, he still kept up his hopes.

On his way back to the gate Bill saw two large limousines approaching him through the archway. He stood aside. As they passed, he noticed that each car carried a bishop, in full regalia, seated in the back. They continued to the central door of the building in which he had his interview. He was told by the gatekeeper that a meeting of the bishops of Ireland was to take place the following day. After the meeting, the bishops condemned, in a statement, British rule in Ireland.

Bill met Marie later and they discussed his interview. He told her about the 'other world' beyond the gates of St Patrick's College. He described the wonderful square with its beautiful flowers and shrubs and, of course, the imposing buildings surrounding it.

She was impressed when he told her of the arrival of the bishops in their modern motors. He explained to her that they were known as the 'princes' of the Catholic Church. One was the Archbishop of Dublin, Dr William Walsh. He may have been a prince of the church but, for thirty years, he campaigned for educational, social and political equality for his flock. (He died in 1921 and a tricolour was draped over his coffin). They discussed if the Carpenter from Nazareth would have approved of this hierarchal system in the church that he founded, two thousand years before.

Speaking of princes, Bill mentioned the ruins of the castle situated just before the entrance to the college and asked Marie if a king or a prince once lived there. Marie told him that it was once the home of the Fitzgerald family, the Earls of Kildare, the last being Silken Thomas, who literally lost his head in the Tower of London. The heads of the Fitzgerald dynasty were later granted the title of Dukes of Leinster. He remembered that Marie suggested he enquire about a job in Carton, which was now the home of the dukes. He told her would go there.

On his next day off, the following week, Bill decided to cycle to Carton House to see if there were any job vacancies. It was a beautiful summer's day and he felt good cycling up the Dublin Road. The trees were in full bloom and a lark sang high above a nearby meadow.

He passed the Black Lion public house, which looked very inviting in the sunshine. He promised himself to enjoy a pint there on his way back. He entered the estate through the main gate opposite Pikes Bridge. He cycled up the winding avenue towards the great Palladian house. It soon came into view, beyond a lake and fulfilled Bill's every expectation where it sat in its splendid setting. He crossed over the narrow bridge of the artificial boating lake and the eccentric Shell Cottage could be seen at the other end. Swans, ducks and geese were busy feeding on the lake ignoring the visitor.

Bill cycled under some fine oak trees and there, half hidden, the fine residence reappeared. It was magnificent. Bill couldn't believe that he had discovered yet another world unknown to him. The large estate spread out on all sides of the house, seemingly for miles. Cattle and fine horses grazed in the surrounding fields and workmen could be seen attending to their daily tasks in the gardens and in far off meadows. He was impressed.

He asked a gardener as to where he could enquire about a job. The gardener looked at him for a moment, stroked his beard, pulled on his pipe, spat, missed the ground and landed on his boot, scratched his arse, farted and finally remarked, 'Ah jaysus, sure the auld jobs are few and far between these days since his eminence, Lord Edward, took over the estate. He bankrupted the place last year and we was all a bit worried about our jobs but we're still holdin' on.'

'So, ye don't t'ink it's worth enquirin', do ye?'

'Ah sure, mister, see the foreman, Tommy Bennett. Just go through that gate there. He'll be the other side, watchin' the gardeners while readin' a paper – a very busy man indeed.'

Bill did as he said and soon found Mister Bennett reading the *Irish Independent*, sitting on a beautiful, ornate, black, cast-iron bench. He introduced himself to the foreman, who invited him to take a seat.

'I suppose you are lookin' for a job, me son?'

'Yes indeed. Anything goin'?'

'Not a lot just now, as the Master has been a naughty boy.'

'I heard the place is bankrupt.'

'And so it is. It's never been the same since Master Desmond was killed in the war. He was a good man; Lord Edward likes to gamble and chase the ladies but we've been short of good labourers because of the war.'

Bill felt hopeful.

'I'll tell you what, can you make hay?' asked Tommy Bennett

'Oh yes, I worked in farms in Rathangan. I can make hay very well sir. I also did other farming jobs, such as milking, cutting hedges, thinning turnips and the like.'

'Very good. We'll be makin' the hay next month so come and see me and there'll be a job for you till at least September. What do ye say?'

Bill said that he would think about it and he would let him know very soon.

Chapter Twenty-Eight
Switching Uniform

For John, the war is never over as he enlists in a new cause,
where his army training comes in useful.

John Brennan joined the ITGWU and continued to work on the building site. The weather was often cold and wet and the work hard enough but he now had three children with the arrival of baby Patrick and he needed the work. He kept himself to himself. He still had a few pints with his friend, Tom Dempsey after work on Fridays. He wasn't happy that anarchy seemed to be creeping into Irish life. Tom was of the same view. Law and order steadily broke down as the police force became less and less effective. The RIC was being targeted more and more. The boycott implemented by the Dáil was having a devastating effect. Recruits were intimidated and shops and traders, who dared to serve police officers, risked retaliation by the republican movement.

John and Mary carried on life as best they could. Unemployment had increased since the return of the war veterans. There was much poverty again in Dublin City. The end of the war saw the end of 'separation' money. Sinn Féin prisoners were released and most were back in Ireland. Life was definitely changing in Ireland and in Dublin especially. Their two older children were at school and Mary was busy with little Sean and the new baby, Patrick. Missus Wilson still called to see them. They often discussed how things might develop.

One summer Friday evening, John and Tom were enjoying a couple of pints in their favourite pub. A young man approached and sat at their table. He was well dressed in a fine suit and wore a cap. He spoke to them, in a low voice, in a more 'affluent'

Dublin accent, 'We know you both served king and country and there's no point in denying it.'

The men were a bit taken aback but said nothing.

'We know you have knowledge of policing, soldiering and the handling of firearms so, if you know what's good for you, you will help in the struggle against British imperialism in this country.'

'What do ye want us to do?' John asked.

'You will wait for instructions from us. We know where you live,' came the reply and the man left.

Tom looked at John and remarked, 'What the fuck was that all about, John?'

'Fucked if I know, Tom. What shall we do?'

They looked around to see where the young man had gone but he was nowhere to be seen. The other customers were chatting and enjoying their drinks as if nothing had happened.

The men wondered what they were going to be asked to do. John had a lot of experience with military firearms and even on the big guns at the front. He knew how to set them up and had some idea how to set the range of fire, etc. He had done so when he returned to the front, following his period of recovery from gas poisoning. Tom, on the other hand, had much experience of policing in his years with the Dublin Metropolitan Police. He had a six-month training period before passing out as a constable. It was an intensive course and some of his fellow recruits did not pass or left before the six months were completed.

John was worried about Mary and the children. Who had been watching the house? He thought that this was getting a bit frightening and he had to seriously consider the situation. He suggested to Tom that they finish their pints, as he needed to see if everything was alright at home. Tom agreed and was secretly worried about who had been watching him as well. He considered taking a different route back to his lodgings.

John arrived home and Mary was a bit surprised that he was early.

'Is everything alright, Love? Why are ye home early?'

'Ah yes, Pet. I am a bit tired today so we decided to call it a night.'

Mary looked at him intensely and stated, 'You're worried about somethin'; can see that, John. Tell me!'

John hesitated and then told her about the stranger who approached them in the pub. He said he would have no option but to co-operate, as he feared for the family. Mary was very upset.

'I don't want ye to go back to war, John. I couldn't bear for ye to be away from home again. It would kill me!'

John gave her a hug and said that, as far as he could tell, they just want him to train IRA recruits on how to operate guns and things like that. He assured her that he would not be in any danger. Mary was not totally convinced but calmed down a little.

They discussed the present situation, with the rise of republicanism and the breakdown of law and order in some towns and cities. John was beginning to sympathise with the IRA but he wasn't sure about some of their tactics. When he mentioned to her that his friend, Tom would be expected to help them with policing, Mary said that she knew of a policeman who lived in Barrow Street not long since. She said she thought his surname was Byrne. John told her that he would ask Tom if he ever knew him.

The IRA consisted mostly of young men in their late teens or early twenties. These young lads lacked military experience and required training and discipline, which included marching and parade ground activities. Veterans of the Great War were ideal candidates to help organise training and share their war-time experiences. They were hardened fighters and had much knowledge of British Army tactics and organisation. Many of

John's comrades were also approached to help in the struggle for freedom. Many were willing to assist but others refused.

During the summer of 1919, the police, more than the military, were targeted by the IRA. The General Officer Commanding-in-Chief in Ireland actually informed the RIC Inspector General, Brigadier General Sir Joseph Byrne, in August that the army could no longer be able to provide detachments to support police outposts. Many weapons were taken from RIC officers and several barracks were raided for this purpose. In March of that year 75 rifles and a quantity of ammunition were stolen from the military airfield at Collinstown, County Dublin.

John was informed, in August, that he would be required to spend weekends training IRA recruits at a secret location. Mary was worried when he told her but she agreed for him to attend, as she knew there would be trouble if he refused.

There was a knock on the door on the nominated Friday evening and John accompanied the young man he previously met to the corner at Boland's Mill. A car was waiting there. He was ordered to get in and he was immediately blindfolded by a second man. He was driven for, what seemed to be about thirty or forty minutes, and arrived at a location somewhere in the Dublin Mountains. It was a fine evening.

He was introduced to an officer who accompanied him to a shed-like building. He was shown several weapons, including three Lee-Enfield .303 rifles, an SMLE short magazine rifle and a Lewis light machine gun. He was asked to identify random items and asked about the different parts of the guns and their calibre, etc. There was also a second machine gun, a Vickers, which he recognised from his war days. He was asked to dismantle and reassemble it. This he did without much effort. He was then taken to a firing range and ordered to demonstrate his skills. The kick from the .303 rifle mildly surprised John as he hadn't fired one in quite a few years. However he was a pretty good shot and the officer was impressed.

The next day John conducted a familiarisation session for fifteen young men, which included loading and unloading firearms, cleaning them and finally firing them. He noticed that there were not sufficient weapons for everyone. Some were quick learners but others seemed to be a bit nervous and a little clumsy. He thought that at least two of them were a bit wary of him because he had been in the British Army. However, the rest of the boys were respectful.

At the end of the day, John was told by the officers that they were pleased with how he conducted the course and of his knowledge of the different weapons. He stayed on site again that night. The following day he gave a revision course. He was brought home in the afternoon, again blindfolded. Mary was very pleased to see him and he later gave her an account of the weekend. He told her that he would be required soon again for a similar exercise. John was happy that all went well and that his knowledge of weaponry did not desert him.

At the end of the month John was again collected from home and brought to the same location, where he conducted a second course. Again all went well and he got to know the IRA officer a little better. The officer, who said his name was Mick, never disclosed his surname for security reasons but he said he was from Westmeath and had been trained by an ex-British Army officer. John didn't believe that his first name was Mick either.

In early September John was again taken to the training area in the mountains. This time he was accompanied by a fellow veteran. They were told to instruct the new recruits in army exercises and it was suggested that they plan a route march for them. The two men were given a map of the local area. This time names of villages were shown on the map, as now they were being trusted, to an extent, by the IRA. However, they were still blindfolded on their way to and from the training area. John and his new friend studied the map and agreed on a route to take. They showed it to the officer, Mick, who approved it.

The march went well and the recruits were beginning to act like soldiers, showing respect for their tutors. Some found it difficult marching at a pace but others were fit enough to keep up. John actually found it quite difficult, as he was no longer a youth and it had been some time since he was on a march. His colleague was younger than him but John noticed that he too was struggling a little. Everything went reasonably well and the officer was quite pleased with the progress of the recruits. On the second day parade ground drills were practised and, due to the lack of guns, hurleys were used instead.

On 8 September the local IRA, led by Brigadier OC Liam Lynch, ambushed 18 soldiers of the King's Shropshire Light Infantry in Fermoy, County Cork. One of the soldiers was killed in a scuffle although Michael Collins, who organised the ambush, emphasised that no one was to be fatally wounded. This order wasn't easy to follow exactly. Lynch himself was wounded accidentally by one of his own men. The IRA got away with 13 rifles in waiting motorcars. They covered their getaway by arranging for tree trunks and boulders to be strewn on the road as they left.

It was the first direct attack by the IRA on the British Army and hailed as a brilliant coup. The subsequent inquest into the incident condemned the attack but failed to reach a verdict of murder as the IRA did not intend to kill the soldier. The result was that the town of Fermoy was sacked by members of the British Army, smashing windows and running amok. John read about it in the newspaper and was shocked that the army, in which he once served, would stoop to such thuggery and disregard for civilians. Some of these men were probably Irish and he may have fought alongside them. He resolved to help the IRA in any way he could and looked forward to an Ireland free of British rule.

The violence against and the intimidation of the RIC continued into the autumn and on into the winter. Resignations from the force increased steadily. The British administration refused to tolerate the situation and, by the end of 1919, they set up recruiting offices in London, Liverpool and Manchester for young men to join the Irish police force. Recruits were offered three pounds, ten shillings plus expenses per week – a lot of money for that time. Farm labours were only earning two pounds, five shillings per week, having just been given a rise from thirty shillings a week, following strikes by agricultural workers. Ninety per cent of the recruits were ex-servicemen and most were from England.

CHAPTER TWENTY-NINE

Dangerous Times

Bill finds that making hay while the sun shines is not always the easy option. He has some difficult decisions to make.

Constable Bill Byrne heard nothing from Maynooth College about employment there. He imagined that the fact that he was a police officer might have been the obstacle. *Never mind*, he thought, he had two weeks leave arranged for late July and he decided to spend it working in Carton if there was a vacancy. Marie was pleased as she was now getting very worried about his safety.

He cycled there one afternoon and again met Tommy Bennett. He told him that he was available for two weeks to help make up his mind. The foreman thought about it and finally agreed. Bill was to receive two pounds ten shillings for a six-day week and then, he was to let him know if he wanted to stay on till September. If he was a good worker, he might even get a 'bonus.'

Bill started work on the following Monday morning at eight o'clock. It was a showery day. He was shown around the farmyard and introduced to some of the workers. Several of the meadows had been mown but the rain had delayed the haymaking. So the first job Bill was asked to do was to cut thistles in a lower field.

He walked there with a young man named Joe Fogarty, from Sallins. They sharpened their scythes and got down to work. Bill hadn't used a scythe for several years but soon got the hang of it. He shared a cigarette with Joe when they had a break. They chatted about the politics in the country. Each offered their own opinion on how events could change daily life in Ireland. They agreed that life would never be the same again.

Bill didn't mention that he was a police officer and said he was just a casual labourer. Joe then told him that he had an uncle in the RIC in Naas and he was worried about him. His uncle had a wife and five children and if he resigned from the force they would probably starve. Bill said he had a 'friend' in the force but he said that he was single, so resigning wouldn't be a major disaster for him but he was concerned about the whole situation. Bill changed the subject to football and they continued with their work. It was quite a pleasant task and they worked at their own pace.

During the week the weather warmed up and the rain stayed away. Further meadows were cut by a team of horses. Bill helped to make haycocks in fields where the hay had already been turned and dried. A horse pulled a rake and heaped the hay in piles along straight lines. The men worked hard and steady, moving from cock to cock. Bill almost enjoyed it but he was not used to hard physical work.

A woman came to the field with a bucket of tea and some scones at lunch time, which was gratefully received by all. Most of the men brought sandwiches. On Saturday afternoons the same woman came with a bucket of cold bottles of Guinness stout, which was even more gratefully received.

After work, on most evenings, Bill found that his body ached and, when he retired to bed, the aches got even worse. However, the days passed quickly and he found peace and solitude in the fields.

One evening he stayed back to help the foreman tidy things up. He and Tommy Bennett talked about the years gone by and how different times were now. They sat under a haycock and shared a cigarette. Bill was reminded of his early youth, making hay in Rathangan as he watched the crimson sun set between the trees. Its red glow told him of a promise of a fine day in the morrow. Tommy told him of the happy days before the war when the estate employed many labourers. The work was hard and the wages poor but, as he said, the craic was mighty. The two men talked for a considerable time and then, as dusk's purple glow fell slowly, they made their way home, friends!

Nonetheless, at the end of the fortnight, Bill decided that this work was not for him. He also considered it to be foolish to give up his steady, if dangerous, job and risk not been kept on at Carton. He went to see Tommy and told him that he would not continue. Tommy was disappointed and said that he was a good grafter and a friend but, as he could not guarantee any work beyond September, it was probably for the best that he quit. He handed Bill his wages and later, when he got to his lodgings, he noticed there was an extra ten shillings in the pay packet.

Bill worked on into the winter with the force in Kilcock. Men were continuing to resign and retire but most of the married ones, as Joe Fogarty had said, had no option but to stay. The news that the British government was setting up recruiting offices in England was a concern for all the remaining officers.

The new year of 1920 brought more bad news for Bill and his fellow officers. RIC barracks all over the country were being targeted by the IRA and soon they were being vacated and closed down. In fact more than 500 had been closed and abandoned throughout the country by March. Empty buildings were often set alight. On one Saturday night in April, 150 barracks were simultaneously burned down in different parts of the country. Courthouses were also targeted. Law and order in many parts of the country was almost non-existent.

When Kilcock Barracks was closed, Bill was sent to Celbridge, a village about four miles south of Maynooth. He still kept his lodgings with Missus Mooney. His relationship with Marie Callaghan cooled a little as he was getting more and more agitated and nervous. He didn't want to be seen with her in the town as he feared someone would recognise him and she would be targeted. Some girls who dated policemen suffered humiliating punishments, such as having their heads shaved for 'walking out with peelers'. Marie had experienced a coolness from some customers in Dawson's shop. She was not sure if she was imagining it or if they suspected something. She was becoming anxious too. One evening, when she met Bill near Carton wall on their bicycles, as arranged, she broached the subject.

'Bill, I t'ink we should talk.'

'What about, Marie? Is there a problem?'

'You know there is and I t'ink it's getting' too dangerous for us to meet like this.'

'Maybe you're right; I'm a bit worried that somethin' terrible might happen to you.'

'And to you. I am very fond of you, Bill but maybe we should take a break for the time being.'

'I always look forward to seeing you, Marie but if t'ings get any worse, we could both be in trouble.'

With that they kissed, hugged and parted. They were both in tears but turned away from each other to avoid any embarrassment. Both were very sad to have to part but it was risky to continue in those violent times. They both also believed that they would probably never meet again.

The first English recruits to the RIC arrived in March, following only six weeks training. The original training period for Irish recruits was six months but, as most of the new men were ex-army, training on firearms and drilling was not required. Anyway, the government wanted to fill the many vacancies as soon as possible. The IRA immediately issued a proclamation, which included a solemn warning to 'prospective recruits that they join the RIC at their own peril.'

Due to a shortage of full police uniforms, these new recruits were issued with half-police and half-army ones and would be given the nickname of 'Black and Tans'. They would later be joined by the 'Auxiliaries', ex British Army officers, whose methods of enforcing the rule of law were controversial to say the least.

Bill had to stay in the barracks in Celbridge for several nights at a time. The RIC barracks in Maynooth was set on fire. The sergeant and his family were first escorted from the building. Bill decided not to return to his lodgings when, in May, the IRA destroyed the town hall in the town by detonating a bomb there. Many of the surrounding houses and shops were damaged. It was planted by a local man, Commandant Pat Colgan, who fled to Domhnall Ua Buachalla's 'safe' house afterwards. Later, during the night, he escaped on a bicycle to Dublin via Dunboyne. Bill was sad to see the lovely hall, in which he danced with Marie many times, completely in ruins.

CHAPTER THIRTY

The Prodigal Daughter

*Martina, the Major's daughter, pays a visit. She finds that her
family's circumstances are as complicated as her own.*

Major George O'Kelly was getting more and more concerned
about the state of the country. He didn't feel entirely safe
anymore. The RIC barracks in Rathangan was closed in early
March 1920 and, with further closures in the county, the nearest
police stations were either in Newbridge or Kildare Town. They
were between seven and eleven miles from his estate. There
were also disruptions on the railway network, sponsored by the
IRA. Railwaymen refused to handle any military munitions and
they also refused to operate trains carrying military or police
personnel. Kildare Town and Newbridge railway stations were
prime targets for this protest.

In September Martina decided to visit her parents. She had not
been to Rathangan for some time and was looking forward to
seeing them again. Her mother had written to her some time
before, to say that her father was suffering from depression. He
had never gotten over the death their son, John. She asked her
to come for a visit, maybe have a chat with him and see if some
medication might help. Martina wrote back to say she was busy
but she would come as soon as she could.

Kingsbridge (Heuston)* railway station was busy that Saturday
morning. Martina brought a light weekend case with a couple
of changes of clothes and presents for her parents. She still had
some clothes in her room at home.

---

* Like Dublin's other station, Connolly (originally Amiens Street
Station – see footnote on page 105), Kingsbridge Station was renamed,
in 1966, after another leader of the Easter Rising, Seán Heuston.

She was now a partner in an accounting company in Dublin, which meant her free time was limited. She had been dating a man for six months, Jonathan Wilde, who was an architect and worked in the city centre not far from her office. She had hoped that he would ask her to marry her sometime in the near future. To her disappointment however, he revealed to her, one evening over dinner in the Gresham Hotel, that he was married. He immediately added that he never loved his wife. He told her that they lived separate lives but still lived in the same house in Foxrock. They had two children, a boy and a girl.

Martina had grown very fond of Jonathan. She even thought she might be in love with him. She was shocked to be told of the marriage and the children. She felt betrayed and very annoyed. She fell silent for a while and then blurted out, 'Why didn't you tell me before now, Jonathan? You know I am very fond of you.'

'And I am very fond of you too, Martina but I was so happy that I met you that I just couldn't pluck up the courage to tell you.'

'Pluck up the courage! Pluck up the courage! Surely, you could have told me before we got serious!'

'I'm sorry, Martina, I should have done; can you forgive me?'

She was close to tears, got up and dashed to the washroom. When she eventually returned, she announced.

'Take me home at once, Jonathan. I have to think seriously about things.'

They broke up for about a month but, in the end, she agreed to continue seeing him. She was unable to get him out of her mind. He had sent her numerous letters, pleading for her to come back. He repeated that he never loved his wife and that the marriage was pre-arranged by his parents, as they wanted him to marry into a respectable and 'very rich' family. He swore to Martina that he was very foolish to go along with it. There were the children to consider. She was a society lady and they employed a nanny to look after them. He loved his kids and he could not leave them. He assured her that he and his wife slept in separate rooms.

Martina lived in a flat in Rathmines. On a few occasions, Jonathan had stayed there, discreetly, overnight. The sex was fantastic. She enjoyed her work and liked to be busy. She loved to go horse riding on Saturday mornings from a stable at the foothills of the Dublin Mountains. Occasionally Jonathan joined her and they galloped together through the woods. It was exhilarating. She put the fact that he was married to the back of her mind. She really did love him despite everything.

One fine Saturday morning he called to the stables and he and Martina saddled up and they went for a ride. Jonathan told her that he was taking her to a beautiful area close to the hills where they usually visited. It was to be a surprise. She was excited. They trotted along the country lanes. The scenery was as lovely as he promised it would be. In the distance Martina could see a building at the top of a hill. She asked what it was called. Jonathan told it was Mountpelier Hill and that the building was known as the Hellfire Club.

'I'm not going into a hellfire club; no way!'

'Don't be silly, my love, it's only a name. I just wanted you to see it.'

She agreed to 'look' at it but she wasn't going inside. She had heard stories about such a club and they frightened her.

They dismounted and tied the horses to a fence. The animals grazed greedily on the luscious grass. She clung on to him as they approached the ancient building. Jonathan enjoyed her tight hug. He took her by the hand and assured her all would be fine. *The 'club' did look quite interesting*, she thought but said nothing.

They entered through the open doorway. She was pleasantly surprised to find that the place was, in fact, not so bad inside. However, the many cobwebs, graffiti and the fire marks on the walls made it a little scary. The morning sun had lit up the room making it a bit less scary. They sat on a bench-like stone and enjoyed the view of the far-off hills through the open window. He kissed her and they embraced. She was happy.

The room was suddenly darkened by a gathering of rain clouds. Martina shivered. She remembered the stories she had heard at Trinity College about this place: the drinking, the drugs, the sex, general debauchery and even devil worship. She put the thought out of her mind. She gazed into his deep blue eyes and told him she loved him. He was about to answer her when, touching her leg, she brought it up and accidentally knocked over an old, battered bucket (She didn't actually kick the bucket!).

Suddenly, there was a loud crash in the adjoining room. They both jumped up startled. They heard movement and a groaning sound coming from the other room. They both froze. Jonathan signalled for her to stay put and, as he inched his way to the doorway, an enormous, bearded, black-coated tramp stumbled in through it. Martina screamed. The tramp dropped his bottle of Guinness smashing it on the floor, tripped over a large beam and fell on his face.

'Ah jaysus, what the fuck are yis doin', frightenin' a poor body out of his sleep?' groaned the big man, as he tried desperately to get to his feet, failed and fell back on the floor.

Jonathan eventually managed to sit him down on another stone. He reeked of booze, mixed with the stench of an unwashed body and equally unwashed clothes. Martina stood well back, covering her nose with her handkerchief.

'Are you all right mister? Are you hurt?' asked Jonathan.

'Ah, I'll be fine. I'm just a bit unsteady on me feet these days. Kind sir, can ye spare a few coppers so a body can get bit of grub in the village?'

Johnathan wondered where the village was, gave him a half a crown, took Martina by the hand and swiftly left the building. They laughed heartily as they mounted their horses.

'You won't forget the Hellfire Club, will you my dear?'

They laughed again.

Martina told her parents that she had a boyfriend but gave no other details. Her mother often pressed her about marriage but she just changed the subject, saying that for now, her job was more important.

The train pulled out of the station on time. She looked forward to seeing her parents and Rathangan again. The train was quite full but her first class carriage was very comfortable and she watched the countryside pass slowly by. The trees were changing into their autumn attire and looked amazing. The colours were awesome.

The train stopped at Sallins and several passengers boarded. When the train arrived at Newbridge, it seemed to wait a long time. There was no sign of any forward movement. Martina continued to enjoy her snack of a black coffee, crackers with a generous helping of Wensleydale. She noticed some passengers had boarded and others disembarked from her carriage. Suddenly, she heard raised voices further down the platform. An upper-class, male, English accent screamed out, 'I'm an army major and I order you to allow myself and my men to board this train, NOW.'

'I don't care who the fuck ye are, sir but you're not getting on my train.'

Martina had a quick sip of her coffee, rushed to the window and peeped out. She saw two army officers and three privates attempting to board the train at the next carriage. The guard was pushing them back but they forced their way in. There was a bit of a commotion with shouts and swearing. The guard emerged and ran past Martina's carriage to the engine. He had words with the driver who immediately stepped down to the platform. The station supervisor approached them.

'What's the matter lads? Is there trouble?'

'Our union forbids us to carry army personal, so if that group who boarded that carriage don't get off, we are staying put,' replied the driver.

The guard nodded enthusiastically in agreement. 'You should know that; shouldn't you?' he added.

The supervisor went to have a word with the army major. A heated discussion in the carriage followed.

Martina looked at her watch, the train was already quite late and had remained in the station for forty-five minutes. The arguments continued next door. Everyone in the carriage was getting agitated and some were a bit concerned. Passengers glanced around and soon they were sharing their annoyances and concerns with each other. The railway company was criticised for having a not very punctual reputation and the republican movement was also mentioned.

Suddenly a shot rang out and a man was seen dashing from the adjoining carriage. All hell broke out – screaming, shouting, crying. A private jumped from the same carriage, revolver in hand. He fired a shot at the fleeing suspected gunman, missed, the bullet ricocheted off an iron supporting beam and broke a window. It just missed a passing woman. Women were screaming, men shouting.

Martina was shocked and upset. She was immediately comforted by a fellow passenger, an elderly gentleman in a bowler hat. He helped her sit down and offered her a slip of brandy from his hip flask. She gratefully accepted and sat down. The man also offered her a cigarette but she refused.

Soon the platform was swarming with police. Statements were being taken and witnesses sought out. Many passengers refused to even talk to the police. Few admitted to seeing the assassination of the Major. It turned out that he was killed by a man who entered the carriage from the empty parallel railway track and made off across the platform. The gate from the platform was mysteriously opened and suddenly closed when the assassin passed through, hindering the chasing soldier.

Major O'Kelly waited at Kildare Town station. Its train was very late. He found the station supervisor, who was enjoying a cigarette at the far end of the platform. He told him that the train had been delayed at Newbridge. He had no further information. Several passengers were also waiting and getting a bit concerned. There had been delays before when military supplies were refused loading by the station staff.

After a considerable time, the supervisor announced that there had been an incident at Newbridge and that the train was delayed indefinitely. There were mutterings of annoyance from the awaiting passengers but the supervisor advised them that their tickets would be honoured on the same service the following day.

A woman approached the Major and asked if he were meeting someone and if so, could she have a lift to Newbridge. George agreed to drive her the seven-mile journey in his recently acquired Morris Cowley motorcar. She said she was meeting her husband who was travelling down from Dublin. They chatted on the way and she told him that two of her sons were killed in the war. George told her about his tragedy too. He was a little grateful that he hadn't lost both his sons, as she did. How would he have coped with that? They wondered what the war was all about. They were under the impression that it was the war to end all wars but there was no sign of peace in Ireland, which was sad. It was doubtful that war would not happen again.

There was quite a crowd outside Newbridge station. There were military vehicles parked close by and many military personnel were present. The RIC were stopping all vehicles approaching the station. George told a constable who he was and that he was there to collect his daughter. His passenger also gave her reason to be there. They were both asked to get out of the car. It was searched by an infantry man.

Passengers who were to travel further were being escorted to buses, to be ferried to an hotel in the town. Martina spotted her father and hurried to greet him. She was still quite upset. George gave her a hug and she told him the whole story. That evening Martina and her parents chatted over dinner. They were all shocked that a murder of the army major should have taken place so near to home.

Martina noticed that her father had lost a considerable amount of weight since she last saw him and that he looked quite pale. Her mother too wasn't her usual bubbly self. They told her of their concerns about the future. Some 'big' houses had already been burned down. 1920 saw the beginning of a republican policy of destroying symbols of British order in Ireland. Nearly 300 houses would be destroyed by 1923. Some houses were burned down mainly because the owners were Protestants.

The Major told them about the two RIC constables who were killed by the IRA in Kill following an ambush. One man was from Offaly and the other from Galway. The police patrol was cycling to guard the Chief Inspector's house. Two of them were taken prisoner. He also mentioned that the public house, The Dew Drop Inn, was wrecked by the police a few days later.

After dinner they retired to the drawing room. The Major seemed to relax a bit more. He lit a cigar and Wilson poured each of them a large Hennessy. They asked their daughter how things were in Dublin and about her new young man. Was she going to take him to Rathangan one day, so they could be introduced to him? Martina just said it wasn't that serious but perhaps, one day, they would all meet. She didn't give away many details about their affair. In order not to be pressed on the subject any further, she said that she was tired and retired to bed. George and Elizabeth were pleased to see their daughter after a long absence. They thought she looked well but suspected there was something troubling her.

The railwaymen's protests and the disruptions continued to December. Some trains were attacked and mail bags stolen – mostly those being sent to Dublin Castle. Kildare Town station was often a target, as it was a junction where the line spilt: one to Cork and the other to Waterford. They were supported by the Dublin dockers. Many workers were sacked because of it. However, it was called off by the union when the British government threatened to close the railways and withhold grants for the railway companies. This would have meant that the workers would not have been paid.

Martial law was introduced that year but only in about six of the twenty-six 'nationalist' counties. The Munster counties of Cork, Kerry, Limerick and Tipperary were the main areas affected. IRA activity was considerably less in other parts of the country. Violence was on the increase. The IRA killed policemen, informers and traitors. Some of victims who were executed were apparently innocent. The RIC retaliated by killing prominent IRA members, often in their own homes. The police were supported by the newly arrived Black and Tans. Sometimes houses of suspected republican supporters were burned down by the police. It was a tit-for-tat situation.

The British government refused to concede that a war (of independence) was in progress and merely attributed the situation to a breakdown of law and order.

CHAPTER THIRTY-ONE

A Deteriorating Situation

Flying columns, Black and Tans, the Auxies, Kevin Barry and another Bloody Sunday.

John Brennan continued his part-time role training republican recruits. As the winter approached the marches got tougher. Rain, wind, frost and snow made mountainous conditions almost impassable but it was excellent training for the young men. They were coming on well. Some had already been selected to act as improvised policemen in areas where the RIC could no longer operate safely. John's friend, Tom Dempsey's part-time job was to train these recruits in policing procedures and he also gave them some insight as to the law of the land.

Mary gave birth to their baby daughter, Joan, on the first of November. They were both doing well despite the hard winter. John now worked at the Graving Dry Dock in Ringsend as he was finding work on the building site a bit too strenuous. His left arm was often too painful and he planned to resign from the job rather than risk being sacked. He still had a pint, when he could with his friend, Tom in the city centre.

As already mentioned, police force numbers were boosted by the Black and Tans in the spring of 1920 and in July they themselves were boosted by the 'Auxiliaries'. The latter became even more feared by the republican movement and the community at large. From May to July, over five hundred RIC officers resigned or retired. The 'Auxies' operated mainly from Dublin but also in the 'troubled' areas of Munster. The year ended with the British parliament passing the Government of Ireland Act, which provided for the partition of the country. It was planned to have one government in Belfast and another in Dublin.

John was disgusted at the atrocities carried out by the police and/or military forces. He never imagined that men whom he fought alongside, in the trenches in France, would now be wreaking havoc in his native land. He resolved to help the IRA in every way he could. The final straw came when, firstly, the eighteen-year-old student, Kevin Barry, was hanged on baby Joan's birthday and secondly, the police and military (Black and Tans) killed sixteen civilians at a football match in Croke Park on 20 November. This was a reprisal for the killing of fourteen British agents that morning in Dublin. It was organised by Michael Collins. It was to be known as Bloody Sunday. That night Auxiliaries killed three IRA men they had captured in Croke Park. They reported that they were shot as they tried to escape. This was in some doubt.

John put himself forward for active duty with the IRA. Many of his comrades, veterans of the Great War, also did so. He did not tell Mary and she believed that he was still training recruits. They had a wonderful Christmas together as a family of six. The older children adored the new baby. John was still getting an army pension and, with the wages he saved from the building job, they could afford to buy decent presents 'from Santy'.

John thought hard about putting himself in danger again but he could not sit back and let the Black and Tans destroy his beloved city and country. Their conduct and tactics were a disgrace, even to much of the British public. Their reputation got a bad press in both Britain and the USA.

In January 1921 John met the young IRA man in the Bachelor Inn. He informed John of an operation that they were planning to ambush a Black and Tan lorry. It was hoped that some Auxiliaries might be on board. The lorry was expected to be on its way back to Dublin from Munster, where the 'Tans' were employed, keeping law and order. The 'military' men were expected to overnight in Newbridge barracks, according to information passed by an RIC sergeant there. John was to join a newly formed Kildare/Wicklow flying column, which was based in Blessington, County Wicklow. The date for the operation would be advised at a later stage. The man told John that he would be contacted by the commandant of the flying column in due course. He reminded him that any betrayal of the plan to the authorities would result in certain death. John assured him that he would not breathe a word to a living soul. They parted.

Work at the dry dock was intermittent but it was less physically demanding than that at the building site. Many widows and families in the city depended much on the army pension and were concerned about the campaign to rid Ireland of British rule. They feared that any new Irish government would not honour the payments. John was a bit worried about that aspect as well but he still believed that Ireland should be governed by an Irish parliament free from Westminster.

John was informed that the ambush would take place on a Saturday in February. He was taken, by car, to an address in Blessington. There he met the IRA Commandant, Sean O'Reilly. He was given details of the planned operation. It was to take place outside the village of Rathcoole, County Dublin on the main Naas/Dublin Road. The road beyond the selected site would be 'trenched' an hour before the lorry was due. This would mean that the lorry would be unable to initiate a swift getaway, as the trench would cause it to overturn. Normal traffic, such as carts and cars, could still pass safely.

On the night before John stayed in a safe house three miles from Rathcoole. In the morning he was joined by the commandant and another volunteer. He was given a Lee Enfield .303 rifle. The commandant had a revolver but he was surprised to see that the other man had only a shotgun. The plan was gone through again in detail. John's position was shown on a rough map of the area. At midday the men left the house and cycled to the village. The firearms were hidden. John's rifle was wrapped in a sack.

On arrival at the site, the men gathered in a copse, not far from the road. They awaited the five other volunteers. The woman of the safe house had given them sandwiches and bottles of milk.

Boiling a kettle and making tea was not an option. Soon the other men arrived: two first and then the final three. No names were exchanged but some men appeared to know others. John was a bit nervous. It brought him back to the trenches in France and the times that he awaited the order to go 'over the top'. He checked his rifle many times and cleaned it again and again. In fact, most of the men showed signs of nervousness, especially the younger ones.

The lorry was due at 1pm. They took up their positions at a quarter to the hour and waited. One thirty, no sign of the lorry. Same at two o'clock. The delay was due to a stop in Rathcoole, when the men decided that they needed a 'hair of the dog' in the local bar. The proprietor didn't want to serve them but the barrel of a revolver pointing at him persuaded him to agree. The street was emptied of shoppers and passers-by when the lorry was observed. The noise level in the bar increased. Finally, the 'Tans' re-boarded their vehicle and the journey was continued, much to the relief of the locals.

Dusk was descending when the lookout whistled from down the road – a sign that the lorry was approaching. John drew back his bolt. He was positioned twenty yards beyond the ambush site. The sound of the engine of the RIC Crossley Tender became louder and louder. The rain began to fall. Slowly it rounded the corner and into view. With what seemed like an age, the vehicle advanced towards the 'welcoming committee'. Commandant O'Reilly dropped his hand, guns blazed, two 'Tans' were hit and fell from the vehicle. Their comrades returned fire, a volunteer fell back into the hedge, dead. The driver revved up and surged forward. John shot a third 'Tan', who fell back into the lorry. His second shot, aimed at the driver, missed him and killed his passenger.

Two military men fell from the back of the lorry due to the sudden acceleration. They rolled for cover into a ditch, clutching their weapons. One opened up with his light machine gun. They too were reliving the Western Front. They picked off two more of the ambushers. The left side wheels of the tender sank into the trench. The driver tried to drive out of it but, sinking further, it overturned into the ditch. Men leapt from the vehicle. Two were hit by the volunteers. The others scrambled for cover and opened up on their assailants.

John continued to return fire but the weapons of the volunteers were no match for those of the army. Also, the experience of ex-servicemen in warfare was far superior to their enemy. Soon Commandant O'Reilly was forced to give the signal to retreat. John and his comrades ran back into the woods and followed a prearranged route to the road beyond the trench, where two cars awaited them. Several 'Tans' followed, firing as they advanced. The volunteers jumped into the cars and sped away. The rear window of the second car was smashed by a bullet but no-one was injured.

The cars raced in an easterly direction along the Dublin Road. At the next junction, one car turned left towards Newcastle and Celbridge and the other, right and headed for the Dublin Mountains. Three of the volunteers never made it. One was definitely dead; it was not known if the other two were dead or alive.

John travelled in the car towards the mountains and soon arrived at the training camp. Commandant Sean O'Reilly also travelled in this car. They disembarked and went to the shed. A debriefing was held. O'Reilly was somewhat disappointed that all the enemy weren't eliminated but was pleased with the bravery of his men. He was saddened that three of them had to be abandoned, including Danny O'Higgins who had lost his life. A prayer was said for the repose of his soul. He hoped that the other two volunteers were still alive. The younger volunteers were obviously upset by seeing men actually being killed. They were told to toughen up. John was thanked for his contribution to the operation and officially welcomed to the Kildare/ Wicklow flying column.

With that, John was taken home. He was physically and mentally exhausted. He never expected that he would use a gun again to kill military men. These men may have fought with him in

France not so long ago. However, the commandant did say that there were at least four Auxiliaries on the truck, so John hoped that he had killed at least one of them. Their reputation was contemptible and they were even not very popular with many of the Black and Tans.

Mary was a bit shocked when John arrived home. He looked drained and untidy. She asked if everything went alright on the training course. He just explained that the marching course was very tough and that he hadn't slept very well. She made him a cup of tea and a little supper of cold chicken and brown bread. He was hungry and wolfed it down. She poured him a decent measure of Power's whiskey, which he swallowed in one mouthful. This worried her a little. Anyway, she knew he was very tired so she suggested that he have an early night. This he did.

Mary fed baby Joan and put her to bed. When she fell asleep, she joined John. He was snoring and she was pleased that he appeared to be sleeping well. However, in the middle of the night, she was awoken by an horrific shout. John sat up and continued to rant and rave, flinging his arms in all directions. Mary had a difficult time calming him down. The children woke up. John was sweating profusely. She gave him some water. She had to go to see to the children. When she returned, John was asleep.

The next morning, there was a headline in the *Irish Independent*, giving details of an ambush near Rathcoole. It said that six military men were killed, including two Auxiliaries. It also said that three republicans had lost their lives. Two of the latter's bodies were found in a field some distance from the scene of the attack. An investigation was launched by the authorities into the incident. A later report maintained that the volunteers were escaping when they were shot. This was much doubted.

Mary showed the headlines to John, who pretended to be amazed and shocked by the news. Mary asked if he had heard anything on the training course about it but he lied and denied all knowledge. He was secretly pleased about the fate of the

'Auxies'. He was never much enamoured with British Army officers.

CHAPTER THIRTY-TWO

Come Out Ye Black and Tans!

Back in Dublin, Bill finds that a policeman's task is not made easier by those who have been sent to help!

Both the barracks and the courthouse in Celbridge were destroyed by fire on 30 August 1920. Constable Bill Byrne was transferred to Dublin. Celbridge had been a difficult barracks to work in. He missed his friends and colleagues in Kilcock. There it was more like a family operation. He knew the sergeant, even his wife and family, and the constables almost like brothers. He even had friends in the town. He knew the local publicans. The principle public house was owned and run by the Byrne family. No relation of Bill's but he had made friends with the proprietor, Billy Byrne. There was seldom any trouble in that pub and not much either in the other bars in the town. On the whole, law and order was respected.

In Celbridge the atmosphere was different. There were officers from all over Kildare newly transferred there following the closure of many country barracks. As RIC men resigned and retired their places were taken, if no Irish recruits were available, by the new 'English' men who had just finished their training – the so called Black and Tans. They did not know or want to know the local community. They were there to do a job – restore law and order by any means. They mostly didn't care how they achieved it. Their reputation was well known even before they arrived at the various barracks. The 'Tans' were as subtle as a brick through a window. They kept themselves to themselves in the large Celbridge Barracks overlooking the River Liffey.

Bill had to stay in a dormitory there, which was shared with several other RIC men. They could not leave the barracks, which meant that they were denied any social contact with the local community. It was too risky to frequent any of the bars, for fear of recognition. Even cycling to a country pub was equally too much of a risk.

The night before the barracks and courthouse were burned down, officers were moved to Lucan, County Dublin and others to the city area. It appears that the RIC intelligence division was tipped off about the attack in advance. Bill was posted to the DMP barracks in Park Gate Street. It was located in a pleasant area of the city overlooking the Phoenix Park. A long-established British military barracks was situated nearby. Known as 'The Royal Barracks', it was later renamed 'Collins Barracks', in honour of Michael Collins, by the Free State in 1922.

Bill and a fellow RIC colleague, Jim O'Shea, shared a room in the DMP barracks. The police officers at Park Gate Street were pleased to have two Irishmen join the staff. They feared the arrival of any English recruits.

The sergeant filled the men in on the situation in Dublin at the time. The Black and Tans were posted to and housed in the nearby military barracks and some were posted to city police stations, due to the shortages of regular policemen. He said that some of these men were interested in policing the city, respecting civilians and taking advice from the local constabulary. However, others were causing trouble. They employed rough military procedures and hassled civilians unnecessarily. They were giving the DMP an even worse name. Since the Auxiliaries (officially known as the ADRIC-Auxiliary Division of the RIC) arrived in the country in July, only a month before, the situation deteriorated. This paramilitary force was not answerable to the RIC, despite its name but instead, they reported to their own commandant.

The sergeant informed Bill and Jim that they would continue wearing RIC uniforms and carry firearms. They were to accompany the local constables and assist them as required.

The two new recruits to Park Gate Barracks went on patrol that afternoon, with two experienced DMP constables. Their beat seemed to be fairly peaceful and Bill was pleased to see a part of Dublin that he had seen, briefly, some years before. He remembered visiting the nearby Dublin Zoo, with dear Kathleen O'Connor, in happier times. He remembered how lovely the Phoenix Park was then. It still was. The trees were beginning to change into their beautiful autumnal attire and deer and sheep grazed contentedly in the open green park. The late summer sun shone lazily through the trees as they patrolled the North Circular Road.

As the IRA increased their attacks on police and military targets the British introduced military courts. These made it easier to convict terrorists. There was no jury. Some police and military personnel secretly took revenge for the attacks. Houses of republicans were ransacked and set alight.

Bill was on duty one late autumn evening when the station got a call to attend a disturbance in Benburb Street. This street was close to the Royal Barracks and ladies of the night frequented the public houses there. Soldiers were good customers for the girls. Bill, Jim and a DMP colleague went immediately. They could hear the din as they entered the street. It was coming from O'Neill's bar. Men were standing outside on the pavement. They could see that some were in military uniform. They recognised them as Black and Tans. One was shouting at a civilian.

'I can drink where I want; back off!' shouted the 'Tan'.

'No you fucken can't, you English bastard!' Came the reply.

The men came to blows. Bill and his colleagues intervened. The men were pulled apart.

'Let go of me, you filthy peeler; let me at the fucker,' cried the barman.

'Leave off. Can't you see I'm a British soldier, you paddy pig?' remarked the 'Tan'.

With that, four more 'Tans' rushed from the door, chased by a group of men. A woman followed, screaming, waving her handbag, her makeup running, blackening her face. Several other 'working' girls escaped and ran up the street. The fight continued on the pavement. Bill and his colleagues had no chance of controlling the situation. They just had to stand back and hope for a backup.

A Black and Tan officer appeared on the scene. He whipped out his revolver and fired a shot into the air. It hit a streetlamp darkening the scene. The fighting stopped. The officer ordered the soldiers back to the barracks, screaming abuse at them. They marched away, many a bit unsteady on their feet.

Bill and his colleagues demanded statements from the participants. The men turned their backs and re-entered the bar. The 'lady' remained.

'I'll give you a statement, Constable. Dem Black and Tans wanted to rape me. I'm a decent woman. I have to do this because me husband was killed in the war and I have four kids to feed.'

Bill listened to her story, sympathised with her and let her go.

The three constables moved away from the bar, as entering it could have proved dangerous in the existing climate. They continued on their regular beat. They walked as far as the Smithfield market area and then turned down to the River Liffey. They headed back along Aran Quay. The evening was relatively quiet. Due to the threat of attacks on the police, the three men kept alert and maintained a good look out. Bill suggested that they return to their station along Benburb Street. His colleagues agreed.

As they turned into Benburb Street, they noticed an army lorry entering it from the other end. It moved down the street towards O'Neill's public house. It stopped outside the pub and suddenly one of the Black and Tans on board opened up with a light machine gun. The front windows were shattered and screams and shouts were heard from inside. The lorry took off along the street towards Bill and his colleagues. More shots were fired into houses again breaking windows. The three men had to dive for cover as bullets bounced off walls and smashed more windows.

When the lorry disappeared around the corner, the men staggered to their feet. There was much devastation in the street. Some of the inhabitants had been injured. Women and children were screaming. Two men in O'Neill's bar were killed and others badly injured. Soon an ambulance arrived. Bill, Jim and their colleague assisted the injured as best they could. Sadly, this kind of incident went on in many parts of the country.

On 28 November the IRA's West Cork Brigade ambushed an Auxiliary patrol at Kilmichael, killing 17 men. The IRA Commandant was Tom Barry, a veteran of World War One. It was a blow for the British Army, as the Auxiliaries had convinced themselves that they were invincible. The IRA, on the other hand, celebrated it as an enormous victory.

CHAPTER THIRTY-THREE

Major Problems

Christmas 1920 and the Major's troubles are worse than he is willing to reveal.

Brian and Mags Byrne were delighted with their new baby son, Seamus. They had a wonderful Christmas together as a family. They went to Mass, visited his parents and relaxed after dinner whilst the older children played with their presents. Brian was a bit worried about the incidents in the previous month: Kevin Barry hanged, Bloody Sunday and Kilmichael. He hoped that his job was safe.

They had invited Bill to come but he was unable to because of the worsening situation in the country. It was becoming more and more dangerous for him to even venture outside the police station. He believed he still was not welcome in Rathangan. He would have loved to see his parents again. The War of Independence was certainly hotting up.

Major George O'Kelly had Christmas dinner with his wife and daughter. They also went to Mass. Martina still had not brought her boyfriend to Rathangan to meet them. She said that it was still quite dangerous to travel and that Jonathan had wanted to spend the festive season with his parents and his brother and sister.

Despite the railwaymen withdrawing their protests, etc earlier in the month, it was believed that the IRA still viewed the railway system as a legitimate target. George junior with his wife and child once again decided not to travel from London for the same reasons. The Major and Elizabeth were saddened that they would not see their grandson, George this Christmas. In fact they had never seen him. They wondered if they would ever see their son and his family again. This added to his depression.

Nonetheless, on St Stephen's Day the Major rode out with the Kildare hunt. Brian had readied his favourite mare and he was proud to ride her to the town to join his fellow fox hunters. It was something he looked forward to every Christmas season.

Martina was still not very happy about Jonathan's situation. He said that he and his wife lived separate lives but sometimes she had her doubts. She believed that he loved his children but surely he could make arrangements to see them, maybe at weekends. She had a sneaking suspicion that he might be using her for sex. He had mentioned his wife's name a bit too often, which fed her suspicions. Her mother asked her several times, when they were alone, if everything was well in her relationship. Martina assured her that she was happy and lied and told her that she thought Jonathan would propose in the New Year. She nearly convinced herself.

On St Stephen's Day Martina and her mother went for a horse ride along the lanes. They did not join the hunt. They chatted as they rode along. The weather was cold but clear. The weak winter sun shone at a low angle, brightening up the day. Martina enjoyed the cool country air and the wind in her hair. It helped to clear her head of the pressures of city life and the worries of the changing political situation in the country.

Elizabeth expressed her concerns about the Major's depression. He was no longer the happy man that she knew and loved. Martina said that he was probably upset with the way Ireland seemed to be heading. The old order was gone and everyone would have to adjust to the new era. However, her mother was very concerned about the new era. What was it going to be like for the middle classes? To her, the IRA and a 'free state' would mean a country run on the lines of communism. Something similar to Russia. The family would probably lose their land and even their house. The Land Commission was already dividing up estates. The O'Kellys were not an English ascendancy family; they were Irish. Why should they have to forfeit their land? Martina agreed that the future was unpredictable and it didn't appear to favour families like themselves.

The two women headed back to the estate and stabled the horses. The Major had not yet returned. The light was failing. They went inside and Wilson poured them both a rather large Hennessy. They were pleased when they heard that the Major and Brian coming up the avenue. Major George entered the drawing room, face glowed and smiling broadly at his wife and daughter, commenting on how beautiful they both looked. They suspected that he had had a tumbler or flask of whiskey too many but they were pleased, as they had not seen him so jolly in a long time. He sat down in his favourite armchair in front of the roaring fire. Wilson served him yet another large glass of whiskey.

'How was your day, girls?' he enquired.

They told him of the pleasant ride they had through the country lanes. He recounted the details of the hunt, the friends he met and how well the old mare had performed. He loved that beast. They chatted on into the evening. Martina played the piano and sang a few songs. Her parents joined in. It was a lovely relaxing evening.

George junior, his wife, Caroline and young George spent Christmas with his wife's parents in Finchley, North London. They had a large Victorian house in the leafy suburb. George and his family lived not far away in Edgware. He was a barrister and was comfortably well off. Caroline was English and was also a barrister. They met at Cambridge University. Although George's accent was more Anglo-Irish than British, he was usually recognised as Irish. Because he was born in Ireland, he was not subject to conscription in the Great War. However, he was often asked his opinion of the unrest and troubles in his native land. Like his father, he was concerned about the fate of landowners there. The newspapers reported on the activities of the new Auxiliary RIC force in Ireland. Several newspapers maintained that the more brutal of these activities were an embarrassment to the British Empire. *The Times* commented on the situation as follows:

The name of England is being sullied throughout the Empire and throughout the World by this savagery for which the government can no longer escape, however much they may seek to disclaim responsibility.

Some IRA operations took place in London and Liverpool in the period 1918-1920 and many IRA activists were arrested. Britain, however, had enough to deal with after the war was over. There were thousands out of work and general unrest. George O'Kelly was spared much animosity for being Irish born.

George would have loved to return to Ireland that Christmas, as he had not seen his parents or his sister in many years. His father often wrote to him, giving him all the latest news and happenings in Rathangan and the country. He decided not to go because of the troubles. It was dangerous to travel and his father advised him against coming for a visit. His father had concerns about the safety of his grandson travelling such a long way. He told his son about the big houses that were being burned down and other activities by the IRA. He said the O'Kelly estate was safe and that, financially, all was well. That was a lie. The end of the war meant that the British Army no longer needed as much supplies as before. The demand for horses and cattle had reduced. The cost of labour had increased. The Major was struggling to make ends meet. He relied on Brian to look after the farming side of things and his horses. He was trustworthy and reliable. The other men that he employed were less so. He had one reliable servant, Wilson; a maid, Agnes, whom he didn't much trust and a very nosey cook, Barbara, who spent most of her time talking. Still, the latter produced wonderful meals. The staff that he employed were only what he could afford and he would not be able to run the estate with any less.

Martina also wrote to her brother. She told him of her concerns for their father's health. He had lost weight and appeared to suffer from depression. Her mother was in good form. She had not visited them as often as she would have liked, due to pressure of work and the dangers of travelling. She mentioned the incident at Newbridge. It was very upsetting for her. She promised to come over soon to London to see them both and especially her little nephew.

One morning in January the Major received a letter from his bank, advising him of his deteriorating financial situation. He was well overdrawn. In fact, he was close to bankruptcy. This he half expected but still, the shock was traumatic. He sat down in his favourite chair and re-read the letter. He thought for a while and then decided not to tell his wife. He filed it in his writing desk and tried to put it out of his mind as he joined her in the dining room. She asked if everything was alright. He assured her that it was. They had breakfast together, he read *The Times* and all appeared quite normal.

A week later there was a loud knock on the door. It was early evening and already dark. Wilson answered it. As before the door was violently pushed open. Wilson fell back and four men entered the house.

'Where's the Major?'

Wilson tried to compose himself and stammered, 'He's ... he's j-just finishing his dinner. Who wants to know?'

The leader again pushed him aside and headed for the dining room. He seemed to know where to find it.

The Major was making his way to the door when it flung open. The leader had a revolver in hand, two of his accomplices close behind. The third stayed with Wilson in the hall.

'Sorry to inform you, sir that you must leave the house immediately; it will soon go up in flames.'

'But why? Why are you burning my home? I have no quarrel with you folks.'

'You are a Sasanach (Englishman) and an anti-Catholic and it must go.'

The man in the hall called for his leader to come out.

'What's the matter, don't you realise we have little time?'

The man pointed to the crucifix over the door.

'Look, look! This man is a Catholic. He's one of us.'

Elizabeth was, by now, slumped in her chair and not believing this could happen again. She was barely conscious. The Major tried to comfort her. She was weeping.

The leader re-entered the room.

'Is it true you're a Catholic?'

'Yes, we both are AND we are Irish.'

With that, the leader noticed a painting of Lord Edward Fitzgerald on the side wall.

'Is that who I think it is?'

'Yes, that is Lord Edward, the architect of the 1798 Rebellion.'

'Right, men, this man is not our enemy. Get out of here.'

The four men dashed from the house, mounted their bikes and headed down the avenue.

The Major and his wife hugged each other; they couldn't believe that they were safe!

Brian Byrne heard about the incident and was a bit disturbed. He was still worried about the fate of many big houses and the loss of jobs when they were torched. A week after the event, he was in the yard preparing the pony and cart for a day of mending fences in the fields. He heard a shot. He rushed to the stables and there, on the floor, Major George Clarence O'Kelly lay dead, his service revolver by his head.

CHAPTER THIRTY-FOUR

The Curragh of Kildare

*John's involvement with the IRA intensifies. Eventually, he pays
the price but it is a familiar terrain for him.*

The New Year of 1921 brought more trouble. Late in the
previous year, the Defence of the Realm Act expired and the
British Government introduced internment. Thousands of men
and women were imprisoned without trial. Ballykinlar, County
Down became the main prison camp.

IRA activity increased however, the army and the RIC became
more aware of their past mistakes. They no longer took the
same patrol routes and they avoided danger areas, where they
could easily become victims of ambush. A guerrilla tactics
training school was set up in the Curragh for British officers.
They even employed military aircraft to monitor any suspicious
movements, both on roads and railways.

In April Richard Mulcahy issued the following General Order
on behalf of the IRA GHQ:

> *The communication to the Enemy of information concerning
> the work or personnel of the Army or the Civil Administration
> of the Republic is an offence against the life of the nation and,
> in the ultimate, is punishable by death.*

John Brennan got more and more involved with the republican
movement. He learned that ex-British Army servicemen
were often suspected of being informers and were eliminated
accordingly. He had to demonstrate that he was dedicated to
the establishment of an Irish Republic, in which he actually
believed.

Mary was getting increasingly concerned about his supposed
training sessions. They often took place after dark and he came

home late, with soiled hands and clothes. He told her he was teaching the recruits about trench construction and night-time manoeuvres. In fact, he was often digging road trenches and felling trees across roads. This was an IRA policy of hampering military movements and disrupting army supply routes.

Mary confronted him one evening when he arrived home very late.

'John, where have ye been?'

'Ah Pet, just doin' the usual training t'ings.'

'Tell the truth, what are ye up to?'

John sat down and asked for a large Powers whiskey. Mary obliged and he swallowed half of the glass in one gulp. He told her most of what he was really up to.

'I'm sorry, Pet. I didn't want ye to know too much in case the peelers arrived and forced anythin' out of ye. They are bad bastards and they will stop at nothin'. I really believe that we Irish would be better off runnin' the country ourselves, without British interference. The 'Tans' are a nasty lot and they must be defeated. I can only play a small part in getting' rid of them, so that's why I must continue helpin' the republican movement.'

Mary joined him on the settee. She held his hand and kissed him.

'You're right, John. We must be rid of them from our land but I worry about your safety and what would me and the children would do if anythin' happened to ye.'

'Don't worry, Pet; I am not getting' mixed up in any direct combat.'

He never told her about the ambush and a few other 'incidents' that he was involved in.

'I'll be alright. Don't ye fear now, love.'

They retired to bed.

John's friend, Tom Dempsey, was now fully employed as an IRA 'parallel' policeman. He worked in country areas, where the RIC no longer patrolled, mostly because their barracks had been destroyed and that patrolling had become a very high-risk activity. Occasionally the Black and Tans would appear on lorries in these areas, park in villages, create a nuisance in the pubs and intimidate the locals.

Tom's job was quite easy. The courts no longer sat as before. IRA suspects were arrested by the RIC and the military. The military courts tried them without any jury. Some were simply interred and others even unlawfully executed by the Auxiliaries and the Black and Tans.

In April John was asked to join his flying column in the village of Blackrock, County Dublin. He was previously asked if he was familiar with high explosives, since he had served in the Great War. John said he had no direct involvement in this aspect of warfare but had some idea about how to set them up. The plan was to destroy the railway bridge in the village. The line ran from the Dublin Station (Connolly) in the city to Kingstown (Dún Laoire) and carried military personnel and supplies to and from Holyhead.*

Commandant Sean O'Reilly and five men, including John and another Great War veteran, Paddy Kearns, examined the bridge. Paddy actually had experience of setting up explosives, as he spent some time with the Royal Engineers in the war. When they had selected the best position to do the maximum amount of damage, they laid the dynamite and connected the detonators. They were in the process of setting the fuses when a military lorry suddenly appeared. RIC officers and Black and Tans leapt from the vehicle guns at the ready. The men had no choice but to surrender.

They were bundled on to the lorry and taken to the local DMP police station on the Main Street. The explosives, detonators, etc were removed from the bridge and taken as evidence. The

---

* See footnotes on pages 17 and 105.

volunteers refused to give their names and were taken to the cells. They were given no blankets. Food consisted of dry bread and water only. They were kept awake by frequent visits by a guard, who made noise by bashing the bars with his truncheon and stamping his hobnail boots on the stone floor. It was a long night.

Next morning the bleary-eyed, exhausted prisoners were interrogated individually. It was noted that one of the volunteers was missing. He had been taken away in the early morning. The remaining men suspected that he may have been the one who betrayed them.

When John was interviewed/interrogated, he was already in a poor state. He was worried sick about Mary and his children. He was told that he would not be allowed to send a message to them until he co-operated. He still refused to answer questions. Finally, he gave his name but refused to give his address. The other four prisoners did the same. They were returned to the cells on two occasions. They still refused to give any further information. After several hours the sergeant informed them that they were to be removed to the internment camp in the Curragh that evening, as there was no room for them in the station.

Mary awoke at two in the morning. John was not in the bed beside her. She got up and went downstairs to see if he was asleep there. No sign of him. Baby Joan woke up crying. She went to attend to her. She was getting very worried. Where can he be at this hour? She gave Joan a bottle and put her back in her cot. She went back to bed but couldn't sleep. Eventually, she dozed off but, in the morning, she believed that she didn't sleep a wink.

She walked to school with Michael and Bridget, pushing her pram in which Patrick and baby Joan looked around them, oblivious of the situation. She didn't know what to think. John always came home. *He must be in trouble*, she thought as she walked to Mrs Wilson's house.

'Ah Mary, what's the matter? Ye look shagged out.'

'John didn't come home last night. He said he was just doin' a few manoeuvres with the lads but he always made it home.'

'Now, now, Mary, don't be worryin'. Come in, sit down and I'll make ye a cuppa tay.'

Mrs Wilson sat her down and brought in the pram with the two children. Little Patrick ran to a cupboard and got busy emptying it of its clutter. The baby was asleep. Mary sat down. Tears ran down her worried face. She blew her nose noisily.

'I t'ought all this trouble would have ended when the war finished and John came home.'

'Ah Pet, there's sure to be an explanation. Maybe their lorry broke down and they got stranded or somethin'.'

'I really hope he comes home soon, Mrs Wilson. What'll I do if somethin' terrible has happened?'

She calmed down a bit and Mrs Wilson made her another cup of tea, laced with Jameson. They had a good chat. After an hour or so, Mary brought the children home, still hoping John would be in the house when she got there.

John and his fellow volunteers were handcuffed, loaded onto a lorry and driven to the new internment camp at the Rath in the Curragh. There were four guards armed with revolvers and light machine guns on the lorry. One was an Auxiliary and the others were Black and Tans. Mean bastards, thought the prisoners.

The weather was wet and cold. The road was rough. The journey was long. The men were very tired. They arrived at the camp in the late afternoon. All were pleased that the journey was over. John thought of his time in Germany and hoped this place was not as bad.

At each corner of the site, a watchtower was positioned. Sentries peered down at them, rifles at the ready, from the towers. The wooden buildings themselves appeared in reasonable condition as the camp had only been open for less than a month. In fact, it was still partly under construction. Rath was now the overflow camp. The original internment prison in the Curragh, Hare Park Camp, had been over filled and some of the 'residents' had to be accommodated in the County Down Ballykinlar camp. That place was now filled to capacity. There were not many prisoners housed in Rath as yet but many were already scheduled to arrive.

The new guests were exhausted and retired to bed. John thought of Mary and the family but fell into a deep sleep when he hit the pillow. Next morning each of them was brought to the camp commandant and interrogated. The men refused to give any information of the operation they had been involved in. They agreed among themselves to give their addresses, as this would allow them to write to their loved ones.

They were not allowed visitors. Later they were allowed to meet the other prisoners. Talking to them lifted their spirits. The camp didn't seem too bad. John thought the food was much better than that in Germany.

On the second day John sat down to write to Mary. He looked out the window and noticed the fine Curragh racecourse directly opposite. He sadly remembered happy days of going to the races at Baldoyle. They seemed like happier days but maybe he was viewing them with tinted glasses. He remembered taking Mary there before they were married. The dances they went to, the fun they had together.

He finished his letter to her after much re-writing. He wondered how he ended up in a 'prisoner of war' camp yet again. He hoped that she would get the letter very soon. It had to be approved by the censors, of course. He remembered what not to write from his previous experience. He knew how upset Mary would be but he felt that he had to do what he did to set Ireland free. He hoped that she would understand. He resolved to hand back his military medals.

Chapter Thirty-Five

Truce

The first, tentative steps towards peace are embarked upon but war has taken its toll on every level.

The situation in Dublin grew worse. The Black and Tans and especially the Auxiliaries were creating havoc. They stopped and searched vehicles and civilians. The authorities had lost valuable agents in the raids and subsequent executions arranged by Michael Collins on 20 November of the year before. Now they were mostly fighting blind as the republicans also had informers in the Castle, which hampered their plans in arranging any surprise attacks and eliminating the enemy.

There was a loud knock on the door as Martina was finishing her breakfast. It startled her. At the door was a telegram boy in a smart uniform. He handed her the telegram and awaited his tip. She gave him sixpence and went inside. She had to sit down when she read of the demise of her beloved father. It said that he died suddenly and she thought it probably was a heart attack. She knew how devastated her mother would be. They were a very loving couple and were always so happy together. She walked to her office and told them the news. Her colleagues were very sympathetic and said there was no rush to come back to work. She thanked them and returned home to pack. She sent a telegram to her mother saying that she would soon be on her way home.

Martina boarded the train at Kingsbridge station. She still felt a little concerned about travelling in these troubled times. However, she had to get home and comfort her mother. Brian Byrne met her at Kildare station. He had the pony and trap as he was unable to drive the motorcar. He loaded her bag and they set off. Martina did not speak very much and Brian respected her. He did sympathise with her when they met. As they headed along the six-mile road to Rathangan she gazed at the Plains of Kildare. She fondly remembered her childhood days, travelling the same road with her parents and brothers. She was particularly pleased to see the Hill of Allen where she played with her younger brother, George and some friends in happier times.

Elizabeth rushed from the house when she saw the trap coming up the avenue. She hugged and kissed her daughter as she alighted. Brian brought in her bag. The two women went to see the Major's body laid out in the parlour. He looked so well, Martina thought, even happy. He was dressed in his military uniform with his medals in display. A candle was lit each side of his bed and he held a crucifix in his hands, which were laced with rosary beads. His head wound was skilfully hidden. Tears were shed. Martina bent over the coffin and kissed her father.

'Was it a heart attack, Mother?' she asked.

It was only then that her mother revealed the true cause of his death. Martina was so shocked that she almost collapsed. Elizabeth held her tightly and led her to a chair. Further tears were shed as the two women embraced.

'Oh my God, mother! How could he do this to us? Why didn't you tell me?'

'He was very ill my dear, very ill. I didn't want to upset you unnecessarily.'

When things settled down, Wilson served the ladies tea and sandwiches in the drawing room. He asked if they would like something a little stronger. They both asked for a Hennessy. They went over the events that took the man, whom they loved, from them. Elizabeth told her daughter of the bankruptcy letter that she discovered in the bureau. She thought her husband was simply depressed but this letter was a heavy blow. She now was so worried about her home and the estate.

Later, Martina revealed to her mother that her relationship with Jonathan was over. She found out that he and his wife were living as husband and wife in all respects and that she was simply being used. Life was cruel!

Constable Bill Byrne managed to stay out of trouble in Park Gate Street Barracks. The Auxiliaries and the Black and Tans did not help his job in any way. Police and military were now looked upon by the public as one and the same. Going on patrol was always stressful. However, there was some safety in numbers.

Brian wrote to his brother giving details of Major O'Kelly's suicide. He was very fond of his employer and he considered him not only to be his boss but also his friend. He told him how surprised he was that the estate had been on the verge of bankruptcy. He realised that the Major had been depressed for some time but he never realised how bad the financial situation was.

Elizabeth O'Kelly was distraught. Her heart was broken. She was now staying with her daughter, Martina, in Dublin. Brian kept the estate going as best he could. He feared that he could have little or no wages soon and he was very worried about his little family. The bank was now his employer.

He said there was a large attendance at the Major's funeral in Rathangan. Both unionists and republicans were there. The parish priest gave a fine oration at the Mass. It included a glowing account of the Major's life and he mentioned his generosity to the less fortunate in the parish. It was very sad. His son, George, was unable to come over from London, which was a disappointment for the family.

Bill was shocked to hear the news. He wondered what would happen to the estate now and he was sure the Major's fine horses would be sold. They were such beautiful animals. He believed that the land would now be taken over by the Land Commission and be divided. What would happen to the beautiful house? He made up his mind to travel to Rathangan, even if it meant that he would have to go in disguise. He would have a word with the sergeant.

His chance to travel came when a truce was declared between the Crown forces and the IRA in July 1921. The year to date had been a violent one. Over 500 of the crown forces had died and around 1000 were injured. About 700 civilians were killed. The British Government, under Lloyd George, threatened to use force and flood the twenty-six counties with troops and fight a 'real' war. The country had been partitioned in June, with two parliaments to be established: one in Dublin and the other in Belfast. The truce was agreed with the British Government by Éamon de Valera, representing the twenty-six counties and James Craig representing the remaining six.

The IRA Chief of Staff, Richard Mulcahy, issued a message to his commanders throughout the country which read:

In view of the conversations now being entered by our Government with the Government of Great Britain, and in pursuance of mutual conversations, active operations by our forces will be suspended as from noon, Monday, 11th July.

The ceasefire did not please everyone in the republican movement but, on the whole, the civilian population was much relieved. The years of violence and disturbances wearied the people of Ireland, especially those in the southern counties. Most had had enough. There was much violence, on both sides, in the days leading up to the truce. On the day before it came into force, another 'Bloody Sunday' took place in Belfast. Sixteen people died in a sectarian conflict in the west of the city and over one hundred and fifty houses were burned down. Sectarian killings had increased substantially in the north of Ireland since partition in June. In many parts of the country police and military personnel and republican sympathisers were killed and injured.

Bill bought an oversized 'newsboy' cap and a long, if too warm, overcoat. The recent truce made it safer to travel by train but there was always the danger of an attack by disgruntled republicans. Nevertheless, he took the chance and boarded a train to Kildare Town. Brian met him and brought to see their ageing parents. Bill had not seen them in several years and there was an emotional reunion. He agreed to stay overnight with them.

There was a lot of talk about the future of the O'Kelly estate and of course, the 'big' house. They were very shocked when the Major killed himself. The old pair worried about his immortal soul and prayed that God had mercy on him since he was not mentally sound. Bill told them that he had asked his local parish priest to say a Mass for his soul. The Rosary was recited.

Brian and Bill were each given a bottle of Guinness. Their father poured himself a Jameson. Brian left soon afterwards and Bill retired to his old childhood bedroom. He was happy to be in his home place, after so many years and it wasn't long before he drifted off to sleep.

Next day Bill was collected by his brother and he went to stay with him for the following two days. He was pleased to see Mags and the three boys again. Baby Seamus was eight months old and a lovely little lad. It was the first time that he saw him.

Bill and Brian discussed the fate of the 500-acre estate. It was eighteen years since the Wyndham Act and now two-thirds of Irish land had become the property of Irish tenants. Brian hoped that he would be able to acquire enough land to make a decent living. Debts had to be cleared, of course but, he believed that Elizabeth O'Kelly might be persuaded to put in a word for him to the Land Commission. He was sad that the estate would be divided but that was the way the country was going.

Bill enjoyed his stay in Rathangan. The weather was generally good and he managed to do a little fishing and enjoy a couple of pints in Dillon's with his brother. Mags looked after him very well. He was sad to have to leave and return to Dublin. He wondered if the truce would hold. He certainly hoped that it would, as a return to violence would spell disaster.

CHAPTER THIRTY-SIX

Escape

Ireland may be on the road to peace but for many, there is still some fighting that remains to be done.

At last a letter arrived at 10 Barrow Street addressed to Mrs Mary Brennan. She had again spent the night waking regularly and wondering what had happened to her husband. She had taken Michael, Bridget and Sean to school and returned to the empty house with little Patrick and Joan. Her heart missed a beat when she saw the letter on the floor. She recognised John's writing and tore it open. She was concerned a bit but so delighted and relieved as she read:

Rath Camp
The Curragh
Co. Kildare

Monday 18th April 1921

Dearest Mary,

I am so sorry I was unable to write to you earlier but I just want you to know, I am in good health and being looked after very well. The food and accommodation is good. In fact they are still building the huts. We were brought here on Saturday, after spending a night in a DMP station in Dublin. I'm afraid I might be here for some time. We are not allowed visitors for now.

I hope you are not too upset and that you are coping well. Give my love to Michael, Bridget, Sean, Patrick and little baby Joan. I miss you all very much. Hoping to see you all soon.

Love you always,

Your loving husband,

John

Mary sat down and hugged her son and daughter: 'Daddy is alright, me loves. Daddy is alright, t'ank God, t'ank God!'

After a cup of tea, she Patrick and Joan went to see Mrs Wilson. 'I told ye he'd be alright, Pet. Now sit down and tell me all about it.'

She told her friend about the letter and wondered what kind of 'camp' John might be held in. The letter said that he was in good health and that the place is nice. However, she said that they have to write this rubbish because of the censors.

'What was he sent to the camp for anyhow, Mary?' Mrs Wilson asked.

'He said he was going on manoeuvres, but I don't know what that even means.'

'He must have been a bad boy if they sent him down to Kildare.'

'Ah no, they send anyone who sympathises with republicans to these internment camps. I t'ink that's what Rath camp is – I read it in the paper.'

'Ah sure, the auld country is upside down, Mary. He might be home in a few days as long as they don't try to stitch him up.'

'I hope so, Mrs Wilson. I really hope so.'

The days went on and John did his best to settle in. The huts were definitely better than those he experienced in Limburg. The food wasn't too bad either. The guards, however, seemed to be paranoid about prisoners attempting to escape. All night, every night, a very bright search light regularly lit up the whole camp. It was often difficult to sleep.

Frequent searches by the guards were made, both of the huts and of the prisoners themselves. In fact, these visits often broke up the day, making life a little less boring. He made friends with several of his fellow inmates. They chatted, told stories and played cards. There was even some talk that a concert might be organised, as some of the lads were good singers and musicians and others could do a bit of acting.

John was pleased when, at last, he got a letter from Mary. She said she was very happy to hear from him but that the whole family missed him so much and they wished he could come home. She did not ask any questions or give any information that might prolong his stay in the camp. She knew her letter would be read by the censors.

John felt very sad that he could not be home with Mary and the children. Spring was arriving and he longed to go with them to the strand, where the sea air was clean and cool and days grew longer. Now all he could do was gaze out the window at the racecourse across the way and wish that he could have a long walk through the Curragh.

The camp was operated by a Scottish regiment. These guards, many of whom were young British conscripts, had little sympathy for the inmates. They swore at them, pointed bayoneted rifles at them and threatened them. However, the prisoners themselves appointed their own camp commandant. Each hut had their own commander who reported to him. It was his responsibility to keep order and to allocate fatigues (menial tasks). The huts had to be kept clean and tidy. This was not a popular job and some commanders quit or moved to a different hut because of the hassle from the men. Some men resented having to do fatigues and were somewhat hostile to strict discipline. Extra fatigues were allocated as punishment. Prisoners were also punished by the guards for various offences. Letter writing and receiving was curtailed and the receiving of parcels stopped.

Escape committees were set up. Two prisoners managed to escape when they were concealed in post office bags, loaded on to an ass and cart and covered in swill. The cart was not checked at the gate, for obvious reasons. Severe punishments followed, including the closing of the canteen and the withdrawal of the right to receive and send mail. Another three prisoners escaped, disguised as workmen, having 'borrowed' passes and overalls.

The digging of tunnels were projects embarked on as the spring turned to summer. John joined in the planning. This activity kept him and many other prisoners busy during the long days. It was hoped that a full hut of about sixty could manage to escape if the right tunnel could be constructed.

John helped to plan and dig a tunnel. He was a big man so he found the tunnel size a bit too tight and, after a while, he developed a problem with his breathing due to the gassing. He had to give up going into the tunnel.

Unfortunately, it was discovered, due to its existence being passed to the army by an informer. It had not advanced very far but the repercussions were brutal. Searches of the hut became more frequent and men were physically abused by the guards. The canteen was closed and, as usual, no letters were allowed out or in. Parcels were opened and food items, such as cakes and bread, were cut open as the smuggling of files and knives was commonplace. John didn't receive a letter from Mary for weeks. He was unable to send her one either.

When the truce was agreed on 11 July, the prisoners hoped that they might be freed. Some were allowed the privilege to return to their families but many were still incarcerated. John was included in the latter. He was very disappointed. He wrote to Mary saying that he hoped to be freed soon but he knew, in his heart, that he might be in prison for weeks, even months to come.

Mary replied, hoping to see him soon. She said that the children were well but they all missed him very much. She said that Mrs Wilson was a great support and that she wouldn't know what to do without her. She told him that the summer was good but without him it might as well be winter.

After the failure of the last tunnel escape, the commanders decided to keep the plan for a major escape attempt secret. Only a handful of the prisoners knew of it. John was one of them. His old commandant, Sean O'Reilly, vouched for him. It was planned for September.

Earlier, several tunnels were worked on at the same time but this time, a single one was planned. Some of the prisoners had mining experience and they were invaluable. Bed boards and other pieces of wood were used to prop it up. The soil was smuggled out at night in pillowcases and spread in different areas, including the recreational/sports field and under the huts. The ditches surrounding the field were ideal for this purpose.

Soon the big day approached and selected inmates were informed to ready themselves for a breakout. They had to swear to keep their mouths shut. This they did. Personal belongings were prohibited. The exact date was not disclosed. The night before the great escape, each escapee was advised of the time of departure and where to assemble. John was selected to be in the second group. He was excited.

It was a dark evening. John made his way to the assembly point. Lookouts were posted at the surrounding huts. The large search light lit up some of the huts in its arc but not the one under which the tunnel was concealed. Soon the men were slipping into the dark entrance. The lookout at the hut door kept his eyes peeled. Everything seemed to be going well. At last the first group of thirty men were gone. A message was received that they had succeeded, there was silent jubilation.

John's group now readied themselves. The men slipped into the tunnel. John was number twelve. He was a bit worried about crawling through the narrow, dark and somewhat claustrophobic underground passage. Thoughts came of the suffering that he went through in the trenches and that horrible gas that nearly suffocated him. He put them out of his mind. Soon he was following the other men into the tunnel. Movement was slow, the air was thin. It was very dark.

Suddenly the man in front stopped and didn't move. John wondered what was happening. Finally, the man whispered to John that a prisoner had smuggled down a small suitcase and had got stuck several yards ahead. He tried to free it but dislodged a support and partly collapsed the tunnel. John felt panic and sweat roll down his face as his lungs gasped for air.

He pushed back, ordering the men behind him to reverse. There was confusion. Others began to panic. Luckily, the man at the head of the tunnel realised that there was a problem and pulled the last man out. The others followed. John just about made it. He climbed from the entrance and collapsed on the floor, gasping for breath. He was given water and a cold towel. The offending escapee was hauled out and given a severe reprimand, which included a whack around the ears from the commander.

Suddenly the whole camp was lit up and sirens screamed. It was discovered by the sentries that prisoners had and were escaping. Dogs barked loudly. Men shouted. Three escapees were captured and shots were fired at others as they bounded into the welcoming darkness of the Curragh.

The commander ordered that the flooring be immediately replaced over the tunnel entrance and the floor swept. Men hurried back to their huts. John struggled back to his. Soiled clothing was swiftly hidden. The guards spent the night searching each hut but failed to find the tunnel. They refused to give up. It took them three days to at last discover it. The usual punishments were implemented. John was very disappointed but there was not much he could do about it.

On 6 December 1921 the Treaty was signed in London. Again, British PM, David Lloyd George threatened war if the terms were not agreed on that date, despite the fact that some of the Irish party had returned to Dublin on 3 December, to consult de Valera.

It was only after the signing that John Brennan was released from Rath Camp. He had hoped, in vain, to be released earlier but, when the time came, he was very relieved. Soon he was reunited with Mary and the children. The children were very happy. John, however, believed that Mary had changed somewhat. The months trying to cope on her own, looking after five young children, had taken their toll. He hoped that he could make it up to her in some way. Money was a little scarce since John had not been working. The IRA had contributed some cash and the army pension helped but there were still some shortfalls. However, John and Mary believed that this was the end of hostilities and that life would soon return to some normality.

The Dáil ratified the Treaty in January 1922 but clouds soon gathered on the horizon. The IRA suffered a split.

Chapter Thirty-Seven

Changing of the Guards

Truce leads to Treaty and a new flag over Dublin Castle. The changeover is a slow process, however.

After the truce was agreed in July, the RIC were instructed to 'coexist' with the IRP (Irish Republican Police). This was not popular with either the British Army or the RIC.

Constable Bill Byrne was a bit mystified with the whole issue. He was, of course, pleased that peace in Ireland was now a distinct possibility but he did not entirely trust his new colleagues. After all, these were the men who had wanted to eliminate the RIC over the past couple of years. Even Michael Collins wasn't much impressed with the IRP. It was thought that they lacked discipline and training. Some of the recruits were frankly unsuitable.

The British Army, on the other hand, soon realised that they would not now all be required to stay in Ireland and that they could soon be heading home. This pleased many of them very much.

Bill continued to work in Dublin. There was some republican activity there but the Republican Police mostly dealt with it. Police, whether RIC or IRP, continued to be suspected by IRA sympathisers and much of the population at large. Respect for the law was something the average Irish citizen was found to be lacking. In the months following the truce, several police officers were injured and others were even killed carrying out their duty. Law and order were wanting in many parts of the country as criminals took advantage of the absence of a trained/ professional police force.

On a day off Bill went for a drink in the city centre. He made sure he wore his 'newsboy' cap and didn't attract any unwanted attention. Walking along the quays he approached the Bachelor Inn and decided to call in. He always remembered the bar in which he proposed to dear Kathleen. This time he wasn't so sad and he thought that he should move on. He would never forget his first love. He ordered a pint of plain porter and lit a cigarette. After a while he happened to notice a familiar face at the other end of the bar. He could not remember the name but then it came to him.

'Hello Tom Dempsey! Is it really you?'

'Ah Bill Byrne! Yes, it is. How are ye doin'?'

'Very well indeed, old friend.'

The men shook hands and Bill slapped Tom on the back.

'Really great to see ye after all this time. Where the hell have ye been?'

Tom told him of his stay with his parents back in Donegal, after he left the DMP and then the return to Dublin to work at rebuilding Sackville Street, including the Imperial Hotel/ Clery's building. Bill told him that he was still in the RIC and then Tom revealed that he was now a member of the IRP. Tom noticed the change in Bill's face. He swiftly added how he was recruited by the IRA man in this very pub and that he had little real choice in the matter.

Bill shook his hand again saying. 'Ah sure, we're all the same now. What does it matter anymore what happened? The past is the past. Let's look to the future and peace in Ireland.'

Tom agreed. Bill bought them both another pint and they continued to reminisce about old times. Tom was back in the old station at Great Brunswick Street. Before they parted the friends promised that they would see more of each other and, maybe, have a day out at the races in Baldoyle one weekend.

In early 1922 it was decided to form a new Irish police force, modelled on the Dublin Metropolitan Police, which were unarmed and apolitical. An armed force similar to the RIC was rejected. Tom decided to join this new "An Garda Síochána" or Civic Guard force.

On 16 January British Rule ended in Ireland when the National Army took over Dublin Castle. De Valera had resigned the presidency of the Dáil and Arthur Griffith took his place. Although the Treaty had been ratified by the Dáil with a majority of 64 to 57, many republicans rejected it. De Valera was one of them despite authorising the Treaty delegation powers to agree a settlement if they thought fit. 'Real' republicans wanted the whole of Ireland to be a republic and not a divided country. There was also the tie up with the British Empire, such as the oath of allegiance to the King. Also, the 26 counties being a 'Free State' and not a republic was not acceptable. Pro-treaty TDs and activists saw it as a means to an end of becoming, perhaps, a republic in the years ahead. Civil war seemed inevitable.

Tom told Bill of his good friend, John Brennan whom he wished him to meet. They finally arranged to meet in the Bachelor Inn. John was a bit apprehensive about meeting an RIC officer and, at first, had refused to do so. In the end, he was persuaded as Tom vouched for Bill as being a true friend and, after all, they were all Irishmen.

Tom intended to exclude a discussion about politics when they met. This was going to be difficult as John was now a dedicated republican and rejected the terms of the Treaty. Tom and Bill, on the other hand, thought it to be the best way forward. They did not want to see any further violence in Ireland if it was at all possible. John had other ideas.

The meeting was pleasant enough. Tom mentioned that Bill once lodged in Barrow Street. They discussed that area of the city. Bill felt that John intensely disliked the RIC and the British Army, even though he fought with the latter. John tried to direct the discussion to the matter of the Treaty but Tom cleverly changed the subject and brought up the recent horse racing in

Baldoyle. The three men were keen racing enthusiasts, so this worked for a time. However, as more drink was consumed John became more aggressive. He called the signatories of the Treaty traitors and British puppets and did not deserve to be called Irishmen.

'That Englishman, Robert Barton, is an Imperial spy and should not have been in the delegation team.'

'Barton was born in County Wicklow. He is an Irish patriot,' replied Bill.

'Well, if he isn't English, he's a fuckin' Protestant.'

'Yes, he is a Protestant but so was Wolfe Tone, Robert Emmett and even our own Erskine Childers.'

The argument went on and became more heated. Finally, Tom intervened and suggested that they go home. John and Bill did not shake hands. John just left, having shaken Tom's. Tom and Bill looked at each other wondering what annoyed the man so much. Tom apologised saying that John was a good friend. He did say that John had been acting a bit strangely since his time as an internee in the Curragh. He reckoned that he was somewhat radicalised there. Many of his fellow inmates were hard-line republicans.

There was also trouble at home, as his wife was not very happy with his involvement with the IRA. His being away for so long didn't help the financial situation and it looked like his military pension would soon end. The Free State would, more than likely, not continue to pay it. John was out of work now, so the future looked bleak.

Chapter Thirty-Eight

Divided Loyalties

Bill joins the National Army when RIC disbands. John remains active in the IRA. Civil war looms.

The new police force, the Civic Guards, was established by 'An Saorstát Éireann' (the Irish Free State) government in February 1922. Bill Byrne stayed with the RIC until it was disbanded in the first half of the same year. Then he was to merge with the 'Guards' but not encouraged to do so. He was not happy to work with the Irish Republican Police in the new force, whom he mistrusted. They, in turn, also mistrusted the RIC officers.

It was at that time that he decided to apply to join the new National or 'Free State' Army. This force was sponsored by the Provisional Government under the chairmanship of Michael Collins, the members of which were, of course, pro-treaty. Only IRA members who supported the Treaty were allowed to join.

On account of his years of experience in the police force and his training in the handling and use of firearms etc, Bill was gratefully accepted. He joined a unit of the army known as the Dublin Guards, which was an IRA unit in the Anglo-Irish War. The army was also referred to as the 'Regulars'. The Provisional Government presented it as the new, modern, Irish security force. Michael Collins was its Commander-in-Chief up to his death in 1922.

As mentioned before, his friend, Tom Dempsey was accepted as an officer in the newly formed police force. He was in favour of the Treaty and believed he could help promote Irish unity in that job. He was worried about his friend, John, as they had drifted apart after their meeting with Bill. They no longer met for a pint. At first he thought that John could not afford to have a drink but one evening he saw him enter another pub in Sackville Street.

After the Treaty was ratified, the split in the IRA became gradually more apparent. In April a Republican Executive was formed and, on the 13th, they occupied the Four Courts in Dublin. British troop withdrawals were suspended, leaving about five thousand still in Ireland. The Northern Ireland Government banned all republican organisations.

Bill and Tom were kept very busy in the city. There was plenty of trouble in the streets and bars between the rival factions. The mood was very ugly. Bill had flashbacks of 1913 but this time he was in the army.

John was active in the anti-treaty IRA. Mary had pleaded with him not to get involved but he told her it was his duty, as an Irishman, to seek a Republic and not to pander to the whims of the British Empire. Ironically, Robert Barton also rejected the Treaty although he had been a signatory. In April John joined his IRA unit in the Four Courts. It was a difficult time for him. Again his allegiances were divided between his family and his country.

In the general election of 16 June 1922 the electorate voted in favour of the Treaty. Michael Collins and Éamon de Valera had earlier agreed a pact to encourage voters to select a candidate either for or against the Treaty, depending on their allegiances. Other issues were to be ignored. The pact failed. It was vetoed by the British Government as the Oath of Allegiance was to be omitted from the Free State constitution. Pressure was put on Collins to have it abrogated as they also feared a return to a demand for a republic. Churchill threatened to send further troops to Dublin. Collins had no choice. However the result of the election was agreeable to the British government.

More pressure was put on the Provisional Government to sort out the occupation of the Four Courts by the 'Irregulars' (anti-treaty IRA) under Rory O'Connor. The British Government was running out of patience. The Unionist MP, Field Marshall Sir

Henry Wilson was assassinated in London by the IRA. Anti-treatyites (IRA) were blamed. The Provisional Government were given an ultimatum to deal with the occupants of the Four Courts. The National Army surrounded the building and on 28 June it was bombarded by two 18-pounder field guns, loaned by the British Army. Initially, the Four Courts were barely damaged. It took over two days for the occupying garrison to yield to the National Army but fighting then spread to the centre of the city.

CHAPTER THIRTY-NINE

Civil War

The sacking of the Four Courts. No longer 'brothers in arms',
Irishmen and Irishwomen are forced to take sides.

John Brennan was inside the Four Courts when the attack began in the early morning. He had been there for fifteen days. Provisions and ammunition were in short supply and the men were now pretty tired. Essentials were smuggled in from supporters. The siege was expected but defence of the building was badly organised. By the end of two days of continuous bombardment the situation was becoming serious. Eventually the republicans remaining were forced to surrender.

Mary was very annoyed with her husband when he told her that he had to meet his unit in the city, on yet another evening.

'What's happenin' to us, John? I need ye here to help me look after the children. You are out most evenin's. We are not a family anymore.'

'Ah Pet! Don't be like that. Sure this business will be soon over and we will have an Irish Republic at last. Then you will t'ank me for bein' a true Irish patriot, not like dem lackeys who follow the Big Fella and his British-lovin' politics. De Valera is the man who will win the day, mark my words.'

He went to the kitchen to kiss each of his children. Michael, now ten, viewed his dad as a hero. He had told his schoolmates that he was unbelievably brave and had killed loads of enemy soldiers. Bridget, eight, hated to see him leave the house and missed him so much when he was away. She always feared that he would not return. Sean and Patrick were not sure what was happening. Little Joan was bewildered but cried, as she knew things were not good. There were tears in John's eyes but he knew he had to go. He tried his best not to show his feelings to his wife as he kissed her and left. Mary was so upset that she simply slumped onto the stair step and wept bitterly. Michael came to comfort her, saying that Daddy was a real hero.

John believed that the occupation of the Four Courts, a major British-built edifice, would persuade the public to see that acceptance of the Treaty was a mistake and that the war against the British Empire had to continue until a Republic was established. He thought, and was told, that the situation would last only a few days. The days passed very slowly. The hours dragged, one into the next.

The National Army encircled the area around the building. There were no shots fired. Men who once fought together in the Anglo-Irish War now watched each other anxiously from their positions. Nerves and exhaustion took their toll. Neither army were properly trained or experienced enough for a situation like this. It was a cat and mouse game. Who would start the inevitable war?

Early in the morning of 28 June John was awoken by an enormous explosion as a shell hit the mighty south-facing wall. Then another soon followed. This was it. This was the fight to the last man standing. There was no let-up of the bombardment. The days turned into nights. There was little sleep to be had in the 19th century, very well built, Four Courts. The IRA garrison was weakening. They were expecting support from the provinces but communications were poor and the leadership was worried. Some of the IRA Executive, including Sean Lemass, a future Taoiseach, managed to escape through a tunnel into Jameson's Distillery. Twelve of the Executive had been present at that time.

On Friday, 30 June, the National Army entered the Four Courts, bayonets fixed and the republicans surrendered. It was around this time that a massive explosion occurred inside the building sending smoke 200 feet into the air. Historical document fragments were scattered over the surrounding streets. John and several of his colleagues seized the opportunity and escaped.

They headed to the centre of the city to join their colleagues in the 'block', an area on the east side of Sackville Street. They had to tread carefully as the National Army was monitoring activities in the city centre. John looked behind as he and his comrades dodged along the quays. He could see the mushroom-like cloud of smoke over the burning landmark that he had just left. This was a godsend as civilians and enemy military were distracted.

The rebels found it relatively easy to enter their headquarters. Their fellow 'Irregulars' greeted them warmly and enquired about the situation they had left. They had an idea that the republicans would be forced to surrender and vowed to hold the city centre until reinforcements arrived.

Private Bill Byrne had been training for two weeks with the National army when he was called up to join forces in Dublin City centre. The occupation of the Four Courts had already happened and further seizures of buildings in Sackville Street were taking place. The anti-treaty IRA had set up headquarters in the street. Bill joined a unit close to O'Connell Bridge and a watch was maintained on the occupied buildings.

Some sniping was happening and there were casualties. He could see the rebuilt Imperial Hotel/Clery's building in the distance, bringing back sad memories of 1916. Once again, the army, this time the Irish army, was setting up heavy (British) guns, which were now trained on the recently restored street.

After the surrender the National Army decided that the best way to end the siege was to bombard the city centre. Once again, Sackville Street suffered severe damage, as it did during the Rising. Bill's job was to watch for escapees and fire on them as the situation dictated. He was not happy about this but he was under orders. It was difficult to determine who were escapees and who were civilians.

Civic Guards officer, Tom Dempsey was also in the city at that time. He was actually on duty in the Trinity College area when the explosion occurred in the Four Courts. He too could see the enormous cloud of smoke in the distance. He realised that the Civil War had begun. This made him quite sad. *What was happening to his beloved country,* he wondered? Was this a second 1916 but Irishmen were now fighting fellow Irishmen?

His duty was to keep back onlookers from the troubled city centre. Many were confused as to what was happening. Tom wasn't sure either. Other parts of the city were unaffected and life went on as near normal as was possible. The sound of gunfire could be heard in Sackville Street. There were reports of injuries and even fatalities. People were asking questions. Tom had no answers. It took five more days for the fighting to cease. The National Army bombarded the areas in the city occupied by the Irregulars. Damage was on a par with that of 1916.

Oscar Traynor, head of the anti-treaty IRA's Dublin Brigade, ordered his men to flee the area and mingle with civilians on their escape. John Brennan was one of them. They made their way to Blessington, by whatever means that were possible. Some even travelled by tram. Many republicans retreated to this town but the National Army troops were already encircling the area and were closing in soon after John and his comrades had arrived.

CHAPTER FORTY

Stepping Stone

*The Irish Civil War is all but over yet, the prospect of lasting
peace hangs very much in the balance.*

The Irregular, anti-treaty IRA troops surrendered in the burning
Sackville Street on 5 July 1922. However, their commander,
Cathal Brugha, made a suicidal defiance, running into the street
revolver in hand. He was shot down and died of his wounds
sometime later.

Private Bill Byrne witnessed this in horror and sadness. How
could this happen only six years after the Rising? The 'war'
appeared be over in Dublin at least. Michael Collins was pleased.
However, Liam Lynch, the anti-treatyite leader was released,
having been captured in Dublin. He was mistakenly allowed,
from a pro-treaty viewpoint, to make his way to the south of the
country, where he established the 'Republic of Munster.'

Bill hoped that things could now return to near normal. He had
been on duty for weeks with little time off. He and his fellow
National Army troops were weary and needed a rest. They
were sent back to their barracks in Beggars Bush. Bill washed
and changed and made his way to the mess. The beer tasted
fantastic. He got chatting to his comrades. They were as puzzled
as he was as to why there was such opposition to the Treaty,
which was ratified by the Dáil and voted for by the majority of
the population in the general election. Bill, having been an RIC
officer, was of the opinion that the legally elected government
should be allowed to rule. He agreed with Collins, believing
that the Treaty was a stepping stone to greater freedom from
Britain and leading, perhaps, to a future Irish Republic. He
didn't see the Oath of Allegiance as a stumbling block.

John Brennan joined his comrades in Blessington. They had arrived there in dribs and drabs and by any means available. Most were very tired after their ordeal in Dublin. Those Irregulars already there were supposed to have supported their units in Dublin but, due to poor communications, they received their orders too late. Nevertheless they were determined to hold the town against the Free State Army. This was never a possibility as the army outmanned them. The British Government supplied the National Army with uniforms, supplies and arms. The Irregular Army's weaponry was hopelessly inadequate. It wasn't long before they had no option but to surrender. John was taken prisoner and sent to Mountjoy Gaol in the city. Some of the prisoners were sent to the Curragh.

Although the anti-treaty IRA had surrendered in the Dublin City area, there were several small-scale attacks on the National Army from time to time. Guard Tom Dempsey was kept busy attempting to keep law and order. Damaged shops and business premises were looted. Much of the population of the city were unemployed while families were hungry and living in atrocious conditions. The fighting had taken its toll.

Tom was in two minds as to what was the right way forward. He felt that the army had been a bit too heavy handed in dealing with the opposition to the Treaty. Many were unaware of the attempts by the Provisional Government to negotiate a ceasefire with the Irregulars and the pressure that was put on them, by Britain, to resolve the situation. Flooding the country with British troops was threatened.

The hardened republicans refused to accept a country partitioned and still a part of the British Empire. Tom felt that the new police force was much more respected than the former DMP force. The National Army was now to be feared more than respected by many. The Dublin Guards Unit was being employed to hunt down republicans and deal with them, not always lawfully. Many republicans fled the city and headed to Tipperary, Cork and Kerry to continue the war. The IRA

Executive decided to move from conventional warfare to a guerrilla fight, mostly in the south.

In August Bill Byrne was sent in a convoy of two ships to Cork, to tackle the guerrilla war in the south under the command of Major General Emmett Dalton. They landed in Cork Harbour on 8 August and by the next day they had taken the city. Over 400 troops were put ashore with an armoured car and an 18-pound field gun. Bill was required to remain in the city. The fighting was fierce and he was thankful not to be wounded or, worse still, killed. Dalton had hoped to be backed up by a land force from Dublin, which might have ended the war. This did not materialise. He set up a temporary police force to keep order.

When Michael Collins was killed in an ambush on 22 August 1922 at Béal na mBláth, those for and against the Treaty were shocked. Major General Dalton was with him in the car. His mistake, apart from leaving the car to confront his foes, was to use the same route to and from Cork. Some say that he was not assassinated but, simply, a victim of guerrilla warfare.

The Provisional Government passed Public Safety legislation a month later, which literally gave power to the National Army over life and death. Executions were carried out under this law, which, incidentally, was technically illegal under the terms of the Treaty. An execution only required the signatures of two army officers and they took place within a month of passing the law.

The legislation was brought in partly because of the successes of the republican IRA flying columns. In August Frank Aiken's unit destroyed the National Army barracks in Dundalk, freeing 300 prisoners. The army was regularly ambushed in the counties of Cork, Kerry and Tipperary, resulting in many fatalities and injuries. The army's worse fear was being booby trapped by improvised mines. There were, of course, many atrocities carried out by both sides. Reprisals took place on a regular basis. A recruitment drive boosted the National Army to 60,000 in the summer. The guerrillas were in trouble.

Under the new law anyone in possession of a firearm was to be arrested and likely to be executed. An amnesty was offered, giving anti-treaty guerrillas a chance to surrender their arms and give up the fight. Not many availed of it.

Erskine Childers, a London-born, ex-British army veteran and importer of German arms for the Irish republican movement, was shot by firing squad on 24 November 1922 in Dublin. His crime was to possess a revolver, given to him by Michael Collins, which was found in his house. He supported the anti-treaty Irregulars. In fact, the Provisional Government would execute 77 republicans between December 1922 and April 1923.

Bill Byrne was ordered to join a firing squad at Mountjoy Gaol at 6am on a Monday morning in early November. He was dreading this kind of assignment. It was one thing to engage in battle with an opposing army but to shoot a fellow human being standing blindfolded only yards away was something else. He attempted to get out of it but he was told that orders were orders and to disobey would mean a court-martial. It could even mean being executed himself.

The morning was cold, wet and dark. The prison looked gloomier than Bill had remembered. He wondered why it was allowed to be named with the word 'joy' included in it. An equally gloomy warder opened the massive door. He was shown to a room where he met the other members of the squad. No words were exchanged. The officer explained the procedure. It was simple; aim at the marker on the condemned man's chest. One gun had a blank round. The guns were given out randomly. No one knew which gun had that bullet. A shiver went down Bill's spine.

Bill was shocked when he recognised the condemned man. He knew it was futile to try to get out of it at this stage. It was John Brennan. Two National Army officers had been killed three days before in a back street in Dublin by a republican hit squad.

This was a reprisal. Four prisoners had been randomly selected for execution. John drew a short straw.

John bravely faced his executioners and did not show any emotion. The blindfold was tied on.

'UNIT...TAKE AIM...FIRE!'

Bill watched in horror as John's legs buckled and he slumped to the floor. He made sure that his aim was slightly off target. John's body, bleeding heavily, trembled where he fell and the officer promptly despatched him with his pistol. The priest approached the body and gave the Last Rites. John Brennan, the ex-British serviceman, Irish patriot, husband and father was no more.

Mountjoy Prison

Sunday, November 5th, 1922

Dearest Mary,

I am to be executed in the morning. I am sad to have to leave you and the children like this. I am proud to die for Ireland. This makes me happy.

I saw the priest this morning and he said I will go straight to heaven. Please pray for me.

Try not to miss me too much, please forgive me. I know little Joan's second birthday was last week. Give her and all the children a big kiss for me.

I love you all so much.

Your dear husband,

John

CHAPTER FORTY-ONE

A Fledgling State

It's a time to reflect on all that has gone before, to rebuild and to re-establish old relationships.

The Free State was formally established on 6 December 1922 by an act of the British Parliament. Two TDs were shot the following day leaving the Ormond Hotel on their way to the Dáil. One of them, Sean Hales, died. Four high-ranking anti-treaty leaders, including Rory O'Connor and Liam Mellows, were executed as a reprisal.

Bill Byrne spent Christmas on duty in Cork. The guerrilla campaign was struggling during that winter, due to many of the anti-treaty IRA leaders being captured and many soldiers taken prisoner. The ordinary civilian was sick and tired of the violence and disruptions of the transport system, etc. Support for the republicans was on the wane. The Press and the Catholic Church backed the legitimate government. The Church issued a statement supporting the government and condemning the IRA for their murdering policies. The press was largely censored but the population wanted an end to the war.

Christmas in a miserable barracks in Cork City was not one that Bill looked forward to. He thought of the happy Christmases and the St Stephen's Days that he spent in Rathangan with his brother, his family and his dear parents. He prayed at Mass, on Christmas morning, that this horrible war would soon be over.

The Christmas dinner was not very appetising. Rabbit was served and other usual niceties were in short supply. However, in the afternoon, a barrel of Guinness was supplied by the officers together with several bottles of Jameson and Powers whiskey. This cheered up Bill and his comrades considerably and the evening was not so bad after all. They even had some improvised music, supplied by an accordionist and two fiddlers and almost everyone joined in a sing-song. Bill retired to bed in a happier mood mostly thanks to the intake of many pints of porter, together with whiskey chasers.

Tom Dempsey was having an equally dismal Christmas Day at his station in Dublin City. He was unable to get leave to return to Donegal, to visit his parents. Even if he had, the railway system had been so damaged by the republicans that getting home and back might have proved almost impossible. He too had a not-so-festive dinner but, again, an ample supply of alcoholic beverages was supplied by the sergeant and the inspector.

On New Year's Day 1923 Tom and Bill met for a drink in the Bachelor Inn. Bill told him about the execution of his friend, John Brennan, in November and how he reluctantly took part in it. He said he had no option and he couldn't believe his eyes when John was marched out. Tom was very shocked. He never thought the war would come to this. He missed his evenings having a pint and a chat with John very much. He had wondered why he hadn't kept in touch. Next day he called to see Mary and the children. She was, of course, heartbroken and there was not much he could say to her to give her comfort. She missed him so much and struggled to bring up her children. The winter months were cruel and Christmas very lonesome and sad. Yet again, Mrs Wilson had helped enormously. Luckily her parents also came to the rescue but life without John was almost unbearable. Tom offered Mary some money for herself and the children. She told him she was alright but he knew she was lying. He made her take it.

Bill Byrne returned to his barracks at Beggars Bush in Dublin that January. The IRA were continuing their campaign of destroying the railway system. Bridges were blown up and tracks removed. However, the new Free State government were determined to prevent the country being brought down by their enemies and put a lot of money and manpower into repairing the lines and the bridges. Bill was employed in guarding these works. Bridges, stations and tracks in Maynooth and Celbridge were damaged and his first assignment was in this area of County Kildare. He was pleased to be back there and happy memories came flooding in.

His unit was stationed in Maynooth where the bridge and railway station were being repaired. On a break he decided to take a stroll down the Main Street. He couldn't believe it when, coming the other way, was Marie Callaghan. He wondered if he should say hello or just pass her by.

'Hello Marie, how are ye?'

'Ah Bill, is it really you? How are ye doin' yerself?'

They got chatting about what had passed under the bridge since they parted. Bill didn't mention the gory bits, such as the firing squad and the killings in Sackville Street. Marie told him she still worked in Dawson's shop, nothing much had changed.

'I suppose you're married now, Marie. Who is the lucky fella?' asked Bill, unable to see her left hand because of her gloves.

'No, I'm not, Bill. Who'd have me?'

'Who'd have ye? Who'd have ye? I would for one.'

'Ah stop; you're makin' me blush,' said Marie coyly. 'I did have a few offers but I'm waitin' for the right man.'

Bill was pleased that she was single and cheekily asked her for a date.

'Well, alright Bill. If ye insist.'

'I do, I do. When can we meet?'

They arranged to meet the following weekend in Dublin. Marie would get the tram from Lucan, as the railway line was still unserviceable from Maynooth.

'Great,' said Bill, 'but I'll meet you in Lucan. Are ye sure you can get a lift there?'

Marie said that her brother had a motorbike and he would take her.

They chatted for a while more but, as they were on their lunch breaks, they soon parted and promised to see each other the following Saturday. Both were very happy that they met again. Marie did exaggerate about the number of offers she had had but she still thought about Bill a lot. Bill was in the same boat. He had no offers but Marie was always on his mind.

As the spring approached, Bill and Marie saw quite a lot of each other. The railway line to Maynooth had been repaired by March and then they could meet more often. Bill was not nervous of being seen in the town with Marie anymore. Now the RIC was no more and the National Army – or just 'the Army', as they were now known – was viewed as Ireland's own security force by most. Marie was also more comfortable about meeting Bill than she had been in the past. He was still a handsome young man and her parents approved of him. They grew closer and closer.

In the New Year attacks on the army by anti-treaty IRA columns, especially in the south, continued. Two soldiers were killed in Millstreet, County Cork in January by a flying column headed by Tom Barry, the ex-World War One British serviceman. Free State senators' houses were targeted and burned down. Army barracks were attacked, as in the Anglo-Irish War. This didn't do their popularity any good.

The 'Irregulars' (the government name that the Press were asked to use) were getting short of weapons and supplies. Safe houses were few and far between. Their troops were weary of living rough. They lacked the facilities to hold prisoners and many had to be released. IRA prisoners were held by the government indefinitely, which wore down morale. IRA families were becoming impoverished. Yet, Liam Lynch chose to continue the war despite having the opportunity to end it in the early part of the year. The killings continued, especially in the south. Both sides committed atrocities. One side were as cruel as the other. Irishmen killing Irishmen.

Liam Lynch himself was killed on 10 April. On the 30th of the same month, Frank Aiken, acting leader, called a ceasefire on behalf of the anti-treaty IRA. On 24 May, he ordered the rest of the guerrillas to 'dump arms'. There was no clear end to the Civil War. Republicans merely 'went home'.

Tom Dempsey continued to work with the Guards in Dublin. There was a clear sign that, at last, the war was coming to an end. In the summer of 1923 he got a telegram to say that his father had passed away. He decided to return to Donegal, take over the small family farm and look after his ageing mother. He had enjoyed his time as a police officer but he looked forward to the quieter life as a farmer in his beloved home county.

In June a Land Bill was tabled to attempt to solve the age old 'Land Question'. Bill went for a short holiday to Rathangan to visit Brian and Mags. They were very pleased to see him. Brian was granted fifty acres of the O'Kelly estate and they were over the moon. Bill revealed that he and Marie were engaged and planned to marry in the following spring. Brian and Mags were delighted. Bill very much looked forward to marrying Marie. He was a bit worried about his job, as the Free State government were planning a cut back of the National Army, as it was expensive to maintain. However, he hoped for the best. There was always the Garda Síochána to fall back on.

In early 1924 Bill wrote to Tom and invited him to his wedding. Tom was delighted to hear from his friend but said that there was too much work to be done on his farm in springtime and, regretfully, he had to decline the invitation. However they promised to keep in touch.

Bill and Marie were married in April in the parish church of her native village of Kilcloon. It was a bright, sunny morning and they considered themselves to be the luckiest people in the world. Bill had joined the Garda Síochána and, by strange coincidence, was stationed in Kilcock.

The fact that the wars appeared to be, at last, over encouraged many to believe in the promise of a new, peaceful and prosperous age in the fledgling Irish Free State. However, the Free State Government continued to struggle to balance the books as expenditure in the wars was considerable. Also, many were disillusioned with the outcome of the Civil War. Much of the decade was taken up trying to avert another war and endeavouring to reconcile the fighting factions. Kevin O'Higgins, a minister for justice in the Provisional and Free State Governments, was assassinated by the IRA on 10 July 1927, in retaliation for the executions that he was responsible for in the Civil War. The IRA had not gone away.

A terrible beauty is born – **W.B. Yeats**

About the Author

A native of County Kildare, Liam Nevin lives in Shepperton, England with his wife Marlene, where he is now retired after forty-one years of working at Heathrow Airport. He is the previously published author of *The Tobacco Fields of Meath* (2010) and *Brightening Over Dillon's* (2016). *The Dawning of the Day* is his third book.

Also by Liam Nevin

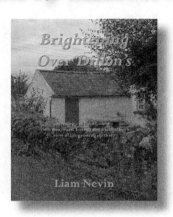

Brightening Over Dillon's

A fictionalised memoir set in 1960s semi-rural Ireland and a schoolboy's view of life growing up there and what he saw going on around him.

Life was not always easy, with few of the mod-cons and creature comforts that we have today. Yet, people were happy and there was little pressure on children to have this, that and the other. Instead, they could play safely outdoors, were free to explore the countryside and to invent adventures.

A picture is painted of a period in Irish life that might now appear to be remote but not so far removed that it has slipped entirely from living memory.

First published in Ireland, in 2016
ISBN: 978-0-9576729-9-4

Available to Buy Online, in print and e-book editions. For further information, please visit:

www.TMPpublications.com

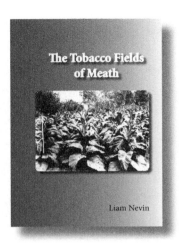

The Tobacco Fields of Meath

The true story of an attempt by Irish families, at the turn of the 20th century, to stem the twin tides of unemployment and emigration, by stimulating industry and enterprise.

Over thirty years of tobacco growing in Ireland (not only in Meath but also the counties of Offaly, Louth and as far away as Limerick) are recorded. The person who looms large is Nugent T. Everard, a progressive landlord who sought to alleviate the hardship he saw around him, mobilising a community in support of this bid.

In relating this account, the author had access to private papers kept by his late grandfather, John Nevin, who was very much at the heart of 'the Randlestown experiment'.

First published in Ireland in 2010
ISBN: 978-1-907522-26-0

Available to Buy Online, in print and e-book editions. For further information, please visit:

www.TMPpublications.com

Printed in Great Britain
by Amazon

20991303R00144